OL[
NEW[

Linda Phillips is in her fifties and lives in Wiltshire. A former civil servant, she started writing seven years ago, when her own two children flew the nest. Her first novel, *Puppies are for Life*, was published by Fourth Estate in 1998. *Old Dogs, New Tricks*, is her second novel.

1

Marjorie Benson was drowning. She struggled beneath the hands, tried to hold on to her breath, fought the cold clamp that clutched the back of her neck. She was about to black out. She was going . . .

But a second later she was allowed up from the sink and the world returned to normal – except that there was still that startling news she'd just heard.

'What was it he said?' she demanded of the young stylist hovering over her. 'That chap on the radio just now?'

Angie tightened the towel around Marjorie's head so that her words, too, came as if from another world.

'Um . . . something about Spittal's closing down, I think . . . Oh –' the girl sucked in a gasp '– that's where your old man works, isn't it? Spittal's?'

'Yes, yes, he does.' Marjorie put up a hand to blot a cold trickle, and found that it was trembling.

'I didn't really take in much of what he was saying,' Angie said. She shrugged. The radio was only on in the background for the music – nobody really bothered to listen to it.

Marjorie frowned. She hadn't paid much attention either. She thought the cheerfully-delivered information had included such time-worn phrases as 'job cuts', 'redundancies', and 'bitter blow to the area', but her ears had only pricked up on the one word: Spittal's.

'I can't believe it, if it's true,' she muttered, allowing herself to be guided across to the cutting chair. Groping for the padded arms she sank down on to the seat, the black cape billowing around her and making her feel like a crow.

The salon's attempt at smart black and white decor did nothing for Marjorie's complexion. She tried not to see the tired pale oval of her face reflected back at her, or the big bare forehead that was normally hidden. Angie always seemed to manage to wash away most of her make-up, she tutted to herself. Or was it the harsh lighting from those spots in the ceiling that was responsible for the bags under her eyes? Perhaps it was the shock that had made her look so haggard.

'Are you sure he said "Spittal's"?' she asked Angie, but Angie could tell her no more, and as the scissors began to snip and slash, to grind and grunt, Marjorie forced herself to pay attention to the matter in hand. Not that she could do much to stop the carnage taking place. She could only sit there and witness it.

She knew from many years of experience that

Angie, like every other hairdresser she had ever come across, was programmed to carry out a certain series of manoeuvres on whatever head lay beneath her hands, irrespective of the wishes that head might try to communicate to her, or what would suit it best.

'Thought any more about highlights?' Angie suddenly asked, perhaps thinking it best to distract her client from the unpalatable news. 'Or how about a coloured rinse – to blend in, sort of thing?'

Marjorie compressed her lips. Every month over the past few years it had been the same sort of suggestion. Yes, she was going a bit grey, but she wasn't yet ready to succumb to it.

'No thank you, Angie,' she said, gritting her teeth in anguish as the scissors hacked into her fringe. It was going to end up far shorter than she wanted. And wasn't it crooked on the left-hand side? Why was there a bit of a gap over one eye, for heaven's sake?

'That OK?' Angie asked finally, her scissors poised above Marjorie's head, ready to swoop for another bite if only given a word of encouragement.

Marjorie nodded and grinned back at her, dismayed at her stark eyebrows, her naked ears and her over-long neck. It would be at least three weeks before she could look in the mirror again with anything approaching equanimity.

But worse was to come. The drier whirred into action and began to scorch her scalp as Angie wielded her fiercest, most root-tugging brush. Tufts

3

of hair were tortured and teased, blasted and blown, yanked this way and that without mercy, as Angie contrived to puff them out where they should have been allowed to lie flat and flattened them where she ought to have puffed. It was all Marjorie could do, not to wrest the brush from the girl's hand and beg to finish the job herself.

'There!' Angie declared at last, adding to Marjorie's agony by giving her a glimpse of ragged neckline with her hand-held mirror. 'That all right for you now, do you think? Yes? All right? OK?'

'Fine. Fine. Lovely. Thank you very much.' Marjorie nodded at herself in the mirror, turned her head and nodded again.

Angie began rubbing her hands together then – with satisfaction Marjorie thought at first, only realising her mistake on finding waxy stuff being fingered through her hair. Why on earth had the girl done that? Now it looked greasier than before she'd walked into the salon.

She wanted to steal home by dead of night; crawl under the nearest stone. No one must see her like this. Instead, she stood up, scattering hair round her feet, and fished in her handbag for her purse. Angie conveyed her usual surprised pleasure over her generous tip, and the frightful ritual came to a close.

Only as Marjorie handed her credit card to the girl at the desk did the news hit her again. Could it possibly be true that Spittal's was closing down?

4

She pulled open the door to the street and stepped out into the late afternoon sunshine of a perfect spring day. No, it was absolutely inconceivable. Spittal's was a successful, modern and go-ahead company. They made microprocessors and other hi-tec components. How could they think of closing down?

And Philip, occupying a senior position with the company, would surely have had advance warning of any such possibility. But he'd not breathed a word about it. Not a single word. So of course it couldn't be true.

At home, Marjorie reached for the flexible spray on the end of the bath and waited for the water to run warm. Kneeling on the bath mat she bent over the tub and set to work with shampoo. Soon she had erased most of Angie's efforts in a glut of medicated foam. Wax, mousse and all kinds of gunk were banished down the plug hole, along with a few more hairs. At this rate, she thought grimly, chasing them round the bath, she would be bald. As well as a little too heavy round the hips. And droopy round the mouth. She sighed. Life could be so cruel.

And what if Spittal's really did close down? Not only would it be dreadful for the hundreds of people who worked there – and God help all of them and their families – but for her, personally, it would be disastrous. Particularly right now. Because just as she'd been thinking events were swinging her way and her months of hard work were beginning to pay off, it looked as though she'd be having Phil hanging about at home with time on his hands while he looked around for another job. Time to get under her feet and throw all manner of spanners in the works. Time to dismantle the plan that she and his parents had been secretly hatching for the past couple of months. He might even – for want of something better to do – try muscling in on her act!

Now *that* simply wasn't to be borne. Phil had always refused to have anything to do with his father's business, so why should he be allowed to step in at this late stage? No, not now that she was about to do that very thing.

Although elderly, Philip's father still ran the three small hardware shops that he'd started as a young man, but recently he had been forced to admit to Marjorie that they were really getting too much for him. Philip's mother was already semi-invalid and had not been able to assist for some while. In fact, had it not been for Marjorie's unstinting efforts in recent times, both with helping Eric in the shops and in doing all she could for Sheila, some other arrangement would have had to have been considered.

Marjorie hadn't planned to help out her father-in-law; it was something she'd fallen into one day when she'd dropped by at the largest of the shops for a bag of rose fertiliser and found him agonising over VAT.

It so happened that she had a talent for all types of figure-work: taxes, book-keeping, cash-flows – all these she could handle with ease. She had worked for a firm of accountants on leaving school and would have trained up to become one herself if Becky, their first daughter, had not put in an appearance. Family life, she had then discovered, suited her even more than accountancy, and she had never felt the urge to go back to doing anything like that – until she saw Eric huffing over his official forms.

'My oh my,' he'd said gleefully, when she'd asked if he needed a hand, 'I'd quite forgotten. This is right up your street, love, isn't it?'

He'd gladly handed her all the paperwork – along with a back-log from an old cardboard box – and from then on she'd been fully involved in all aspects of the business, learning as she went along.

And now the plan that the three of them – Eric, Sheila and herself – had been working on was that, since neither Philip nor his siblings had ever shown any interest in the shops, Marjorie would take over the complete running of them from the beginning of next month. She was to accept a proper salary, which she had never been offered before and wouldn't have dreamed of accepting if she had, since she was only too happy to help out, and she would be allowed *carte blanche* to make of the business what she could.

Eric and Sheila would take things more easily

from then on, although Eric said he would still 'pop in now and again to keep an eye on things'. And they would only draw from the business what little they felt they needed to live on.

'But –' Marjorie's face had clouded a little after her initial burst of euphoria '– what are Colin and Chrissie going to think of all this?' Her brother-in-law and sister-in-law might raise all sorts of objections to their inheritance being 'taken over' in this way, even though they wouldn't want anything to do with the shops themselves.

Both Philip's brother and his sister had elected to go their own ways, just as he had done. In fact, much to his father's disgust, it was Philip who seemed to have set the trend, paved the way, made it easier for the others to stand up to parental authority and say no. Heedless of Eric's protests, Colin had gone into the leisure industry and Chrissie was married to a trout farmer in North Wales.

'Colin and Chrissie can think what they like,' Eric grunted. 'They've had their chances and blown 'em, as far as I'm concerned. They've not been forgotten in our wills, if that's what's bothering you, and that's all they can rightfully expect.'

Marjorie noticed that he'd not included her husband in his condemnation. Philip had always been his favourite in spite of everything, though he would never admit it. Did he still harbour a hope that his firstborn might yet one day step into his father's shoes? And was Marjorie merely the next best thing?

But she swept the notion aside. Eric's proposal had touched and flattered her; why should she look a gift-horse in the mouth? She had always felt as much loved by the couple as their own children were – perhaps even more so since her own parents' tragic death – and to be trusted with Eric's pride and joy... well, it was surely to be taken as an accolade. An accolade that she had been hoping for all along but one that she'd dared not expect.

She'd not whispered a word to anyone about her troubles of late, but the truth was that she had been feeling a little low and oddly insecure, what with it being *that* time of life when a woman feels less than her best and society conspires to make her feel utterly useless – fit only for the scrap-heap. The future had begun to look so empty and she had been desperately seeking something she could look forward to, with pleasure or even zeal.

Next year she and Phil would be celebrating twenty-five years of marriage; and with modern medicine being what it was, and people living longer and more healthily, it looked as though they stood a fair chance of maybe twenty-five more together. What on earth were they going to do with all that time? Or more to the point, since he at least had a busy career for a while, what was *she* going to do? These were the thoughts that had begun to haunt her, even before their two daughters had left home and her 'caring' role had already begun to dwindle. Since the girls had physically removed themselves from the family home and needed her even less, a kind of panic had set in.

But she had not let her concerns remain mere thoughts. No one could accuse her of sitting back, bemoaning her fate and wailing that there was nothing to be done about it. Instead she had started sowing seeds. And it wasn't entirely by chance that Eric had come up with his proposal, if she was honest about it: she had been slowly and carefully working on him as she helped him in his shops, slipping in the odd suggestions here and intelligent comments there, and making herself pretty well indispensable, until one evening, just after Christmas, he'd hung up his overall, turned to her with a grave expression, and said he had something to say.

He had then proceeded to put forward what were essentially her own ideas for the future of the business as though they were all his own. It seemed not to have occurred to him to promote one of his managers to do the job in his place; his only thought was of her. And what a boost it had given her! Especially when she realised the size of the salary he was considering paying her, and the degree of control she was to be given. It was all far more than she'd ever imagined.

So now her life was mapped out. With the shops to keep her occupied and the prospect of grand-children on the way, she could happily spend her remaining years here in London where she'd always lived, amongst family and friends, and not ask for anything more.

But what if Spittal's closed down?

Whipping a towel from the radiator she scrambled to her feet. She must see Eric and Sheila at once.

By the time she reached her in-laws' house, two blocks away from her own, the half-heard news about Spittal's possible closure had become hard fact in Marjorie's mind, and the only possible outcome a dead certainty. Grimly, her keys rattling in the lock, she let herself in at the front door.

She had had free access to the house for many years, but only in recent times, when Sheila's joints had begun to grow too painful for her to greet guests at the door, had she taken advantage of it.

Stepping into the wide, well-polished hall with its thick Indian rug she never ceased to be impressed by her surroundings. She tried not to be because Philip always referred to the house – behind his mother's back and well out of earshot – as 'hideous'.

Never, he had been known to say, his eyes narrowed against the clashing wall-papers, the gaudy paint work and the eclectic assortment of ornaments, had so much money been squandered to such disastrous effect.

Certainly Marjorie would not have chosen such

bold patterns either, or so many of them crowded together in quite the way they were – above the dado, below the dado, outlined with borders, panelled with borders; nor would she have considered the over-large crystal chandeliers as fitting for such a house. She would not have lain inch-thick ornate rugs on top of deep-piled patterned carpets. And the swags and drapes at the window were way over the top. Yet the whole was immaculately kept and gave out a sensation of luxurious comfort. Stepping into number fourteen Rosewood Gardens was like entering a secure, well-padded sanctuary.

Marjorie slipped off her shoes, as was the custom in this household, and waded across yards of Axminster in search of her mother-in-law, calling out as she went. She found the stout little figure of Sheila Benson sitting in the breakfast room, as usual, busy with her needlepoint.

'Thought you were going to the hairdresser's,' the older woman said, blinking up at Marjorie through glasses that magnified her eyes.

Marjorie gave a weak smile. 'Oh . . . yes, that's right,' she said vaguely, her hand straying up to her hair. 'But first I've some mind-blowing news for you.'

'What? Not the baby already?'

'No, no!' Marjorie fluttered her hands at the idea. Her first grandchild wasn't due for another ten weeks at least.

'Wow, you gave me quite a turn.' Sheila had

struggled half-way out of her chair; now she fumbled her way back to it. 'What is it, then, this news? You're looking rather upset.'

Marjorie flopped into the large wing chair on the other side of the French window and sat with her feet tucked up under her skirt. A smell of spring and fresh-mown grass wafted through the open door, but she was hardly in the mood to enjoy it. For a while, ordering her thoughts, she watched the gardener that her in-laws hired for two mornings a week plough up and down the long lawn, making the first striped cut of the year. The man's irritation with the ungainly cupid that had been cemented to the centre of his work area since last autumn was obvious by the way he kept hurling aside the electric cable.

'Well,' she said at last, 'I suppose you haven't had the radio on? And perhaps it wasn't on the local TV news. I could hardly believe it at first. But, really, it must be true.' She turned wide, incredulous eyes to her mother-in-law. 'Spittal's is closing down.'

Sheila let fall her embroidery frame. She dropped her scissors as well. 'But . . . but surely that can't be true?' She put a hand to her chest. 'My but you've given me another turn!'

'I'm sorry.' Marjorie knelt down to retrieve the scattered items, barely managing to locate the tiny scissors amongst the swirls of leaves and flowers. 'I didn't mean to alarm you. I should have broken this to you more gently.'

13

Sheila waved the apology aside and put a hand on Marjorie's arm. 'It was just the thought of all those poor people. Not to mention Philip. Whenever I hear of places closing down and folk being put out of work I'm reminded of my childhood and my father losing his job.'

For a moment her face reflected her bad memories but she quickly rallied. 'Anyway, let's not look on the black side. These days there are redundancy payments, aren't there? Help from the government too. Not that it'll matter so much to Philip; he won't be needing it, will he?'

Marjorie was about to lay down the horse-and-cart tapestry in her mother-in-law's lap, having first admired all the tiny stitches, though she had no patience herself for anything involving needles and thread. Now she glanced up sharply at Sheila's words.

'What do you mean?'

'Well –' Sheila spread her hands as though she thought an explanation superfluous '– it looks as though he will be going in with his father after all. I mean to say, he'll have no other choice now, will he? No one will give him another job at his age. So you see, it's an answer to all our prayers – and not a minute before time. Just what we've always wanted.'

'Oh, I see what you mean.' Marjorie's voice was faint.

'It's what he should have done long ago,' Sheila went on, 'when his father reached retirement age.

14

In fact he should have done it right from the start, the minute he got his degree. But what he should do and what he wants to do, are two different things to Phil.' She gathered up some loose ends of wool, took off her glasses and chewed on one of the arms. Absorbed in her thoughts she failed to notice the dismay in Marjorie's expression.

'What makes you think,' Marjorie said, trying to keep her voice calm, 'what makes you think that Phil will agree to take over the business even now? Maybe he'll have other plans.'

'Well, I can't think what they would be. This must have come as a shock to him; he won't have had time to plan anything. My feeling is that he'll be only too glad he has this to fall back on. Ha!' She let out a chuckle, still oblivious to Marjorie's agony. 'Life's full of nice little surprises, isn't it? There you were, thinking you'd have to soldier on alone with all the shops, and what happens? Suddenly there's Phil beside you, free to help after all. And Eric will be so thrilled when he hears the news.'

'But – but I thought we had it all planned . . .'

Marjorie watched helplessly as Sheila wrapped her tapestry frame in an old pillow case and stowed it with her wools inside a hinged footstool. Something in Marjorie's tone must have penetrated at last; she paused before shutting the lid, then put it down at half-speed.

'You don't sound very happy about this,' she exclaimed with concern and surprise.

Marjorie looked away, embarrassed, hardly

trusting herself to speak. *Well*, she silently scolded herself, *what else could she have expected?* Phil was Sheila's son after all. It was perfectly understandable that she should be more pleased at the prospect of having him run the shops than anyone else on this earth. Certainly more than a mere daughter-in-law, no matter how much they loved her.

And perfectly right it was, too. The way it should really be. Yes, really. Who could deny it? Blood was thicker than water, when all was said and done.

Right or not, though, it was cruel. A 'nice little surprise' it was not. How easily she had dismissed the possibility of such a thing happening! How silly to have assumed that Philip would go more or less straight into another job. For of course Sheila was right, wasn't she? No one would take him on in another firm now, not at his age. There was nothing else he could do but kow-tow at last to his parents.

But where did this leave her? She had never for one moment pictured Phil working alongside her in her new venture. Not that that would be the case; if they attempted to run the shops together she was sure he would immediately assume control of everything – see himself as her superior.

He wasn't as bossy as his father could be at times, but he undoubtedly had that streak in him. He wouldn't have got where he was today without strength and determination. Which meant that she wouldn't get a look-in. In no time at all she would find herself relegated to the more menial tasks; not

16

even allowed a say. As they were in their marriage, so it would be at work. How could she expect it to be different?

Oh, the idea was quite intolerable. She had wanted so much for herself. Had wanted to prove her capabilities and show Phil that she was no longer the dependent appendage that he had always seen her as; she was a person in her own right.

Glancing at Sheila she forced a smile. 'Events are moving too quickly for me. I need to get used to the idea. And perhaps, before we speculate any further, we'd better see what Phil has to say. He doesn't even know what we've been planning yet.'

'No.' Sheila gave a little shudder to emphasise her disapproval of this fact; she didn't like secrets between spouses. They were unhealthy.

Twiddling her wedding ring round her finger Marjorie could only agree with her. She glanced down at the gold band that had once had a pattern on it but had now worn smooth; both it and the diamond engagement ring had channelled grooves in her flesh. Married all those years, she thought with a pang of conscience, and she'd been keeping secrets from Phil because he wouldn't have liked what she was doing. Whatever would that old vicar who'd married them have to say about that?

Of course he was probably pushing up daisies by now, but recently, for some strange reason, his words had been coming back to her. Not so much about being honest with each other – presumably he'd thought that went without saying – but all manner of other unasked-for advice that he'd seen fit to offer them on the run-up to their wedding day. For example, it was his view that in all their future life-decisions the final word should be Philip's. He should be the one to wear the trousers and Marjorie should defer to him.

Sitting side by side on the musty vicarage sofa as he delivered this instruction, they had stared at him in silence, hardly able to believe their ears, for even in those days such notions were so out of date as to be laughable.

Marjorie had sensed Phil's suppressed mirth bubbling up, his hand tightening round hers as they solemnly nodded their heads, and she'd found it hard to keep a straight face. They had escaped from the interview as soon as they could, running hard to get well away from the vicarage before their laughter came spluttering out.

Nevertheless, a few days later Marjorie had found herself promising to obey her husband for ever more until they were parted by death. And she had largely adhered to the vicar's words through-out her marriage; she had let Philip wear the trousers and had always deferred to him, even if at times he had jokingly had to threaten her with hell-fire and brimstone.

At least it had had the advantage that Phil had no one to blame but himself whenever things turned out badly – a neat cop-out for her, to be true, but it didn't always suit. It certainly wasn't going to suit her now if his plans clashed with her own . . .

'Come and have dinner with us this evening,' she urged Sheila. 'I'm going to tell Philip everything. It's time to sort all this out.'

2

Philip Benson hurried out of the lift and crossed the glossy foyer of Spittal's admin. building in ten easy strides. He was far from being a vain man and would have been surprised had he been told that at least a dozen female heads turned to follow his progress before he disappeared through the revolving doors.

This owed nothing to the fact that he was the sales director; the MD himself could have stripped naked on top of the reception desk and no one would have batted an eye. But Philip Benson was 'something else', according to most of the women who worked at Spittal's; he was generally considered by young and old, fat and thin, married and single, to be more than 'a bit of all right'. Even though he was hitting fifty. Even though he'd gone grey. Even though he would soon be a grandfather. None of that mattered a jot. As for Mrs Benson, well, wasn't she the lucky one?

Many a time had the phenomenon that was Philip Benson been thoroughly analysed, but no satisfactory conclusions had ever been reached. He was not conventionally handsome – whatever that might mean. Some said it was his slow, shy smile that did it; some his affable nature. Others considered his selflessness was the charm, for what could be more attractive than an all-round decent bloke, they argued, who had no idea that he was?

Philip's ears would have burned with embarrassment if he'd had any knowledge of these discussions. Either that or he would have assumed that the subject of them was someone else. Happily heedless of turned heads, longing glances or wagging tongues, he ducked into the pub next door to Spittal's in search of a much-needed drink.

Spotting his old friend in one corner, slumped over a glass of beer, he grinned that slow, charming smile of his.

'Thought I might find you here, Tom,' he said, jerking a stool from under the table and straddling it. 'Things getting too hot for you back there?'

Tom almost choked as Philip clapped him on the shoulder. He looked up sourly, licking foam from his bushy moustache.

'Bloody chaos, it is,' he complained with a despairing shake of his head. 'Here, let me get you your –'

'No, no, I'm buying,' Phil insisted. He caught the barman's eye above the row of backs hunched round the bar and was soon well into a glass of Guinness, with another pint lined up for Tom.

'Not exactly a good place to be in at a time like

this,' Phil said, loosening his tie. 'Personnel, I mean.'

'You can say that again, man, indeed you can. You can imagine what it's been like. Nothing short of a riot.' He pretended to mop his brow. 'I've come in here to escape, though I expect the hordes will soon catch up with me, demanding to know why they've been laid off with only a pittance when some other sod's being kept on, and how the devil are they going to go home and break it to the wife? Like it's all my bloody fault, you know?'

He eyed his companion morosely, and since Phil rarely nipped in for a quick one on his way home asked, 'And what're you doing in here, pal? Turning over a new leaf?'

Philip drank down a few more mouthfuls before adopting a wry expression. 'Wondering how I'm going to break it to the wife, actually, just like everyone else.'

'She doesn't know?' Tom's surprise revealed the whites of his eyes. They were stained with red threads of tiredness.

'No,' Phil admitted reluctantly, 'she doesn't know a thing.'

'But I thought . . .'

'That I would've told her days ago?'

'Well . . . with your prior knowledge . . . and surely you could have trusted her?'

'Of course I could have trusted her. She wouldn't have leaked it.' Philip waved that line of questioning aside. 'It was just that – well, I suppose I couldn't broach it.'

Tom snorted his disbelief. 'Don't tell me our sales director is scared of his wife? But . . . but it's not as if it's even bad news for you, is it? Won't this just suit your Marjorie down to the ground?'

Philip's expression darkened. 'You're assuming I'm taking redundancy, Tom. And all things considered I suppose . . .'

'Be plain daft, not to, wouldn't it?' Tom demonstrated his ideas with his hands. 'Take the money – nice tidy sum –' he grabbed air and clutched it to his chest '– and straight into your father's business.' He made a throwing motion. 'Isn't that what Marjorie's always wanted? Not to mention your mum and dad.'

Tom knew the history of Philip's rebellion very well – mostly as related by Marjorie, the ubiquitous 'girl next door'.

She would have been about eight and Philip nine when his father's local hardware shop had begun to make money. 'Real' money, that is, as opposed to scraping a living. Eric Benson was about the only person not surprised by his success. He had worked damned hard for it, he was quick to tell anyone who would listen, and he lost no time in putting his profits back into the business and buying himself another shop in the adjacent borough. He soon repeated his earlier success and bought yet another shop before calling it a day.

Three shops, he decided at the end of a

particularly busy week, hardly left him with time to draw breath. And being the kind of person whose powers of delegation were nil – although it was unlikely that he'd ever realised that fact – he told himself that enough was surely enough.

After the purchase of the second shop the Bensons left their crowded flat and came to live in the house next door to Marjorie and her parents, by which time Philip was eleven and taking the dreaded 11-plus.

Not that the tests presented Philip with much of a problem – he sailed through them all in less than the allotted time and wondered what all the fuss was about – but it brought the Bensons' attention to the whole question of secondary education, and Eric, his new-found wealth growing steadily in the bank, began to get ideas above his station.

The upshot was that Philip, his sister Chrissie, and later his brother Colin, were forced into private schooling. Forced being the only word for it, where Philip was concerned: he resented the whole idea and dug his heels in as hard as he could. He didn't want to have to walk in the opposite direction to his friends every day and be called a toffee-nosed pansy, he complained in Marjorie's sympathetic ear.

Already he had a lot to live down. Since moving into the new house he'd been compelled to witness vulgar displays of his father's newly-acquired wealth, as all manner of goods found their way from the high street stores to the family home.

There had been a huge new television with shiny double doors, a radiogram with record auto-change, a tape recorder that weighed a ton, and a snazzy food-mixer that worked miracles. Even a shiny new car – the latest thing on the market – appeared outside the house one day. That neither of his parents could drive was neither here nor there.

As for his mother, well, she went mad on a whole new decor for the house and ordered a truck-load of tacky knick-knacks.

Philip was endlessly ribbed for all this by his slightly awe-struck friends, and then – horror of horrors – his father had come up with the idea of sending him off to a snobby school! But at least his mother had some sense left: she drew the line at putting any kind of distance between herself and her firstborn child. He must come home to be properly fed, she insisted. The school had to be a local one.

And so Philip had had to grit his teeth – for no one could stand for long against Eric Benson's domineering manner – and make the best of a bad job. No amount of telling him how privileged he was made a scrap of difference to young Philip as he trudged up the road each morning in his immaculate red blazer with gold and blue braid; he made up his mind to hate every minute of his new way of life. Absolutely every minute.

But of course he hadn't. He'd gradually settled in to the school, even distinguished himself, and left at eighteen with a batch of certificates that were more than good enough to take him on to university for an engineering degree.

It was only on leaving university that the final stage of Eric Benson's master plan was revealed, and Philip realised he was expected to take over the hardware businesses from his father.

'With all your qualifications, lad,' Eric had told him, throwing out his chest as he stood behind the shop counter, 'you'll be able to build all this into an empire for yourself. People are keen to do their own home improvements these days, and there's big money to be made.' He made it sound as though Philip ought to be eternally grateful, as perhaps he should; not many could expect to have such opportunities handed to them on a plate.

'But Dad,' he'd protested, already planning to go back to university and try for a master's degree, 'I didn't spend years studying for decent qualifications just to sell spanners and plastic buckets! I didn't, and I won't. I'm sorry. But I won't!'

This time he withstood the pressure from his father and the emotional blackmail from his mother. From that day on he'd had nothing to do with the family business.

Philip nodded at Tom over his Guinness. 'Oh yes, yes, I can always go into the family business.' His tone was heavy with scorn. 'It's what everyone's always wanted. Everyone, that is, except me.'

'Well . . .' Tom swung one short leg over the

27

other and drummed his fingers on the table, '. . . I know you've never been keen. But at least you have that to fall back on, haven't you? Damn lucky you are, really, you know. Considering the alternative.'

'The alternative,' Phil stated unnecessarily, 'is to move down to the Bristol office with what's left of the London mob. And in spite of the amalgamation I can even keep my position . . . *if* I decide that's what I want.'

Tom blew out his cheeks; Philip sounded as though he were actually considering the choice. Personally, he had soon told Spittal's what they could do with their Bristol plans.

'But Phil, you wouldn't be wanting to move, would you? Not at your time of life?'

Philip met his friend's incredulous gaze. His time of life? Did Tom see him as an old man? He didn't feel it.

'I don't think this redundancy idea's something to rush into without giving it serious thought,' he hedged.

'No . . . no. Maybe not.' Bemused, Tom stood up and went to the bar for refills, leaving Philip alone with his thoughts.

Philip sighed when he'd gone; he had hoped Tom would understand, but he hadn't really expected him to. Tom wouldn't know anything about how he'd begun to feel lately, because feelings weren't things they discussed. The trouble was that unlike Tom he was nowhere near ready to hang up his hat.

He needed a change, that was certain; needed to climb out of the rut that his life had sunk into, and Bristol seemed like an answer. The Bahamas would have been better, admittedly, but Bristol would have to suffice. Anywhere away from the area in which he had been born and bred would do. For too long he had felt as though he was still tied to his parents; still under their watchful eye. What a ridiculous state of affairs at his age!

For a long time he had wanted to escape to pastures new but it had never been practical, or so Marjorie had said. Each time the subject cropped up she had constructed a case against it. Usually it was because of the girls: they were at a crucial stage of their schooling, or too bound by their social lives. When weren't they? But the girls had long since finished their schooling and gone on to make lives of their own. So nothing tied him and Marjie to south London any more. Nothing much would be missed.

Oh, how he longed for change! Life had become so predictable of late, with each year following the same pattern. Everything revolved almost entirely round the family circle, because Marjorie liked it that way. A great one for family, Marjorie was, particularly on birthdays and at Christmas. Birthdays demanded a slap-up meal together in a restaurant, and Christmas was celebrated at their place or at his parents' or – a recent innovation – with their daughter Becky and her husband Steve.

Holidays, at least, they took with friends: usually

Tom and Beth but sometimes with Val and Ian as well. And it nearly always had to be Spain because Beth claimed she loved it and didn't want to try anywhere different.

They would spend most of the first week listening to Val's long list of complaints about the hotel or scouring souvenir shops for Beth, who tended to get lost in them. The second week would pass in endless discussions on where to go next year – as if it would make any difference – and Ian would invariably make himself ill from too much beer and sun. Marjorie's nose would turn red and start blistering towards the end of the holiday; Tom would stop speaking to Beth; and they would all come home wondering why they'd bothered to go in the first place.

When all their children were young it had been even worse, but that was thankfully in the past. They'd had a few good laughs it was true, yet one holiday inevitably became blurred with the previous one and none stood out in the memory.

Philip longed to go off with Marjorie on their own somewhere. Anywhere. It didn't matter. But whenever he'd suggested it, Marjorie had looked at him as though he were an alien.

Philip shifted on the pub's padded stool. His feet fidgeted beneath the table. The upheaval at Spittal's had dug up feelings long since buried and almost forgotten. But now he must do something about those feelings before old age crept closer and it was too late. Spittal's was showing him a way out. He would never get another chance.

'Tom,' he said when his friend returned, dripping their drinks over the carpet and across the table, 'I want you to promise me something.'

'Oh?' Tom fixed him with a wary eye; Phil's tone had alerted him. 'And what would that be now?'

Philip looked away. Explaining wasn't easy. 'If you happen to bump into Marjorie, I'd rather you didn't say anything to her about any of this kerfuffle. About the redundancy package I mean. And don't tell your Beth about it either; the two of them are bound to get together before long, and then it would all come out.'

'What? You mean . . . ?' Tom's jaw began to drop. 'But I'm taking redundancy, no question, so how . . . you can't . . . Marjorie's bound to wonder why you're not leaping at the chance to do the same.'

Phil had thought about that. 'Look, you're two – nearly three – years older than I am. Let's pretend there was a cut-off point and that you were given the chance of redundancy but I wasn't; that the powers that be consider there's still life in this old dog and they expect me to soldier on.'

'But – Marjorie's not stupid, Philip.'

'She's a little unworldly though.'

Tom knew what he meant. As with his own wife, Marjorie had never been out in the cut and thrust of big business. Both women had been content to be mothers and housewives. Marjorie would probably accept Phil's word as gospel, not dig about asking questions. But that didn't mean Phil could ride rough-shod over her the way he seemed intent on doing. She ought to be consulted over this important issue, given a chance to air her views, and certainly have some say in the final decision.

Tom looked this way and that, planted his stubby hands on the table and gasped like a landed fish. 'Now let me get this straight, Phil,' he finally managed to say, his neck reddening round his shirt collar. 'You haven't any intention of taking redundancy, have you? And you're sitting there and telling me that you're going to lie to your wife about it?'

'Yes,' Phil said quietly, 'I'm afraid I have to. For the time being at least. Maybe when she's come round to the idea . . . oh, I just *cannot* work for my father!' His warm brown eyes pleaded for understanding. 'I've never deceived Marjorie before, you know. It'll be for the very first time. And I'm sure it'll all work out for the best in the end.'

A difficult silence fell between them.

Tom rubbed his moustache with one hand. It made no difference to him whether it was the first, the hundredth, or the last time Phil deceived Marjorie. He might even tell a few porkies himself. But Phil? Phil, whom he had always thought of as a fair, honest sort? The man was tumbling in his estimation.

'Well, then –' Tom's voice, when he finally spoke, crackled with ice '– perhaps it's a good thing we'll soon be separated, then, if you're really going to do this. I *had* thought we were going to have some good years ahead of us, life-long buddies that we are. But if you're set on going, and – and treating your wife like this, well . . .'

Phil might have guessed he'd have trouble with Tom. In truth he was having trouble with himself. 'You don't understand,' he said, draining his glass and rising. He would like to have gone into all this more fully, unburden himself to Tom, but he could see he hadn't handled the matter very well; Tom didn't look ripe for listening any more.

'No,' came Tom's surly response. 'I bloody don't understand.' Then, as Phil started to walk away, he growled, 'I just hope your Marjorie does, the day she learns what you've done.'

Oliver Knox checked his watch. Why did Jade always have to be late? She'd turned being late into an art form. And there was no excuse this time. He knew her aerobics class had finished punctually.

Having completed his routine in the gym he'd stopped on his way to the changing room to peer through the glass panel in the studio door. The advanced aerobics session had been drawing to a close and the class – mostly women but there were a few men – had been sitting cross-legged on mats. They had reached the stage where they rolled their heads round on their necks with their eyes closed, which meant they hadn't much more to do. He knew that soon after that the instructor would creep over to her tape recorder, switch off the snippet of classical music to which her flock was supposed to relax, and clap her hands. Then – rather stupidly, Oliver thought – everyone else would start clapping too, smiling foolishly at each other as though they had just been brought out of hypnosis.

He had stood admiring Jade for some time, for she was by far the most beautiful girl there, even with her long blonde hair scraped into a knot on top of her head. Her stylish aerobics gear – lime green crop-top with black cycle shorts – flattered her superb figure, and her amazing legs went on for yards before they ended at the ridiculously expensive trainers she'd bought last Saturday. In comparison to the other women she was an Aston Martin among a car park full of Ladas. Even the teacher appeared clumsy beside her.

Grinning to himself, and rippling his developing chest muscles – the work-outs were certainly doing the trick – Oliver had slipped away for a shower. Then he had gone on to the club bar in the basement, ordered himself a lager, and waited.

He was on his second pint before Jade turned up. She glided into the chair opposite him smiling her dazzling smile and tossing her freshly-washed hair. But by then Oliver had forgotten his pride in her; he had sunk into a brooding mood.

'You'll be late for your own effing funeral,' he told her. He was sitting with his chin propped on one hand, a small cigar poked between the second and third fingers, and was unaware that he appeared to her to have smoke coming through the top of his boot-polish-black head.

'Oh dear,' she soothed, trying not to smile, 'have we had a hard day?' She leaned across the table and pecked his pouting lips.

Oliver glared at her all the more. He hated not

being taken seriously. 'It was going all right until I heard about Benson, but then–'

'Benson?' She plucked up the little menu, glanced over it and transferred her attention to the 'Specials' listed on the wall. 'I don't think I know Benson. I'm going to have the venison this time. What'll you have? Oh, and some of that lovely wine we had the other day. Which one was it, do you remember?'

'The most expensive one on the list,' he growled. 'Have you seen my Gold Card statement? It came in yesterday's post.'

'No.' Jade turned down the corners of her mouth. 'My Visa was bad enough. Why should I want to know about yours? Horrors! But so what? I could eat a whole horse.'

She studied the menu more closely, but she'd already made up her mind. She called out her order to the barman – whom they both knew well since they spent at least two, and often three, evenings at the country club – and sat back looking around.

Oliver grew more disgruntled at this blatant lack of attention. 'You do know who Benson is. Philip Benson. Remember? I told you all about him. He's one of the London mob. A rather significant one.'

'Oh. Yes. Of course.' Jade looked faintly put out. 'Well, I beg your pardon, Olly, but I can't be expected to remember everything. My head's full of company law at the moment.' But she was wasting her breath. It was no excuse, as far as Oliver was concerned, that her law exams were less

37

than a year away and that there was such a lot to cram in: she should have remembered who Benson was.

Oliver had made a lot of fuss about Spittal's restructuring plans over the past few months. He had been fully counting on promotion to sales director in place of Platt, who was retiring. Instead, although yet to be officially confirmed, it looked as though this bloke Benson might be coming down from London to take the job and Oliver would have to stay put as his assistant.

'There's no justice in this world,' Oliver complained into his glass of lager before tipping the contents down his throat. 'No justice at all. I mean, he's fifty, for God's sake. Why would they want to keep on an old wrinkly like him?'

Jade decided it would be prudent not to speak her mind. It was obvious that the powers-that-be thought Benson the more able man.

'You know what your MD's like,' she reminded him. 'He's hopelessly old-fashioned. Moralistic. Stuck in his ways . . . He's bound to go for an older man, isn't he? One of the old school.'

'Well, I only hope he knows what he's playing at, bucking current trends. And how the hell did I come to be lumbered with an anachronism like that? I tell you, Jade, if I'd known what the set-up would be like I'd never have joined this firm.'

'Your time will come, Olly.' Jade put out a comforting hand.

'Oh yes. When I've one foot in the grave and no teeth.'

Jade hooked one side of her hair behind her ear. 'I suppose . . .' her blue-green eyes flickered over Oliver's face '. . . I suppose this Philip Benson's a married man?'

'How the hell would I know? Though come to think of it maybe he is. There was a discussion in the office as to where he might live, and someone suggested that one of those big new houses on the Brightwells estate might suit him. Personnel are sending him the details, anyway.'

'God, no!' Her eyebrows arched. 'Not that hell-hole. He'd have to be out of his skull.'

'Yeah!' Oliver managed a smile; it amused him to think of his new superior, whose guts he already hated on principle, coming to live with the plebs. True, some of the houses were quite desirable if you liked that kind of thing; but the ambience was all wrong. Brightwells was nothing but a huge town over-spill. Accommodation for the masses. A sprawling nonentity hastily thrown up to meet the ever-growing demand for executive-type housing.

Oliver dragged at the cigar and blew the smoke over their heads. 'So I suppose he must be married,' he concluded, 'if they think he needs a place like that. What difference does it make, anyway?'

'Well . . . I was just wondering. Perhaps it helped him get the job. I mean –' she hurried on '– it might count with your MD, mightn't it, whereas . . . now don't look at me like that, Olly, I'm not advocating that you and I should be married, even after your divorce has gone through.' She flushed, tossing her hair again. 'You know I'm not.'

Olly regarded her carefully. Did she really mean that? You never could tell with women. Most of them couldn't be trusted. They would swear blind they didn't want something, when all the time it was the very thing they did want. Like babies. *Goodness me, no,* they'd protest. *Whatever would I do with one of those?* And half the time they'd be glued to the Mothercare window. Same with marriage. *Who'd want to be married these days?* they would claim. *It's a perfectly meaningless institution. Only a piece of paper . . . oh look, what a gorgeous ring! And I just love white weddings, don't you?*

Jade, to be fair, hadn't been like that so far, and they'd been living together for nearly six months. But then, he had made things crystal clear to her from the start. Since his first shot at marriage had been such a failure, he told her, he believed that 'open' relationships were a safer bet, and had gone on to explain exactly what he meant by that. He was nothing if not honest.

'I love you, Jade,' he'd said, 'but to be perfectly frank with you I can't promise to be completely faithful. I'm not that kind of man. I need to feel free to – er – engage in other relationships from time to time. Nothing permanent, mind. Just the odd fling. I'd always come back to you . . .'

Seeing Jade's startled expression – the involuntary

parting of her lips, the narrowing of her cat-like eyes – he had hastened to reassure her. 'Of course, it would work both ways. You'd be free, as well, you know. To go with other guys.'

Jade said nothing.

'And if, on the odd occasion,' he blustered on, since he appeared to have blown his chances and had nothing more to lose, 'if on the odd occasion the opportunity of a swap came up – you know, at a party or something – well, it could be great. Really. It would. I mean – have you ever tried it? Afterwards you compare notes. And that's the best part of it, you know, telling each other about different experiences – in bed – and – God,' he'd wound up, hastily adjusting his trousers, 'I'm getting horny just thinking about it.'

Two plates of venison arrived and Oliver stubbed out his cigar. 'Our not being married hasn't bothered H J up until now,' he told Jade.

'H J?'

'Holy Joe. Big boss. Jocelyn Hemmingway-Judd.'

'Oh, him. Well, no, maybe not, who knows?' She shrugged, so that her baggy cotton sweater slipped to one side revealing a naked shoulder. 'But it *might* have affected your promotability without your realising it. In his eyes –' she made her own goggle '– I presume, we're living in sin.'

Oliver waited while the barman finished glugging wine into their glasses. 'Living in sin,' he muttered in disgust. 'What a load of cock. It's the job

41

that counts, surely? The way you do it; the results you achieve.

'Cheers, Tony,' he dismissed the barman, and began to attack his food. But his mind was still with H J.

'Perhaps this new guy's not married,' Jade said in an attempt to lighten his mood. 'He could be gay, you know. H J wouldn't be happy about that.'

Oliver considered the matter. He would like to think it a possibility, because Jade was right: H J wouldn't be able to stomach that. 'Now how am I supposed to know whether Benson's gay or not? I've not even met him yet. If it's anything to go by, word's come down from London to the women in our office that he's quite fanciable. The secretaries are wetting their knickers in anticipation.'

'Really?' Jade grinned. She had become inured to Oliver's coarseness. 'I thought you said he was old.'

'Not too old for that, apparently. Even you might fancy him.' Oliver chewed, emptied his mouth, and stabbed the air with his fork. 'Hey, that's not a bad idea!'

'What?' Jade had a quick brain, but couldn't follow his thoughts on this occasion.

'Well, how about –' he began to chuckle at his idea '– how about we invite him over to dinner when he moves down here and that you get on rather well with him – follow my drift? And then, when he's nicely drooling over you and making a complete arse of himself, it's somehow spread around the office that he's been pestering his junior's girlfriend. Even tried to force himself on her. Hey presto! One disgraced sales director's booted back to the smoke. And then yours truly steps in to fill his shoes.'

Jade let out a gasp, nearly choked on a sip of wine, and sat back fanning her face. 'Oliver B Knox! Really! You'll be the death of me.'

'It would be worth trying it on, though. Think of the extra money.'

'Only you could be so daft as to dream up such a preposterous scheme.'

'Full of imagination, I am. And it isn't all that daft. Or original really, as you must know in your line of work. Women are doing it all the time, aren't they – claiming harassment and rape, and no one can prove a thing?'

Jade glanced coldly across at him. 'I hope you aren't suggesting that women make up things like that – just for revenge or compensation? And in any case, you know I'm not allowed to handle that type of work.'

Jade never missed a chance to air a grievance about her job: she wasn't yet a qualified legal executive and, as soon as she was, she wanted to go on from there to become a solicitor. It was a long, hard, highly competitive road on which she had set herself – especially having to work and study at the same time – and all the experience she was gaining at Hart, Bruce and Thomson's was in con-veyancing. She longed to move on to more interesting work; saw herself as the star role in court dealing with the more contentious side of the law – criminal, perhaps, or marital. Something to sink her teeth into.

'Jade,' the doddery old senior partner was always telling her, 'you cannot run before you can walk.' Some days she felt like kicking him out of the way; she would soon show him her mettle.

Oliver still had his gleaming black eyes fixed on her. 'Would that be a definite "no" then?' he prompted. 'Do I take it you don't want to play at being a *femme fatale*?'

He waited for her to say something, but she carried right on with her meal, wrapped up in her own private world. She obviously didn't think he deserved an answer. Which was a pity. He was rather taken with the idea himself.

44

4

Marjorie sat up in bed trying to read her library book while waiting for Philip to return from taking his parents home. What a ghastly evening it had been. Normally she would have been half-way through her latest thriller by now, but with the day's events blotting everything out she was stuck on page three and had no idea of the plot. She kept staring up at the wallpaper, not seeing it. But all she could think of was Bristol.

Bristol? Oh, no, no, no. Not now. Not when she was on the verge of an exciting new challenge in her life – one that she needed with increasing desperation the more she thought about it all.

After years of looking after Phil and the girls – enjoyable though that had been – she yearned to exercise her brain, to use her skills, and to achieve, in doing so, a degree of personal satisfaction. More than that: she had a deep-down need to assert herself and prove to Phil that she wasn't as dependent on him as he'd always seemed to think, that she was an equal partner in the marriage with independent ideas and a life of her own to be lived.

But of course he knew nothing of her recent way of thinking, so as soon as he came back to the house she would try to explain. Would it make any difference to his plans, though? Could she get him to change his mind? He'd seemed so adamant that they had to go to Bristol, but even now she could hardly believe he was serious. They had lived in London all their lives.

To be honest, their suburb was no longer the place it had been – in fact it had changed almost beyond recognition like most of suburbia had done – but it had always been their home. How could Phil think of moving away? The matter of the shops aside, how could he expect her to leave Becky when she was about to have her first baby? How could he expect her to abandon this house with its comforting familiarity, their relatives and friends. Moreover how could he take her from her much-loved garden? If nothing else occurred to him, surely he must realise how much *that* meant to her?

Why, only that afternoon, inspired by Sheila's gardener and urged on by the glorious sunshine she had hurried home to give the grass its third cut of the season. There would just be time, she'd surmised, to fit it in before her in-laws arrived. Their meal had already been taken care of: she had one of her home-baked pork pies lined up in the fridge, and the pastry had turned out deliciously golden and buttery – exactly as Philip liked it. With a salad prepared and new potatoes waiting to be boiled there had been practically nothing left to do. She'd only hoped that the subject they would be discussing would not spoil everyone's enjoyment of it.

Marjorie turned back two pages, wondering how many words her eyes had travelled over without her brain making any sense of them. Pork pie, indeed! If she'd only had the success of the meal to worry about!

Although the garden had slipped into shadow and was rapidly cooling to a chill, the sky remained light and high. A peacefulness lay over everything, save the odd bird flapping from tree to tree and chattering to its mate. She would have loved to carry on pottering about on what promised to be a heavenly evening, but Philip was due home any minute.

She'd opened the garage door in readiness for him, hurried into the house, and checked that his slippers were by the back door – this last duty being performed with a guilty glance over her shoulder, as though her daughters were in hiding, watching.

'*Mum!*' they would have chorused had they been there, raising their eyes at each other. They agreed on very little, being opposites in character, but on one thing they did concur: their mother was a hopeless case.

'This has nothing whatever to do with feminism,' Marjorie had vainly tried to advise them whenever they bemoaned the way she lavished attention on her man. 'It's simply a matter of common courtesy.' At which the girls would giggle behind their hands until their mother went on to remind them that she had carried out much the same little acts of loving kindness for them as well throughout their childhood, and didn't they intend to do the same for their families when they had them? She sincerely hoped they would.

Marjorie had often fretted after these exchanges, wondering what selfish little monsters she had brought into the world. Had she failed in her duty as a parent?

But, back in the kitchen and arranging the salad in a bowl, she'd consoled herself that the girls seemed to have turned out well enough after all: Becky *had* found herself a husband, in spite of her dreadful bossiness – a trait that she had unfortunately inherited from her grandfather. And Em, eighteen months her junior, had astonished them all by plumping for a 'caring' profession. She whose favourite back-chat throughout her teens had been 'see if I care', had suddenly decided to do precisely that. She was now in her final year at nursing college.

Marjorie crushed a sliver of garlic and whisked up a vinaigrette dressing, her thoughts suddenly changing track. Why hadn't Philip told her about Spittal's closing? She was sure he must have known before the local media got hold of it. Why had he kept it to himself?

Well, all right, she had kept her little secret from him, as Sheila had reminded her, but she didn't think him capable of doing the same. How well, though, could you ever know someone – even someone you had lived with for nearly twenty-five years? It was a disconcerting thought. She was still frowning when Philip's car swooped on to the drive.

It was soon apparent, by his slackened tie and the whiff of rotten apples on his breath, that he was guilty of something he rarely did: he'd been drinking on the way home.

'When did you find time to do that?' she asked, nodding toward the wrought iron clock above the kitchen table. The clock was in the shape of a sunburst and had jerked out the seconds for them with its distinctive throaty rasp since the day they'd moved in. Like the contents of the rest of the house it had a dated look about it, Phil's early distaste for materialism having stayed with him. Nothing was ever replaced in this house unless it fell apart – and even then Phil thought twice about it.

Marjorie had never much cared about the state of the house. As long as her garden was in immaculate order she was happy. Let one of the girls gouge a groove in the dining table and she would hardly turn a hair; let one of them drop a doll in her display of daffodils and she would turn purple.

'Find time to do what?' Philip was gazing up at the clock, not seeing any connection.

'Find time for drinks in the pub on your way home. You're only a few minutes later than usual.'

49

'Oh . . . there wasn't much going on at the office today, so I left a little early.' He shrugged off his jacket, hung it on the back of a chair and stood looking down at it. He slipped off his tie and coiled it. When he glanced up he had a lost look about him. It seemed he had something to say and had no idea where to begin.

Suddenly remorseful, because she'd been so busy thinking about herself that she hadn't realised quite what his firm's closure would mean to him, she went over and put her hands on his shoulders. 'Oh, Philip! Don't worry about how to tell me the news. I know about Spittal's already. I heard it on the radio. And I'm so sorry that it's had to happen to you; I know it must be a shock, but –'

'You know?' Alarm was plain in his eyes. 'Good grief . . . I suppose it was bound to get around. Honestly, love, I meant to tell you all about it myself. I wanted to break the news gently.'

'Well, now you've nothing to break. And your parents know about it as well. I went round and told your mother, and she'll have explained everything to your father. And they'll be here any minute, as it happens. I've asked them to come round so we can all have a talk about it.'

Philip pushed back his hair. It was thick, even if it was grey, and was unruly. Normally it didn't trouble him, unless he was ill at ease. Then he would rake it with his fingers or try to smooth it down. 'Talk?' he repeated slowly. 'About what?'

'About your redundancy, of course, and what

you're going to do now that Spittal's is closing. And about what we've all been thinking . . .'

Her voice trailed away at the sight of his grim expression. She put down the dish of coleslaw she'd been giving a quick stir, dropping the spoon with a clatter; suddenly it no longer seemed to matter that the mayonnaise dressing had collected at the bottom of the bowl.

'Spittal's isn't closing,' he said, his lips set hard in a line.

'Yes it is, Phil. I told you, I heard it on the radio.'

'No, Marjorie, no. It isn't, strictly speaking, closing.' Then he'd uttered the words that had sent a chill crawling up her spine. 'It's moving its premises to Bristol.'

Marjorie closed her library book and let it drop to her lap. All hell had broken loose a minute later when Eric and Sheila arrived for their meal. Phil had been horrified and angry at what they'd all been planning for him behind his back. Everything had come spilling out, even before they sat themselves down at the table – about how helpful Marjorie had been in the shops and how they'd decided she should take them over now that Eric wanted to retire – it was all laid bare.

Phil had turned an unpleasant shade of red, and had made it clear in no uncertain terms that it simply wasn't on. Neither he nor Marjorie would be able to take over the shops, he'd told them; he had to go to Bristol in accordance with his employers' wishes, and that was that. Redundancy?

51

Not for him, and he couldn't have afforded to take it anyway.

The pie was cut but no one enjoyed it. Marjorie had sat stony faced, Sheila pink and embarrassed, while Eric expressed his feelings at length and grew so agitated that he drank his wife's glass of wine by mistake as well as his own, and then helped himself to more. In the end Phil had to run them home in his own car because his mother's health prevented her from walking even the two blocks back to their house, and his father's swimming head prevented him from driving them himself.

Marjorie snatched up her book once more, Phil's return being heralded by the dull thud of a loose paving stone beneath the bedroom window. Propping the book open against her knees she tried to focus on the print. Perhaps, if she took no notice of him, he'd give the matter a rest. She'd made it clear that his plans didn't suit her; he just needed time for the fact to sink in.

But he couldn't leave the subject alone. He came into the room, walked round to her side of the bed and sat by her legs. She could no longer ignore him because she had to shift her balance on the mattress.

'Why on earth didn't you tell me?' he asked after a while.

'Tell you what?'

'About working for Dad all this time.' He gave an incredulous gasp as though he still couldn't take it in. 'What did you think you were doing?'

'What do you *think* I was doing? Helping out, of course.'

'I didn't mean that. I meant, what did you think you were up to, not telling me about it? I realised you helped my mother a lot, but I had no idea you were working practically full-time for my father too. You've made me look such a fool.'

Marjorie bunched up a piece of frill on the edge of the duvet cover, her hands beginning to tremble with suppressed anger. Could he think of nobody but himself? And couldn't he at least give her credit for the way she'd managed to pack so much in to each day? She'd obviously succeeded in making him feel as pampered and cosseted as he always had been – not an easy task on top of doing every-thing else – otherwise he'd have noticed something amiss.

'I always meant to tell you. I would have done . . . but it's your own fault, really. If you'd been more reasonable, where your father's concerned . . . And anyway I was bored with being at home all day. Couldn't you see that?'

'You never said you were bored.' He sounded miffed; insulted that being his wife hadn't been fulfilment enough for her.

'What would you have done if I had? Suggested I join the Women's Institute? I already belonged to that. And the Housewives' Register. And the PTA when the girls were still at school.' She gave an impatient shake of her head. 'These things are all very well, Phil . . . Oh, I suppose I just outgrew

53

them. I never meant to work for your father. It just sort of happened one day when he needed some help with his VAT.'

A weary sigh whined from him. 'It's made everything so much worse!'

Getting up from the bed he walked over to the window and looked out. Marjorie had been loath to close the curtains against the setting sun, but the huge orange ball had dropped behind the houses opposite some time ago and it was dark. Nevertheless, Phil still stood looking out.

'Fancy coming up with this crazy idea of taking over the shops! Don't you think you should have consulted me before putting impossible notions in Dad's head?'

'What's crazy about it?' She thumped her fists into the duvet. 'And why should it be impossible?'

'Well –'

'You're surely not implying that I'm incapable.'

'I didn't say that, now did I?'

'You didn't need to. It's what you were thinking, though, wasn't it?'

'I hadn't actually got that far. What I'm saying is . . . well . . . that you *can't*.'

'Well, of course I won't be able to *now*. Not if you insist on taking me to Bristol. But I wasn't to know about your plans beforehand, was I?'

'I didn't mean that, and you know it.'

'No?' Marjorie was lost. 'Well, what do you mean, then? I don't get it.'

But as she glared into his face she saw, to her

astonishment, that he'd adopted the taut, pitying expression that she recognised all too well. It was the one that came upon him only rarely, at such times as he could not avoid the usually unmentioned subject of her parents' demise.

Marjorie's mother and father had died from carbon monoxide poisoning fifteen years previously. A faulty water heater had been responsible, although Marjorie had never been able to look at it that way. She saw it as largely her fault and constantly blamed herself for not being in the right place at the right time.

To add to the horror of it all it had been Marjorie's misfortune to discover them. She had called round to see them one Saturday morning with some school photographs of Becky and Em. Fortunately the girls had not been with her – they were out doing 'ballet and tap'.

Certain that her parents would be at home she hadn't even taken a key. She had knocked and rung with no result and eventually spotted them through a window at the side of the house. The tableau was one that would for ever be printed on her mind: the pattern the sun was making on the black and white tiled floor, the day's post half-opened on one of the work-tops, two untouched cups of coffee on a wooden-handled tray, and the horribly familiar clothes that the two inert figures were wearing as they slumped together by the back door.

Later it was realised that the key had been removed from the keyhole, probably for safety reasons following a spate of burglaries in the area, and hidden under the biscuit tin. If Marjorie's parents had ever been conscious of their possible fate, the locked door and the missing key had effectively sealed it.

But, Marjorie now wondered, if this is what Phil was thinking about, what had it to do with her ability to run the shops? Unless . . . was he alluding to the fact that she had had a breakdown after the event? A perfectly understandable breakdown, surely, under the circumstances? And if so did he really think it had any bearing on her present-day capabilities?

It proved to be the case as his next remarks showed.

'The responsibility. The stress. The long hours . . .' he was saying.

'But I've been doing most of the work for months!' Oh, how exasperating he could be at times! He stifled her with his over-protectiveness. It was like being a child not allowed to grow up. A prisoner driven mad for escape. 'Phil, I really don't need molly-coddling like this. That was fifteen years ago. Just because I cracked up a little then, doesn't mean I can't handle a bit of stress. A certain amount of stress is essential in life. It keeps you on your toes and functioning. I *know* I can manage those shops.'

'Well, I'm afraid you won't get the chance to prove what you can do, one way or the other.' He drew the curtains across the window. 'And I won't be doing it either.'

'Phil!' She growled his name through clenched teeth. Her dream was slipping from her grasp. The shops had been her escape route – in fact, her only means of escape. Because what could possibly replace them? No one else on this earth would put her in charge of three shops. No one else would put her in charge of anything. She had no formal qualifications. No CV. She would never get past the first post.

Clutching at straws, she found herself willing to compromise where only hours before the idea had been abhorrent.

'Look,' she said putting one finger and a thumb to her temples where a muzziness signalled the start of a headache, 'OK, so you haven't been made redundant, but couldn't you resign from Spittal's instead of going down to Bristol? Then you'd be free to take over the shops and we could both run them together.'

'Oh really?' he scoffed. 'And live on what, may I ask? They don't bring in that much profit, you know – and there'd be four of us to support. Anyway, even if it were possible I could never take over from Dad. He simply wouldn't let me, and you know it.'

'But of course he –'

'He wouldn't. Not in reality. Oh, he'd willingly hand over the reins, I know that, but he'd still be there, breathing down my neck, telling me what to do. He would, you know he would.' Arms gesticulating he paced the room. 'You've no doubt experienced it for yourself. He can't keep out of it, can be? Can't trust anyone but himself. As soon as he's set you to carry out a task, he starts forcing himself in on the act.'

Marjorie's silence, her compressed lips, told him he was right. Working for Eric could be frustrating.

'You see, I do know what goes on in Dad's little empire; he made me work there in my holidays, remember? Even as a young lad I could see that staff turned over at an astonishing rate, and that managers came and went. I don't suppose anything's changed. Many's a time when you would have had to bite your tongue in front of him, Marjie, and try to smooth people out behind his back. Tell me if I'm wrong.'

But Marjorie couldn't do that. 'What you say is true,' she agreed, 'but I'm sure he'd stay out of the way now. He isn't a young man any more and he'll need to take things easy.'

Phil came back to the bed and fished under his side of the duvet for pyjamas. Finding none there he went to a drawer for a clean pair and began to undress.

It isn't fair, Marjorie thought morosely as his lean legs were stripped bare. Phil could eat what he liked – and he liked all the 'wrong' things – and still not put on any weight. He had much the same slim figure that he'd had the day they married, which was more than could be said about her. She slipped down on the pillows pulling the duvet up to her chin.

'No,' Phil went on, ferreting in the wardrobe for a trouser-hanger, 'what Dad should do is sell up and get out. Think about it intelligently: the shops are all too small and they're in the wrong places. "Little shops round the corner" are a thing of the past. People would rather drive out to a superstore any day. Get more choice and pay less.'

Marjorie sank further down the bed. What he was saying had a ring of truth. Each year was proving more of a struggle than the last, but only because Eric refused to get up to date. She felt sure there was room for a lot of improvement. But all Phil seemed to want to do was to go on banging nails into the coffin containing her dreams.

'And when he's sold them off – though who would want them now heaven only knows – he should invest whatever they bring in. If he's careful he should have enough money to buy professional care for the two of them for the rest of their lives.'

'So that you can wash your hands of them?' Marjorie was open-mouthed. To think that Phil could be so mean. Was it right that his parents should have to pay for care? Shouldn't it be provided freely by their children? But of course, the world wasn't like that any more, although she had thought Phil, being of the old school, would have seen things differently. Increasingly she had the feeling she no longer knew the man she had married.

She watched him screw up his underwear and toss it on to the heap in the bottom of the only built-in cupboard that the room possessed. In spite of his words she thought she could see him struggling with his conscience.

'I have no intention of washing my hands of anyone,' he said. 'I'll help them to find someone reliable to manage the shops so that Dad can retire if he really wants to, though I don't believe for a minute that he will, and we'll get someone to help Mum as well. OK? I shall always be around for them when there's a crisis.' He paused before shutting the cupboard door. 'Bristol isn't so very far away, you know.'

5

With the entire contents of their home somewhere between London and Bristol, Philip and Marjorie checked into a hotel for the night. Falling into what purported to be a four-poster bed – well, it did have four rough posts meagrely swathed in cheap curtaining – they groaned with exhaustion.

'Soon be there,' Philip said in the awful hearty tone he'd adopted ever since Marjorie's last bastions of defence had crumbled.

She had resisted this disruption in their lives with all her strength. Childishly she had at first adopted the attitude that if she ignored Phil's plans they would go away, but of course they hadn't. He'd continued to be as determined to move as she'd been to stay put. The arguments they'd had over the weeks! None of which had done any good.

She had had to leave everything in the end, because what alternative did she have? Break up the marriage and leave Phil – or bow to his judgement as per usual? But of course leaving him was unthinkable. She had loved him since the day she'd set eyes on him and still did.

She thought she'd lost him once, years ago when he'd gone off to university. Surely that was the end of their close, but entirely innocent and platonic friendship, she'd thought. Never would he return to her, still unattached, and see her in a romantic light. And yet the unlikely had happened. He'd sown his oats and come back to her.

What had been the attraction of 'the girl next door'? she had asked herself at times in later years. But she hadn't enquired too closely: she'd merely been grateful for the fact.

No, she could never leave her husband. But he did deserve to suffer a little for dragging her away from all that she knew and loved, so at the moment he was firmly consigned to the dog-house.

'Just think,' he went on remorselessly, 'tomorrow night we'll be sleeping in our brand new home.'

'In our dreadfully saggy old bed,' she grunted. Shame had seized them when the removal men, in full view of the neighbours, had carried out the cumbersome double divan. Neither of them had realised quite how decrepit it had become.

Perhaps Phil saw his wife in much the same way, Marjorie thought, adjusting her pillows for the night; she had been around so long he simply didn't notice her any more. Because if he looked at her with just one ounce of interest wouldn't he realise how unhappy he'd made her?

She'd tried to tell him, tried to explain her

feelings and her needs, but when she'd come out with words like 'escape' and 'challenge' it had sounded to him as though a move to new pastures was exactly what she needed. He'd even admitted somewhat sheepishly that he'd been feeling a need for change himself. He'd not been able to see – or hadn't wanted to see – that her ideas were not at all the same as his.

New pastures! Tears collected under her eyelids as she thought about her lovely old garden and Phil's apparent indifference to it. Maybe it had been stupid of her, but she had mown and clipped and tidied, right up to the last moment. Philip, seemingly so easily able to shed all his old attachments, had been irritated to find her dead-heading the last of the tulips while the men were carting the dustbin away.

'There won't be anyone here to appreciate your efforts,' he told her, gazing around for the last time at the immaculate scene. He might have been surveying crop-damage, judging by the look on his face. 'Anyway, the relocation company will be taking care of all this. It's their responsibility now.' He glanced up at the guttering as though, in accordance with sod's law, it might come clattering down at this crucial stage of the transaction and he would yet have to see to its repair. He really couldn't wait to turn his back on it all, it seemed.

Running a hand for the last time over the perfect globe of her favourite *Chamaecyparis obtusa 'Nana'*, Marjorie had doubted that anyone would lavish as much loving care on her prized specimens as she had. Over the years she had painstakingly cultivated every inch of the hundred-foot plot to create a miniature paradise. It was her proudest achievement – after the girls, of course.

When she and Phil had first moved in, the garden had contained only a rectangle of grass, one cherry tree, a grave-like island bed and a straight concrete path. It seemed inconceivable that a 1930s semi could have remained so unaltered throughout its previous ownership, but there it was. And it stayed that way for the first two years of their marriage. Philip had mown the lawn, when pressed, and Marjorie had weeded the bed.

Her passion for gardening had not begun until Becky's first summer. Having rocked the baby to silence in her pram, she would stretch herself out under the cherry tree beside her and try to grab a little sleep. But while her body craved rest from the hard work that one small child seemed to generate, her mind could not ignore her surroundings. She found herself longing to conceal the bare wood fence, to grow something against the house, to erect a trellis against a too-keen-to-gossip neighbour.

Soon she found herself doing more than pulling weeds. She scattered seeds, cadged cuttings, scraped money from the housekeeping for minuscule shrubs. And Philip was nagged into doing a bit more than just the mowing; he put up trellises, screened the dustbin, and relaid the path with stepping-stones. In time the garden took shape.

Now largely Marjorie's preserve since Phil had been far too busy in recent years, it was the envy of all who saw it . . . or had been.

A tear trickled towards her ear, threatening to dampen the hotel's lumpy pillow, and as she reached up to wipe it away Phil went on in his bright, bracing tone: 'It's going to be fun, you know.'

Lying snugly within the confines of the four-poster he set out his plans for their future life. There would be new places to investigate, new friends to be made, new neighbours to meet. A number of the neighbours would be Spittal's employees. 'Brightwells is so handy for them, you see.'

None of them was known to Marjorie though. The only Spittal's people she knew were the redundant ones being left behind in London. And new friends? How would they make new friends? It was something they hadn't had to do for a long time, and those they'd had up until now had been acquired with no conscious effort that she could recall. They'd just happened.

But she must stop this destructive line of thought; it wouldn't get her anywhere. Looking backwards was pointless. She must start addressing the future. Be positive. Take life by the scruff of the neck and make it work for her. Yes, that's what she would do: find herself a new role and build a whole new life. Somehow she must be able to claw her way back to the state of happiness and hope that had been hers until so recently. Couldn't she? Surely it wasn't that impossible?

And certainly her problems appeared less daunting the following morning as she spread sweet jelly-like marmalade on cold triangles of brittle toast. The sun was shining in a cloudless haze of blue, and she could almost feel in holiday mood as she gazed through the hotel window.

Phil drummed his fingers on his place mat, impatient to take her to the new house. 'First you complain they've brought the toast before you're ready for it,' he grumbled, 'then you wolf six slices.'

'Moving's given me an appetite,' she said, and went on crunching slowly.

'Aren't you keen to see the new house?' His eyes danced as though he had a huge, mysterious Christmas present waiting for her.

So far she had not set eyes on their new home. Philip had acquired it entirely on his own, having seen it briefly on a visit to his new place of work. Such had been Marjorie's resentment that she had steadfastly refused to go down to Bristol with him on that occasion, nor had she been anywhere near it since. She'd been curious about it, naturally, and now the thought of it gave her a fluttery sensation inside – what woman wouldn't feel stirrings of interest at the prospect of a brand new house? – but she wasn't going to let on to Philip.

She'd merely sniffed when he'd first shown her the artist's impression of Plot 19, The Paddock, Brightwells. He had thrust the estate agent's brochure at her the minute he'd arrived home from his trip, crossing his heart and swearing to die that the house he'd found for them looked just like the picture on the front. It was ready for immediate occupancy, too, he told her, the couple who'd originally intended buying it having dropped out, and the builders had set an incentive to exchange contracts within a month – an incentive that Phil told her he was keen to take advantage of.

'Why have the couple dropped out?' Marjorie asked, drying her hands on the kitchen towel and studying the picture. It was a classy-looking place, admittedly, and she quite liked *looking* at houses even though she had no intention of moving out of the one she was in, so she took the details into the through-room and spread them about her on the settee.

Phil followed her like an eager puppy. 'I don't know why they dropped out, exactly. The agent didn't say. People do change their minds, you know.'

'Not usually at so late a stage,' Marjorie argued. She smelt a rat already. There must be something wrong with it, although it certainly looked fine on paper.

'A spacious lounge,' she muttered to herself, skipping through the blurb, 'ample dining room *and* a Victorian-style conservatory?' Not only that but a study, too, where Phil could keep his astronomy books. And the kitchen was an absolute knockout. Enjoying cooking as much as she did, it was hard not to feel a thrill.

She studied her husband for a moment. 'You say those people had even chosen the bathroom tiles, and all the fittings and carpets?'

'Yes, yes, they had. But nothing we wouldn't have chosen ourselves. That's the beauty of it all: we could move in straight away.' His eyes glazed over. 'Just imagine! No more worries about this jerry-built heap. No more patching up the roof, or the dodgy bit of guttering round the back . . .'

'Bit on the pricey side for the provinces, isn't it?'

Phil waggled his hand judiciously. 'So-so.'

Marjorie frowned; events felt as though they were racing along at a rate of knots beneath her reluctant feet. Phil had told her the other day that they wouldn't even have to sell their own house before buying the new one: the relocation company would take it on. All they had to do once the legal side had been completed was to move out with their furniture.

He'd been drip-feeding her such tit-bits of information for days by then, no doubt hoping to wean her towards full acceptance of his plans. Aware of his tactics, she had armoured herself well against them.

'You can manage to afford this –' she flapped the brochure '– but you can't afford to go in with your father? I don't quite see your logic.'

'I've told you a hundred times –'

'*Three* bathrooms? *Three?*' She pounced on a black and white room plan. 'What would we need three bathrooms for?' In her mind's eye she saw a lorry load of Harpic trundling up to the front door, a trailer of toilet rolls dragging behind. 'And five bedrooms!' she gasped. It would be like running a boarding house. She looked up at her husband as though he had taken leave of his senses.

'You were worried about leaving our friends,' he reminded her. 'Well, that's why we'll need extra rooms – for when they come down to visit us. And for the girls, of course.'

'Our friends?' Marjorie snorted. 'If Beth and Tom are anything to go by we'll never see any of them again.'

The house details forgotten for a moment, Marjorie stared into space. 'I simply don't understand it. Beth and Tom were so . . . well, uppity, I thought, when we saw them the other day.'

They had met up by accident at a mutual friend's house the day after Spittal's closure was announced, and the minute Tom and Beth had put in an appearance the atmosphere had noticeably chilled. Naturally Spittal's plans had been first on the list for discussion, but Tom and Beth had stood to one side looking awkward, even frosty, and had hardly attempted to join in.

Marjorie had come away puzzled and not a little hurt. Philip had gone quiet too, so she presumed he was feeling the same. 'It's almost as if they were jealous of us,' she remarked on their way home in the car, 'jealous because you've been given the opportunity to move with the firm and Tom hasn't. Funny, I never would have thought they could be like that. Would you?' But Philip, offering no comment, simply stared at the road ahead.

Marjorie had smiled grimly; she would have liked to reassure Beth that she'd be delighted to change places with her any day, and would have said as much if it had just been the two of them having a cosy chat, without Phil there, ready to glare his disapproval. As it was, she had pretended a resigned acceptance of her fate and said little.

Turning back to the brochure she wondered what Beth would do if confronted with a huge new Tudor-style house at Brightwells. She peered more closely at the artist's impression and feigned an innocent expression

'What sort of trees are these?' She knew that as far as new gardens went, two rolls of turf and some chicken wire were all you were likely to be given.

Phil fixed her with his most quelling expression. 'You have to plant those yourself.'

'This one's bigger than the garage.' She jabbed her finger at a large, impossibly green willow tree, arching over a perfect lawn. There were none of those messy bits of twig and leaf lying about underneath it either. 'Take all day to dig a hole for a tree like that,' she scoffed, 'and then you'd need ten men.'

'Marjorie. Please. Don't be tiresome. I know you're going to miss the garden here, but just think what you could do with this plot. You'd have a whole new canvas to make your mark on.' He rustled through the leaflets in search of a plan of the entire 'paddock'. 'Look, the garden's going to be a bit smaller than we're used to, I know, but you've been saying lately that this one will soon be too much for you to keep up with, and I'm sure you could make the new one just as nice . . .'

'Oh yes, I'm sure I could. Given twenty-odd years and a fortune. We'd have to go back there on day trips from our nursing home to see how it was all coming along.'

Phil flung down the specifications.

'I can see there's no pleasing you,' he snapped. 'I don't know why I bother to try.'

She jumped up from the settee. 'You know how you can please me,' she wailed back at him. 'You can tell me we're staying put. You know how I hate the thought of moving. At our time of life it's ridiculous. And you know how much I'll miss my lovely garden. I'll miss all our friends as well!'

She stood up, letting the brochure and its contents scatter. 'You don't seem to give a damn about me any more. You don't give a damn about anyone. All you think of is yourself.'

Tears had not been far away. She'd stormed back into the kitchen where she had been scrubbing the grids from the cooker and started clanging them about.

It must have sounded as though the bells of hell had been let loose, Marjorie thought as she popped the last piece of toast into her mouth. She put down her knife, wiped her fingers on her napkin and sat up straight. The moment could be delayed no longer. Her new life was about to begin.

Sunshine warmed the back of Jade's neck as she paused in front of the antique shop. She hadn't meant to come down this street today. She need not have done so. The firm of Bath solicitors for whom she worked could be reached just as easily by any number of back street routes. And yet here she was, balanced on the balls of her feet as a gesture towards making her stop a brief one, but knowing full well that she would not. She had passed this window before and knew that in the middle of the tasteful display sat a wonderful Moorcroft vase. A vase that she fiercely coveted.

Her eyes gleamed; her lips parted. A hunger gnawed at her stomach. Oh, but it would look so good in their little hallway! The yellow ochre of the walls and the tones of the rug that she had chanced upon last month at the antiques market, would complement it perfectly. She had to have it!

Her ankles relaxed; her heels touched the pavement. The decision had been made. Fending off a fleeting vision of Oliver's dark displeasure she swivelled one fashionable navy blue loafer towards the entrance to the shop, and the other quickly followed.

OK, she told herself as she pushed on the heavy glass, so it costs a lot of money. A hell of a lot. Far more than I ought to lash out. But it's my own money, isn't it? What's it to do with Oliver?

It was almost as though she were echoing her sister's words of the previous day. Jade had complained to Selina that recently Olly seemed to be growing twitchy with regard to her spending too much money and that he hadn't been like that when she'd first met him.

'What's it to do with him?' Selina had said, adding rather nastily, Jade thought, 'Don't tell me your blinkers are wearing out. I always wondered what on earth you saw in him.'

Jade had glared back at the shorter, dumpier version of herself and not answered. But she had sometimes wondered the same thing herself. What had she seen in him? Especially after that crazy speech of his, when he had suggested they move in together. The conditions he'd set down!

Right at the beginning she had had no doubt as to his attractions: intelligence, energy, ambition. He was a mature man with knowledge of the wider world, and she couldn't abide silly, inexperienced boys just starting out in life. He might be a bit on the short side, admittedly, but she'd never liked wearing high heels anyway. And he did have rather nice dark sweeping eyelashes.

But that speech! Eyelashes notwithstanding, she had nearly ditched him there and then. Strangely it was his honesty that had stopped her; his frankness and his 'openness'. How refreshingly, wonderfully different he was!

In those early days he'd been generous with presents too – remarkably so, since he had an almost-ex wife and two children lurking in the wings. They must be making demands on his salary, she guessed, even though he was earning quite well. But he still managed to make her feel cherished.

She didn't like to dwell too much on Oliver's past. He rarely mentioned it himself. And while it was a little disconcerting to think that he'd ditched his whole family, she had the impression that it was not something he had done lightly or without good reason. His ex must have been pretty awful to him, mustn't she, to have merited being dumped like that? It wasn't as though Oliver had had someone else lined up either; it was only months after the event that he'd met Jade.

Having thought over Oliver's crazy speech for a little while she had realised that what he was proposing might suit her. After all, the last thing she wanted was to be tied down. She didn't want the complications of marriage and children because of the career she planned to pursue. She could quite understand that Oliver might have had enough of that level of commitment too. And while the thought of 'other partners' was a bit hard to swallow, at least she would know where she stood.

All in all it seemed a sophisticated, responsible, modern and thoroughly practical idea. The way things were heading everyone would be going in for detailed marriage contracts before long, so why not 'living together' contracts too? Infinitely sensible. With both eyes wide open, where could she go wrong?

But she hadn't bargained for him turning miserly the way he had. Well, to hell with Oliver's meanness . . .

Within ten minutes Jade had secured the Moorcroft vase and made the fawning young salesman's day – not to mention her own.

Godfrey Hart, her boss – a gentle, quiet man in his early sixties – was less thrilled. He had expected Jade in the office over an hour ago. In the ordinary course of events he wouldn't have minded so much, only today she was supposed to have sat in on an interview with a particularly interesting client in order to gain valuable experience.

He would have liked to point out, too, that since her flat, in one of the lesser-known Georgian crescents, was but a stone's throw from the premises of Hart, Bruce and Thomson, she really ought to be able to get to work on time. Particularly as other members of staff managed perfectly well, though they had to commute into town.

But he was a weak individual where Jade was concerned. Her wide-eyed delight in her purchase, in the sparkling spring morning and in life in general, rendered him, as usual, powerless. All he could find in his heart to say as she proudly held out her vase for his approval was, 'That's really beautiful, my dear. Shall I lock it away in the safe?'

6

Marjorie wound down the passenger window for a closer look. 'Yes, that's definitely a brick wall out there. No doubt about it.'

Philip ground his teeth. He had had about enough of Marjorie's sarcasm lately, her hurtful little jibes. And she had obviously made up her mind not to like the house, no matter what its merits might be. Resting his elbow on the sill of his own open window he rubbed a hand over his mouth. He mustn't let himself be drawn into an argument when on unsafe ground, he told himself. Marjorie had every right to find fault with things; she had never wanted this move. It was all down to him. He just wished she would keep quiet about every little setback, although even her silences somehow managed to convey disapproval.

'Well, there wasn't a wall here before,' he snapped, unable to keep tetchiness from his tone. He loosened a button on his shirt. Although not yet mid-morning the car was already uncomfortably warm. The thermometer on the dashboard showed that the outside air temperature was unusually high for late spring and he wondered, as he surveyed the garish red brickwork silhouetted against the powdery blue of the sky, whether they were in for a scorching summer.

'I suppose,' he said, having turned the car in the lane, 'the woman from the site office brought me to see the house this way as a short cut.' Canny bitch, he added silently. She'd certainly seen him coming! A lot of building had been done since that visit, none of which he had been aware of at that time. And now that he could see the way the development was going he realised that nobody in their right mind would want to spend the price being asked, to live on such a cluttered site. It would have been far better to have gone for something more exclusive. Aloud he said, 'That wall must belong to our garden. Look, you can see our roof on the other side.'

Marjorie craned her head for the first glimpse of their new home as the car bumped back down the lane. The roof – their roof – with its rows of raw brown tiles, looked solid enough even for Philip's peace of mind; the black plastic drainpipes equally so. She must try to like it for his sake. It wasn't fair of her to keep longing for their old place when it had been such a worry to him.

She would try not to spoil his pleasure, really she would, and it could only be half an hour, after all, since she'd made vows to herself about being positive. How quickly her intentions had slipped!

But it wasn't easy. Her trepidation was increasing with each passing minute

Having rediscovered the site office, Philip took his bearings and set off down what they soon realised must be the main and only thoroughfare into the estate, and as he drove, the silence that accumulated in the car with the passing of each block of houses, pressed down on them.

Marjorie found a song running through her head. What were the words? Something about little boxes made of ticky-tacky. She recalled it from years ago but its message, sadly, had not reached the ears of the architects. She glanced across at Philip, who had his hands fixed doggedly on the steering wheel, and wondered whether he was finding it difficult not to turn the car round again and head back the way they had come.

'Didn't see any of this lot,' he managed to murmur, 'when the woman showed me the house. Think some hedges must have been ripped out too.'

'Oh?' Marjorie lifted her eyebrows as she looked from side to side. It was hard to imagine how all these houses could have escaped Phil's notice, hedges or not. There were hundreds of them. Simply hundreds. Spreading in every direction. And yet the plans they had been given had shown only fifteen in all. A select little development, they'd supposed The Paddock to be.

'I thought . . .' she began to put her question to Phil but he anticipated her.

'Obviously there are other builders here. Ones I

knew nothing about. Of course, they don't show you those on your plans.'

'No, but –' Her tone implied that he should have made more enquiries. Heavens, couldn't he have *seen* what was going on? 'Somehow –' she scrutinised the plots more closely '– they don't exactly look as though different builders put them up. I suppose they *are* different in little ways, but overall they tend to look much of a muchness. Even ours isn't all that different from what I remember seeing in the brochure. Where is it now, by the way?'

They were speeding away from the completed properties now, bumping over rutted mud left behind by countless works vehicles. The unmetalled road continued its relentless march across a pot-holed field and Philip followed it, his eyes fastened on the horizon. And now Marjorie realised that the solitary house looming ahead of them was their new home – the only one of that particular phase to have been built.

'What's happened to the rest of The Paddock?' she demanded, bewilderment setting in.

The car had come to a halt on a slab of bare concrete which would be their drive when the work was finished, only at the moment it fell two feet short of the garage and didn't quite meet the road. Twin panelled doors faced them beneath a grand pointed roof; their cars – Phil had promised her a new one – would be sheltered in a detached property of their own, large enough to house several homeless families. But that, and the adjacent house, were the only buildings around them.

'This is the first of The Paddock to go up,' Phil said, patting his pockets to locate the keys to the front door. 'The builders'll start work on the rest of them as soon as people put down their names.'

'You mean, we have no neighbours yet?' Adopting the attitude of a stranded sailor Marjorie shielded her eyes and squinted at the 'ticky-tacky' estate shimmering through the heat haze in the distance. Civilisation lay miles away across a sea of reddish, dried-up mud. 'How many people have put their names down?'

'Really, Marjie, I can't be expected to know everything, can I? Look, I've found the keys now. Let's go inside. I'm sure you're going to be thrilled when you see this.'

And she was. She had to admit it. She fell in love with the kitchen at first sight; couldn't wait to unpack her utensils and start cooking something. But Phil, laughing his first real laugh for weeks, took her hand and wouldn't let her put her head in another cupboard until she had seen everything else. By the time they returned to the kitchen her cheeks were flushed with excitement.

If only he'd thought about the boiler!

'Oh, Phil . . .'

He turned from his investigation of the fuse box to find her pale and trembling behind him. Moisture gleamed on her lip. Her complexion resembled candle wax.

She pushed him into the utility room and showed him the white appliance on the wall. 'It *is* a gas one, isn't it?' Their previous house had been 'all electric', which had suited Marjorie just fine. She had managed to overcome her fear of gas sufficiently to enter other buildings where it was installed, but she couldn't bear the thought of it in her own. The lighting of it, the way it blipped into life, the roar of it under a grill – none of this could she bear to contend with.

'Oh, Marjie, I meant to warn you.' But clearly he hadn't given it a thought. In his efforts to get her to make the move at all it hadn't even entered his head.

'How could you?' she whispered. 'How could you?'

'I'm sorry, really I am . . . don't look at me as though I've done this deliberately. But it's all new and perfectly safe. Look, we can have special detectors fitted.' He tried to take her in his arms. 'What happened to your mother and father – it'll *never* happen to us.'

But he knew that that wasn't the point. Marjorie could do without gas appliances as a constant reminder. So could he as well if he were honest with himself. Marjorie wasn't the only one still haunted by the event; nor was she the only one to have the occasional nightmare. The whole family still suffered. Naturally it had been worse for Marjorie as she had been the one to find them, but he'd been devastated too. He had known her parents for most of his life and a lovely couple they'd been. Then there had been the two girls, mere youngsters at the time, who couldn't begin to understand. And his own parents who had lost good friends. And the milkman had been so cut up about it because he thought he should have noticed something, and – well – the list went on and on.

Phil looked up from his morbid musings to glimpse the removal van trundling towards the house across the landscape which, only a few minutes previously, they had been looking down upon from the landing window and jokingly nick-named the Red Sea. There was nothing more he could say to Marjorie now, or do for her, except suffer a gross black mark for his gaff and get on with the work in hand.

'Your money,' Oliver said flatly that evening, watching Jade as she swept aside a Tiffany lamp that had been a 'must have' four months ago, but which was now apparently out of favour, and installed the vase in its place.

'That's right.' She darted a chilly glance at him, noticing that he'd already changed for the country club. Leaning against the door frame in his track suit he looked full of pent-up vitality, but hard-faced and narrow-eyed as well.

'Do you mean you bought this with your salary or with the savings from your modelling work?' he went on in the tone she'd come to know so well: the tone that was ninety per cent geniality but ten per cent heavy sarcasm. 'Because the first can't possibly cover it and the second's been spent ten times over.'

Jade's pleasure in her purchase drained away. She flounced into the bedroom and began stripping off her navy suit. 'Trust you to take the fun out of everything.'

She was well aware that her savings had long since gone. Did Oliver have to keep reminding her? He'd even begun to hint that perhaps she should take up modelling again, do a bit in her spare time to help cover her expensive life-style. What spare time? she asked herself, pulling a leisure suit over her bra and pants.

She picked up a brush and ran it down the long shafts of her hair, then clipped back the two front sections of hair with blue combs. Suddenly she looked ten years younger than her twenty-six. Yes, she thought without conceit, checking her reflection in the glass, she could certainly still do some sort of modelling work if she wanted to. But she didn't want to. She'd had more than enough of all that.

She had begun a career in modelling at eighteen when she left school. It had been entirely her mother's idea. Her mother had practically pushed her into it because she had always wanted to be a model herself, instead of which she had become pregnant before she left school and had to marry Jade's father.

Jade had gone along with the idea at first, being

attracted by the possibility of making a little money to set her on her feet. Pointless to expect her no-good father to give her a start in life; he'd never had a bean himself. Well, not for long anyway. And perhaps she owed her mother something for the struggle she'd had bringing up Selina and herself; with their father flitting in and out of their lives she'd had a rotten time of it. Dad had drifted in when he needed money to fritter on horses and out again when he'd cadged all he could.

On leaving school Jade hadn't decided what she wanted to do with her life. It wasn't modelling, she knew that as soon as her mother suggested it. Modelling, she was inclined to believe, was not all it was cracked up to be. But it would be something to be going on with – just supposing she could actually find someone prepared to take her on . . .

To her surprise, the first agency to which her mother accompanied her accepted her without hesitation. The agent could hardly believe her luck as she eyed Jade up and down. It wasn't every day that a girl of this calibre walked in off the street. She promised Jade great things and apparently knew what she was talking about. By the end of Jade's first year, work was flooding in at such a rate that she could pick and choose what she did.

Someone suggested she ought to apply to a bigger agency in London, and soon after taking that advice Jade found herself smiling from the covers of increasingly glossy magazines. There was talk of the big fashion shows – London, Paris and New York.

She knew she wasn't happy with what she was doing but she threw herself into the work, telling herself all the time how lucky she was. Her mother kept telling her, too. Millions of girls would give anything to be in her shoes, she was constantly reminded, and just think of the money she was making! Jade, though feeling trapped, could only agree. She found it impossible to call a halt. With so little time to stop and take stock of herself she couldn't plan what she wanted to do next.

Time ticked on and Jade did nothing to alter the course of events, but after three years of hectic schedules and living out of suitcases she began, to her mother's chagrin, to make real noises of discontent. Jade questioned what they were doing, fell into gloomy silences and continually dragged her heels.

During one particular scramble behind the scenes she found herself in a space that would have confounded a pixie, having to wriggle out of one complicated and – in her opinion – ghastly outfit, into another equally hideous creation, and emerge looking beautifully immaculate. Inside she was screaming with frustration. This, she decided, was ridiculous; this was not the way she wanted to spend one more minute of her life.

'It's degrading, superficial and monotonous,' she told her mother later. 'A nonsensical way to live. In fact it isn't life at all. And what will I do when my looks fade? What shall I have to fall back on?'

Besides, she didn't like the way 'normal' people regarded her – like some kind of mindless freak. Especially men. To them she was so much meat and didn't have a brain, whereas in reality she knew she was bright and intelligent.

'I've decided to jack it all in,' she'd announced, wiping off her make-up for the last time. 'I'm going to do something in law.'

Oliver had been standing in the tall bay window overlooking the street, his thoughts presumably still on money. 'Perhaps, we should come back here to eat after we've been to the club,' he suggested. 'Is there anything left in the fridge?'

Jade made a face in the mirror. 'Even if there is I don't feel like cooking it. I'll feel even less like it after advanced aerobics.'

'But –' Oliver got no further. Down in the street a dark green van had been cruising backwards and forwards along the crescent. Now, having abandoned hope of finding a parking space the driver stopped in the middle of the road, jumped out and began to unload large flat packs of frozen food. Oliver read the words *Gardiner's Gourmet Foods* that were stretched along the side of the van in gold Gothic print.

'Have *you* been ordering food?' He turned to Jade as the bell for their flat was pressed.

'And don't you think you've overdone it a bit?' he put to her five minutes later. He couldn't help grinning at his impossible girlfriend across the growing stack of boxes. Even he, in his current drive for economy, was enjoying the prospect of plenty, the warm Christmassy feeling that the sight of so much good food induced.

He had only had a ham-on-the-bone sandwich for lunch and his eyes bulged as the delivery man dumped trays of fat pink juicy prawns on top of thick-cut rashers of bacon. Ready-made meals of *coq au vin* soon topped dainty lamb noisettes. *Boeuf bourguignon* followed poussins packed in rows; duck breasts joined shoals of rainbow trout.

'Grief!' Oliver muttered when he saw the invoice, but Jade, already signing for the goods, was dismissive of the cost.

'I beg your pardon, Olly, but we do have to eat,' she was quick to remind him as she began to cram the stuff into the freezer, 'and now at least we've something for tonight. How about these two portions of *boeuf en croûte*?' She held them up like weights.

'Wonderful. That only leaves us with precisely forty-six portions to get through.' He snatched up the invoice. 'Forty-six beef Wellingtons, four dozen *coqs au vin*, and God knows how many of those titchy little chickens by your feet. Really, Jade, how long do you expect all this lot to keep?'

But Jade refused to have the stupidity of her extravagance pointed out to her. When the leaflet advertising the delivery scheme had dropped through the letter box it had seemed a brilliant idea.

She still thought it was. No more trips to the supermarket! She hadn't imagined it could work out so expensive but . . .

There was no doubt about it: as far as money was concerned Olly was becoming a pain.

7

Damn!

Philip cursed himself repeatedly as he made his way to Spittal's new premises. It was his first morning in the Bristol job and he'd not left home in a good mood. How come he'd overlooked this business with the gas supply? He wished to goodness he hadn't, particularly right now.

Anxious to impress his boss, he had decided not to take any more time off work than was absolutely essential for moving; consequently, just when he felt he should be supporting Marjorie through the trauma that he had undoubtedly stirred up again, he found himself compelled to leave her to struggle on alone with a colossal headache and packing cases everywhere.

The last thing he needed at the moment was a wife on the verge of cracking up. Now, if she only had a friend or two – a little company to rely on – it would be useful. Then he wouldn't have to worry about her so much. Could he somehow help her in that direction?

Pushing on the massive doors of the tall silver and glass building that now housed Spittal's employees he resolved to do something for Marjorie if he could. After all, he needed her, almost as much as she needed him. She was the one who made sure everything in their private life ran smoothly.

He was never without clean socks, for example, and she kept the home neat and comfortable. She remembered people's birthdays, dealt with Christmas as though it were a military campaign, packed him off to the dentist at regular intervals and sent his suits to the cleaners in rotation. She was a good cook, too, when it came to the entertaining that his job required of him from time to time, and managed very well as long as she remembered to let him do most of the talking and tried not to voice an opinion.

He glanced across the building's tiled concourse, appreciative of its airy ambience and palm-like plants that stood the height of modest trees. Yes, this was a smart move on Spittal's part, he decided: far better accommodation than the old place, convenient for rail and air links as well as lying close to the M4 corridor: ideal for their plans for expansion. And just the shot in the arm that he needed personally to put back the sparkle in his eye.

Pressing the button for the fourth floor, he rehearsed the coming scene in his mind. He had, of course, already met his new colleagues but could hardly claim to be well acquainted with them. His brief visit had left him with only a sketchy impression.

He certainly remembered Oliver Knox, though, as the short dark man sprang forward to greet him. That knuckle-grinding hand-shake of his was obviously designed to show the world what a tough little nut he really was in spite of his lack of height. But it didn't fool Philip. And that all-too-wide-to-be-true smile of Jocelyn Hemmingway-Judd . . . no, that didn't endear him much either.

Suppressing a shiver of apprehension he allowed Oliver to reacquaint him with the room he'd been allocated – Spittal's disapproved of open-plan offices – then listened with half an ear to his platitudinous speech of welcome before dismissing him as quickly as was decently possible.

'I'll be keeping my head down for most of the day – er, Oliver – reading through some paper work.' He laid a hand on top of a pile already awaiting him on the desk. 'So I'll not be needing anything much today. Tomorrow, perhaps, we can get together for a chat and see where we carry on from there.'

'Fine,' Oliver said with a firm nod of his head, sounding for the first time in Philip's short experience of dealing with him as if he genuinely meant what he said. No doubt their feelings for each other were mutual and he was glad to make his escape.

Phil had already summed up the younger man

as an obnoxious little turd with a chip on his shoulder as big as a telegraph pole, and all because he had not been given a promotion when he thought he deserved one. Quite a ridiculous attitude, in Phil's opinion, because Oliver had already progressed rapidly in his short career. He was a whiz-kid with a great talent for the job – a talent that had served him well even though he had few qualifications on paper. Why couldn't he be satisfied with what he'd achieved? It had taken Phil years of study and patient plodding to get where he was today.

Oliver left the room with alacrity, shutting the door behind him in a way that Phil found particularly irritating. Instead of turning the handle to move the catch, thus causing the least possible noise, he'd jerked it hard against the mechanism so that it *ker-plunked* into place.

Must be getting old, Phil told himself, frowning at the wood-stained door. Or was he just unlucky with his new colleagues? It wasn't only Knox he had to deal with. How about this Hemmingway-Judd? Could he ever get along with him? Rumour had it that he was a highly moral and principled man. Well, maybe. But he hadn't exactly struck Phil as someone he could immediately take a shine to.

He couldn't imagine himself, for example, confiding to him that he thought the National Lottery a good thing and put a fiver on it every week. Or that in spite of his private education he had never actually read *War and Peace*. Or that he preferred old Beatles' hits to opera and made sure he never missed *The X Files* on TV.

As for working with so righteous a mortal ... well, he suspected it would be like treading egg-shells all the time: say the wrong thing, or crack a joke that might be misconstrued as being in the least bit blue, and heaven help you.

Drawing the pile of paper towards him Philip shook his head. What a pair! Talk about being between the devil and the deep blue sea. With one thing and another he was going to have to be on his toes.

He flipped the corners of a thick report, the little ripping sound so satisfying that he did it several times. It was better than reading the stuff, anyway.

But wait a minute. Why bother ploughing through it all? Rather than banish young Oliver to his room, why not put him through his paces? See what he really knows? Now *that* was a good idea.

When Philip had brought Marjorie a cup of tea that morning she'd been lying flat out in bed with a cold mask strapped over her eyes. Her headache threatened to be a real humdinger.

'You can manage all right on your own?' he'd asked anxiously, placing a glass of water and two pills beside the tea.

Marjorie lifted a corner of the mask to chill him with one eye. Since he could hardly miss his first day at the new office there was little he could have done about it if she'd said no.

'I expect I'll be all right,' she sighed. So long as she didn't blow herself up trying to light the gas hob, or suffocate for the sake of having hot water. She still couldn't believe he had gone ahead so thoughtlessly and bought a gas-run home. Now, trying to limit the damage, he was drowning her in a deluge of his remorse, pussy-footing around her as though she might disintegrate.

The gas wasn't the limit of his guilt: the telephone that he'd promised her would be installed immediately, had failed to materialise. To be fair it wasn't his fault, but he was behaving as though it was.

The site foreman had crossed the Red Sea at knocking-off time the previous evening expressly to inform them that there was a slight hitch over the telephone cable.

'Don't tell me!' Phil had said wearily, worn out with the problems of the day. 'You haven't put one in.'

'Oh, we put one in all right,' came the cheerful reassurance, 'but it's yet to be connected to the system.' And he couldn't say when that would happen.

It was a good job, Marjorie decided as she drained the last of the tea, that Phil had gone to the office; at least any news about Becky could reach him there.

Would it though? Something was bound to go wrong; she'd had a premonition about it right from the start, that they wouldn't be available when needed. Wasn't it dreadful of them, she'd argued with Phil, to leave Becky when she was about to present them with their first grandchild? How could he think of such a thing? But he'd pointed out that Becky herself had no such qualms about their moving away, so why should she?

Unfortunately it had appeared to be true.

'There's no need to worry about *me*, Mum,' Becky had said one day before the move, following a shopping trip. 'You've enough to think about, with going to Bristol.'

Bending with difficulty she'd rolled herself into her father's favourite chair, where she'd sagged like a shapeless bean bag, her breath coming fast with the effort of bringing an assortment of carrier bags from the car that she'd parked only yards away at the roadside.

'But I do worry about you,' Marjorie told her, wondering how much more her daughter could expand; she was already huge and still had several weeks of her pregnancy to go. She lifted Becky's feet and shoved a stool underneath for support. 'And it's only a *possible* move. Nothing's settled yet.' At the time she'd still held hope of a miracle.

'Well, Dad seems to think –'

'Bristol, indeed. I ask you! I don't know what your father's thinking of, wanting us to move down there. And how will you manage when the baby comes – without me, I'd like to know?'

'Well, I can always send for Steve's mum, can't I? She's only a mile away.' Becky scraped back a strand of hair and began tucking it into the short plait she wore at the nape of her neck. Intent on the task, and perhaps forgivably absorbed in her 'condition', she'd given little thought to her words; not noticed how her mother had winced at them.

Marjorie twisted her wedding ring round. She didn't want Becky to call on anyone but herself, and was amazed that the girl could consider such a thing. Steve's mother, Elaine, was of course entitled to an equal interest in the affair – she would be the other grandmother after all – but the thought that she might be first on the scene was totally inconceivable.

All Marjorie's competitive and jealous instincts came rushing to the fore. *She* wanted to be the first to see the new baby, the first to hold it, the one to be ready with advice. The idea of someone sharing the event was just about bearable, but the possibility of Elaine ruling the roost while she, Marjorie, was stuck miles away down the motorway when the baby arrived, was not to be borne at all.

The more Marjorie thought about it the worse the scenario became. With her and Phil in Bristol the child would see far more of Steve's parents as it grew up than it would of them. Jim and Elaine would be popping in and out all the time; the child would be bound to grow to love them almost as much as it loved Becky and Steve. It would be they, not Phil and herself, who would bask in the first smile; they who would spot the first tooth. They would feel the chubby little arms around their necks, relish the first wet kiss, hear the first attempt to say Nan-nan. They would witness the struggle to sit up, the first toddling steps. Oh! Marjorie's heart twisted over in her chest.

And no matter how many visits she and Phil fitted in, there would never be enough. She would not be able to strike up anything like the same rapport. She could picture the child now on one of their rare visits, staring up at them with tear-filled eyes, its lower lip trembling because it had no idea who they were.

'I know you can call on Elaine,' Marjorie said, trying hard to keep a whine of self-pity from her voice, 'but – but it isn't quite the same, is it? I mean, wouldn't you prefer me to be there when the baby comes? To help and – you know – everything. That was always the plan.'

Becky looked up sharply then, her mother's tone bringing contrition to her lips. 'Oh, yes, Mum! Of course I do! And you *will* be there, won't you? Dad's already promised you that.' Anxious to escape the subject, she began to poke about in her shopping bags, brought out a baby's sleeping-suit and spread it over her 'bump'.

'Do you think this is going to be big enough? It looks so very wee.' She glanced up again to find her mother still full of fear and doubt. The subject wasn't easily dismissed. 'Look, Dad said that the minute you get the signal from me or Steve he'll have you both in the car before you know what's hit you. You'll be back here long before the baby puts in an appearance, and you won't have missed a thing.'

'I'm not so sure . . .' Not wanting to cast a gloom over the forthcoming event Marjorie tried hard to see it all happening that way. Babies, though, were a law unto themselves. 'But supposing . . . oh, any number of things could prevent me reaching you in time: it's almost bound to happen in the middle of the night, isn't it? Or maybe more quickly than a first one usually does. Or anything.'

She rubbed her forehead. Oh, she'd had all this argument with Phil but he wouldn't listen, any more than Becky seemed to want to listen. Becky obviously thought her a fuss-pot. Making something of nothing.

Marjorie had been counting on both her daughters as allies in her battle to stay put, but Em, over the phone from her hall of residence at college, had barely expressed any interest in where her parents chose to live, let alone raised objections.

'Go for it, Mum,' was how Em had greeted the news. 'It's time you both had a change of scene.'

Becky was now saying, 'In a way, I'd like to know whether to buy blue or pink for the baby.' She stroked the impossibly small white garment with its appliquéd fleecy lamb. 'But I also want it to be a surprise. Do you think we were right to say we didn't want to be told the sex? What would you have said?

'And,' she went on, 'how hard should I resist if

they tell me I ought to be induced, do you think? I mean, how will I know whether it's absolutely vital for the baby's sake, or they're just saying that so that they can be sure of a free weekend?'

Marjorie dragged her mind round to considering these questions. She guessed that Becky had only put them to her in a belated attempt at making her feel needed and involved. Unfortunately all the girl had succeeded in doing was in adding to her mother's sense of uselessness.

'I'm afraid I really don't know what to think,' Marjorie confessed. 'I don't recall having so many decisions to make twenty-five years ago. Mostly we did as we were told.'

Discarding the eye mask, Marjorie pushed back the covers and rolled herself out of bed, praying that the baby wouldn't come today when she was feeling sick, incompetent and ninety-nine years old.

'Look it, too,' she told her reflection, having dragged herself to the bathroom washbasin. She rummaged in her toilet bag for a pill of another kind – her little blue one. Cupping her hand for water from a smart brass tap she gulped it down.

She had had high hopes of the blue pills. Some women claimed they had wondrous effects: made them feel great and took ten years off their age. Well, they had stopped the hot flushes, which *was* truly wonderful, but they hadn't achieved much else. Why did her hair feel dry and dead? Her skin like that of an ancient Egyptian mummy? Where was the promised youthful figure, the renewed energy and drive?

Her gaze wandered to the open window as if the answer might be there. Instead her attention was taken by a collection of flower pots basking in the rapidly strengthening sun. They contained cuttings from her favourite old shrubs and she had been nursing them along with great care. But the removal men, with little regard for their survival, had dumped them down just anyhow in a corner of the back garden.

Garden? Her gaze roved the rough patch of ground. It was marked out on three sides by a sturdy but naked fence, and on the other by the wall that had blocked their access the previous day. Chunks of brick and pieces of jagged metal were scattered here and there. A man-hole stood two feet proud in the centre, and a deep murky puddle stagnated nearby. How was she going to make anything of this? It would take for ever and a day.

She ought to be out there with a spade, making a start. But she still needed to sort out the kitchen. And their clothes were jammed together in hanging cartons. There was still so much to be done.

Willing some strength into her body for the daunting tasks ahead, she took an extra pain-killer, splashed her face with water, and hunted for something to wear.

8

Marjorie found herself in the big echoing kitchen, confronting the cooker hob. The gleaming white metal winked chinks of sunlight back at her, almost painful to the eyes. Never had she seen so beautifully clean and shiny a cooker hob, nor one that could appear so alarming. The very thought of making those jet black holes blip into action was enough to churn her stomach, and no amount of telling herself she was being silly about it did any good. Well, she need not touch it right now. Later, she would. Not now.

She pulled open the fridge. It contained the remains of their much-travelled cool-box: a scrap of dolcelatte cheese, two Granny Smith apples and half a carton of milk. A shop was desperately called for.

She stood for a moment listening to the appliance's motor as it hummed into life. In that vast, silent house it could have been the engine of a ship. A ship bobbing gently in the middle of the Red Sea. Taking her nowhere.

Straining her ears for some evidence of life in the vicinity she heard none. Not a voice came faintly on the breeze, not a car swished by along the road, not even a bird sang for joy this bright morning. Not in The Paddock, at any rate. The double glazing worked so well that not even the builders' machinery could be heard.

Upstairs, leaning from the bathroom window, she had been able to catch the far-off bleeping sound that the machines made when going backwards – and had come to the conclusion that they rarely worked in a forward direction – but apart from that she might have been entirely alone on the planet.

She let the fridge smack shut. This would never do. If she didn't do something constructive she would go mad. Her priority, and her *only* priority should be finding some way to replace what had been so savagely snatched away from her. She must get a job of some sort; do something useful with her life. Anything. She had to get out of here.

To take full advantage of her expedition Marjorie filled an old shopping trolley with clothes that she should have ditched before the move but hadn't managed to summon the enthusiasm, and trundled across the baked mud field to the site office. With a small roller-blind tucked under one arm and feeling foolish for not already being in the know, she enquired of the woman in charge of house sales as to where she might find some shops.

The woman eyed her trolley with as much

distaste as Becky and Em had always done whenever it had fallen out of the hall cupboard. For years they had been telling their mother to get rid of it; such a thing might have been acceptable once, before most women learned to drive, but nowadays nobody under sixty would be seen dead with one.

Looking down at it, Marjorie had to admit they'd been right. It wasn't quite the thing. And the sales assistant must have thought her a little senile too, when she explained who she was and where she lived.

What sort of person would move house with a load of junk? And who in their right mind would have bought a house without first finding out where the local shops were?

Marjorie lifted her chin and concentrated on the directions she was given. As it happened there was a small parade within reasonable walking distance and it was in the process of being expanded to cater for the new estate. She soon located the charity shop where she intended to off-load her clothes. And it was there, much to her surprise, that she made her first real friend.

Stella Ericson worked at the shop on two mornings each week. When Marjorie walked in she found her puzzling over a computer print-out. It transpired that she could account for only half the bought-in stock that should have been there. Not that it seemed to bother her much.

Marjorie, smiling into the woman's long pale

face, felt she had never before met anyone so placid and laid-back as this one. At first she'd appeared sad and remote but she had rallied a little and even laughed at Marjorie's description of how she and Phil were having to crawl about below window-level in their new house in order to get into bed.

'Not that we have any neighbours,' Marjorie finished wistfully. 'There's really no one to see in.'

It was then that Stella, perhaps sensing Marjorie's loneliness, had suggested that she, too, might like to help in the shop now and then. Marjorie hadn't committed herself. Assistant in a charity shop? And unpaid? She didn't say as much, but she had been hoping for so much more for herself. Nothing like her father-in-law had been prepared to offer her, naturally, but at least a proper job. Promising to bring more items when she'd sorted them out, she took her leave and headed for the job centre.

Later, as she dragged her trolley back to the house Marjorie counted the windows. All those rooms, she thought. Perhaps we could take in lodgers. Well, it was now patently obvious she would never get a job outside the home, so why not? But she could already see Phil's face if she were to suggest such a thing. No, that idea was definitely a non-starter.

She skirted a pot-hole and recalled the news-paper ads she'd tracked down in the library: they were nearly all for cleaners, care assistants, can-vassers – nothing suitable for her. And without the all-important CV she could hope for nothing much else.

The woman in the Jobcentre had been pleasant enough; more than willing to help. But Marjorie felt all along that she was merely going through the motions of considering her client's plight.

'There are *some* employers who positively favour – er – the more mature person,' the woman told her, 'but I'm very much afraid . . .' She'd taken off her glasses at that point and shaken her head a little.

'The government says we should be flexible,' Marjorie pointed out, 'and be prepared to develop more than one skill in our working lives. Two or even three different careers, they say, we should expect to manage. So I wonder, d'you think I could train for something . . . ? I don't know exactly what.'

'Well, of course, there *are* plenty of courses . . .'

Marjorie had waited while the woman gathered together pamphlets that might be of use, but probably weren't, and as she sorted through them began to see that it was all rather pointless anyway. Oh yes, she could gain some qualifications – book keeping, perhaps, or secretarial – but by the time she had acquired them she would be that much older and that much nearer to the dreaded brick wall of ageism. Heavens, most people were thinking of retiring by then, not starting out on a career. Education, education, education. Lifelong education. That's what the government trotted out.

Did it know what it was talking about?

She had taken the leaflets and escaped, wondering whether she could persuade Phil to cadge a job for her at Spittal's; get her in, so to speak, by the back door. After all, he surely owed her that much. He wouldn't like it, of course. But perhaps, she thought, rummaging in the pocket of her denim skirt for the door key to the new house, he would feel shamed into trying, at least.

She suddenly realised, walking along the plank that served as a path, that she was not alone. Two elderly women were standing on her door-step, smiling benignly at her, the blue Mini in which they'd arrived parked by a heap of rubble some distance away.

'We were about to give up,' one of them said, nodding her snow-white head. 'We would have phoned beforehand if we could, but your husband explained about it not being connected. He said you were sure to be unpacking cartons, though, so we thought we'd find you at home.'

'My husband?' Marjorie said faintly.

'Yes,' the other woman put in. She wore a thick coat and a hat with a pin in it, although Marjorie was finding her sleeveless sun-top just about bearable in the searing heat. 'Perhaps we should explain who we are.'

Marjorie listened with growing dismay as they eagerly filled her in. She could hardly believe what they were saying. Apparently Phil had been asking among his colleagues at work for some of their wives to befriend *his* wife! And it had been suggested that she might like to join a sewing group that someone vaguely knew about.

'We're making a montage of our district,' the grey-haired woman was saying.

'A collage,' the other corrected. 'It's really awfully good fun. We're using felt, appliqué and all sorts – something to inspire just about everyone. What would be your forte, Mrs Benson? Needle-point? Cross stitch? Or perhaps even a bit of stump? Stump work seems to be the latest thing, you know. It certainly fascinates *me*.'

While Marjorie cast about for an answer, she seethed inwardly. How dare Phil do this to her! How dare he! She hated anything to do with needle and thread, and he surely must know that by now. And she was perfectly capable of making her own friends, thank you very much. Oh, this was really too bad!

'If you can spare us a minute of your time, we could tell you all about it.' The women looked hopefully at the door, no doubt desperate for a cup of tea. And Marjorie had no option but to let them in.

9

The first thing Oliver saw when he arrived home
from work was not the yellow ochre walls or the
antique rug or even the Moorcroft vase; it was the
letter. It lay on the mat looking ominously official
and he immediately sensed trouble.

Of course he had been expecting trouble for
some time. Everything was bound to catch up with
him one day. But, oh, he wished it hadn't.
Especially not right now; he'd had such a hell of a
session with new-broom Philip Benson and he
couldn't face much more aggro.

And it didn't help, either, to know that he had
brought his problems on himself. Well, no that
wasn't true: he'd been blameless in the beginning.
After all, it was Sally who'd left *him*; he hadn't
walked out on *her*. That's what made it all so unfair.
Why should he be lumbered with this hassle?

With a heavy heart he picked up the letter and
made for the kitchen, but a scrabbling sound
diverted him to the dining room where, much to
Jade's dislike, he kept a pair of chipmunks.

'Glad to see me, you little rogues?' He hurried to

the floor-to-ceiling cage that he had built into one of the recesses next to the fire place and put his face to the glass front. 'I can't let you out to play at the moment,' he told them, 'Daddy has things to do.' He checked their food store and feeding dish. They certainly wouldn't go hungry, whereas he himself was famished.

He passed on into the kitchen, threw the offending letter on to a work top and began raiding the fridge. Jade wouldn't be home for hours yet; it was her day for evening classes. He took out a cold cooked chicken breast and defrosted four slices of bread. Finding the lager had run out – why hadn't he remembered last time they went to the supermarket? – he poured himself a large gin and tonic and carried it all through to the sitting room, where he flicked on the television and waited to be mesmerised.

But his mind wouldn't relax. Not because Jade would abhor the way he was scattering crumbs over the blue and white striped knowle sofa, but because of the letter. He must open the dratted thing.

His snack finished, he forced himself to fetch the letter from the kitchen and slit it open with the vegetable knife. Armed with another gin and tonic he returned to the sitting room to learn the worst.

The worst proved even more shattering than he had feared. If he hadn't seen it with his own eyes, set down in black and white, he would never have believed it. Could this really be done to him? He stared at the wording again. Yes, they meant it; their warnings had not been empty. They were going to slap an attachment of earnings on him. A large one. And he had no say in the matter whatever.

That anyone could take your hard-earned money away from you like this appalled him. He sat back, the letter on his knee, feeling sick and dizzy. Then blood rushed up in anger. He wouldn't let them do it. He sprang to his feet. He wouldn't let them get away with it. There must be something he could do. Yes, and Jade would be able to tell him how to go about it. Even if she hadn't yet studied this particular aspect of the law she was bound to have information on it in one of her books.

He strode into the dining room to the recess that was chipmunk-free. Here Jade's law books had been gathering over the months in increasingly impressive rows. But where to start looking for the information he wanted? He needed Jade to help.

He checked his watch to see how soon she might be home. Ages. Then suddenly, thumping his forehead with his fist, he sat down on one of the window seats. Stupid! Jade was the last person on earth he could ask about any of this. The very last. Because, before she could help, she would need to know the whole sad story including the bit he found difficult to face up to.

Up until now he had led her to believe that it was he who had left Sally; not the other way round. Well, what kind of pathetic berk would he have looked if he'd admitted to having a woman walk out on him? Didn't look too good, did it? Having revealed himself as a loser, any woman in her right mind wouldn't have given him a second glance. So, as far as Jade was aware, it was a case of 'unreasonable behaviour' on Sally's part and he didn't like to talk about it much. And it went without saying that she should keep the kids. Unreasonable or not, the law tended to think children should be with their mother.

The truth was that Sally had run off with a squaddie. He let out a groan and let his head fall back against a cushion. The nightmare was starting again, parading remorselessly behind his eyelids. It seemed that he was never to be allowed to forget that fateful afternoon when he had slipped home early from work.

He had been scouring his desk drawers for a computer disc – not his Spittal's desk; one that went with the job he'd had at that time – but he'd eventually realised that he must have left it somewhere at home, which was a pain because he badly needed it. In fact he couldn't attend the three-thirty meeting without the information it held. He only hoped, as he dashed from the office and across town, that Billy hadn't posted it in the video machine or dropped it in the toaster.

Leaving the car engine running in front of the house he ran indoors via the kitchen door at the side. As he had expected, the door was open. But the place struck him as strangely quiet. No kids in sight; presumably they were asleep. And no Sally.

But a radio played softly upstairs. Music. By Enya. A haunting, dreamy piece. His disc forgotten, he crept upstairs, thinking Sally must be napping too, or at least lying on the bed.

He was right about the latter. Sally *was* lying on the bed, flat on her back with a man in her arms. He would never forget their faces as, aware of a third presence, they turned to find him in the doorway.

The scene froze like that for – he had no idea how long. Long enough for it to scar his mind so that he would never be able to eradicate it. Nobody spoke a word. They seemed to be expecting him to say something, and, looking back, he supposed he should have said something. But all the time he was expecting *them* to speak. He couldn't think straight, let alone from sentences. And he had no idea what to do.

He found himself running; running to get away. Down the stairs, out into the street, and hurtling along the pavement. As though he were the guilty party. Not her. Not the bloke. But himself.

It took him a long time to come to his senses. When he did, he realised he'd been sitting in a park for hours, shivering, sobbing, and feeling sick.

He finally dragged himself home to find that Sally had her mother with her. The children were there, too, strapped in their matching feeding chairs and cramming jam doughnuts, of all things, into their mouths.

Apparently her mother had brought the kids

back; she'd had them for the afternoon 'to give Sally a break'. Sally, in her mother's opinion, had taken on too much, having the babies so close together – only a year apart. They were wearing her out.

Of course even she must have been a bit miffed with Sally over the kind of break she'd been taking, but she didn't let on. She'd never had much time for Oliver and blamed him for everything, saying it was all his fault for never being around for Sally and the kids; that he was always too busy; that he was wedded to his work.

He hadn't bothered to waste his breath on the silly old bat by explaining that he'd been working damned hard for Sally and the kids, putting a decent roof over their heads and food in their mouths. She wouldn't have seen it.

Sally chipped in too, between her floods of tears, complaining he was too ambitious by half, far too relentlessly driven. But he didn't believe that was the real reason for what had happened. She was only echoing her mother, the way she usually did.

And he was so angry – not only with her and her mother and the other bloke, but with himself. He felt so hurt and ashamed and inadequate because Sally had had to go to bed with someone else. That was all he could think of: that Sally had gone to bed with someone else. If her mother hadn't been there he would have killed her. Instead he threw her out. Told her mother to take her slag of a daughter and get out.

Seeing he was livid and in no mood to talk, they

started to gather up stuff for the children, sorting out coats and toys and things, but he said oh no, they weren't going to take the children. They were to stay with him. He would see a solicitor in the morning about a divorce and would apply for custody too.

The women were astonished. Clearly they didn't believe him, and he wondered what he was saying too, because both children seemed to have cottoned on to something pretty devastating going on by then and began to bawl at the tops of their voices, slobbering masticated dough down their bibs and holding out their stubby little arms to be comforted. They had sugar all over their cheeks and blobs of jam in their hair, and he didn't know how to stop them crying, or where to start cleaning up the mess. But the women took the view that they would leave it like that for now. Wait for him to cool down. He would see reason in time.

But it took a long time. Months of acrimony, of Sally begging to be taken back, but all the while, he suspected, with her lover still in the background. Months of fighting over the children without upsetting them too much which, of course, was impossible. Young as they were they knew what raised voices and slanging matches meant.

At first, determined to take care of them himself, he had taken leave from work, and done everything for them. He would soon find a full-time child-minder, he told himself. Anything rather than hand them back to Sally.

But of course it hadn't worked out. He couldn't look after them properly; his employer ran out of sympathy; the child-minder turned out to be hopeless. So when Sally and her mother tried to get the children away from him they won hands down.

From then it was all down-hill. He'd even agreed, eventually, to change the house for something smaller so that Sally could move into it with the children and they wouldn't have to suffer any more disruption. He would still have to pay the mortgage, of course, though it would be less than before, leaving him with a few crumbs to support himself.

Sal kept telling him her affair was over, which he was more inclined to believe by then. But he did sometimes wonder: who was the guilty party in all this? It seemed that *he* was the one being made to suffer. All he was left with at the end of the day was rented accommodation and a struggle to make ends meet. Whereas Sally was OK, wasn't she, set up in a cosy little house in Gloucester with their children and claiming maintenance from him? And there was nothing more he could do except go to see the children twice a week as adjudicated by the courts.

Only that didn't work out either. He would turn up at the allocated visiting time only to find that the children weren't there; they had been taken out for the day by their Granny, or some such. Often Sally wasn't there either, and he would have nothing to vent his wrath on but a silent, closed-up house. He had never felt so enraged, frustrated or impotent as he did on those occasions.

At every turn he found himself banging his head against a brick wall. The system seemed weighted in women's favour. Solicitors were useless, judges were prejudiced. Everyone was against him.

He couldn't call on his parents for help either. He'd turned his back on them years ago. His father had been a lay preacher and they had rowed during his teenage years.

Then he suspected that the lover had resurfaced, but it was impossible to prove. By then he had changed his job to the one he now held at Spittal's, because it paid more, and had moved to Bath to be closer to it, which meant he was no longer near enough Sally to keep checking up on what might or might not be going on. The round trip on access days proved difficult enough. But the thought that Sal's boyfriend could be trying to take his place infuriated him beyond endurance. Here he was, slogging himself to death, shelling money out for a family he wasn't allowed to see half the time, and probably lining the pocket of his wife's lover!

So his answer to Sally had been to dig his heels in and refuse to pay up any more money. But that had been stupid of him. No matter what he wanted, no matter what his intentions of starting afresh on his own, there was no way that he'd be allowed to. He had responsibilities. He simply couldn't escape.

Then he'd met Jade. He hadn't thought he could ever love anyone other than Sally, but Jade put Sally in the shade. Now he had even more reason to hold on to whatever money he had. He wanted to set up home with Jade, redecorate the run-down flat he'd had to take on and begin a new life. Start all over again. Even bow out of the children's lives, much though the thought choked him, because his popping in and out confused them too much, and it seemed like the best thing to do.

But he'd decided from the outset that he wouldn't marry Jade, even when his divorce was finalised. It wouldn't be fair to her, because her money would be seen as his, to be dipped into by ghosts from his previous life, and he couldn't abide that. What's more he didn't want her to think that children could ever be on the cards. He couldn't bear the heartbreak of more children.

From all this had been born his ridiculous proposal to Jade about having an open relationship. It was the last thing he wanted really, but all he'd been able to offer her.

Oliver found himself back at the fridge contemplating the tail end of the tonic bottle. It held just enough for another drink and would only go flat if he didn't finish it tonight. Funny how the gin had run out. Usually it was the tonic and you had to open a new one, which meant you had a lot of *that* begging to be used up and you were soon on a slippery slope.

Faced with the problem of not wanting to waste a dribble of tonic he began to search the flat. He would have to find where Jade was keeping the replacement gin. She had been to Paris recently, looking up a pen friend she had met face to face on one of her modelling trips, and with whom she now kept up a regular acquaintance. On her way through customs she had picked up some duty-frees.

But he could find no sign of them in the kitchen, nor anywhere remotely logical. In the end he was reduced to searching Jade's half of the large mirrored wardrobe that took up one wall of their bedroom.

Her half? he grunted to himself, batting aside coats, suits and dresses. More like her seven-eighths. And why did she need all these shoes? For heaven's sake, there were even clothes in carrier bags: new stuff she'd not bothered to hang.

If Oliver had been a worried man before, he was an even more troubled one by the time he located the gin bottle. Hell. What should he do about this?

Joe French looked up as Jade opened the door to the lecture room, his questioning glance changing to one of lofty superiority on seeing who had arrived. Ever since Jade had refused him a date he'd been set on making her college life as unpleasant as he possibly could, and it showed in every contour of his face.

'So sorry I'm late,' she cooed, gliding past her least favourite lecturer with eyes averted and nose held high.

Under cover of the amused tittering of her

fellow-students she ignored the caustic response that her 'apology' brought forth and crossed the room to an empty desk by the window where she organised her books and settled herself, with calm disdain. She had some thinking to do. Serious thinking. Too serious to permit the likes of that ginger-haired nerd Joe French to crawl under her skin.

Biting the end of her pen and opening her notebook she feigned absorption in the resumed lecture, but her thoughts were fixed on Oliver. He'd phoned her at lunch-time, incensed over the arrival of his new boss. He'd been determined not to like him and by the sound of it he hadn't even had to try very hard; animosity had flared between the two men like a forest fire.

She had listened dutifully to Oliver whingeing on, wondering what on earth she could do about this. He had been sunk in gloom ever since hearing about Philip Benson and might even do something stupid.

Or perhaps it wasn't a work problem at all. Was money bothering him even more? He was always going on about that too lately. Or it might be something to do with his wife and kids.

Perhaps – and she hardly dare allow the thought – perhaps it was the thing she feared most of all: that he had wearied of her and found someone else, or – worse still – was carrying on with his ex-wife!

She stared at her virgin notepad, her knuckles to

her mouth. Ever since moving in with Oliver she had tried to imagine how she would deal with such a situation if and when it arose. How would she react? Because although she had verbally accepted his terms and conditions, and in theory they had sounded reasonable, in her mind she still baulked at them.

How much easier life would be if she could really adopt Oliver's idea of openness! But she couldn't. She had tried, but when it came to the crunch, she knew she couldn't. She wasn't made that way.

Even her parents hadn't been like that. Oh, Dad had been no saint but he'd not taken up with other women. Horses had been his sole weakness. He had always remained faithful to her mother, and she to him, although no one could have blamed her for looking for someone better.

No, this notion of openness was not for Jade, and she couldn't see how it could work for others. How could anyone with a shred of self-respect put up with being treated like that? How could they cope with the awful feeling of rejection when they found themselves temporarily out of favour and someone else taking their place? How could you kiss someone good-morning, knowing they'd be kissing someone else good-night? How could a woman carry on loving someone who was prepared to let you go with other men?

Of course, in the beginning she had felt confident of holding Oliver's interest; of never having to face up to the fact that he might dally elsewhere. He wouldn't *want* to look at another woman, so long as he had her. That was what she had thought. And so far she was sure he hadn't. So far.

He *pretended* he had flings. Yes, pretended. Why, she had no idea. But he would sometimes snuggle down in bed with her and regale her with tales of his supposed conquests. As he had once told her, talking about sex turned him on – and that much proved to be true. So far he'd never asked her to contribute on these occasions, for which she was thankful. She couldn't imagine how she would deal with it if he ever did. Fortunately he seemed content to do all the talking. And it was harmless enough, she decided. The whole thing was a harmless bluff. And wasn't it better to tolerate this minor peculiarity than be faced with some other turn-ons she could think of?

Usually, lying in bed listening to him, she could scarcely suppress her mirth. Surely he had taken chunks of such mind-boggling exploits verbatim from men's magazines? After all, he spent hours down at the hairdresser's, claiming, when he returned, that his preferred salon was busier and more popular than most; probably he'd been poring over their dirty mags while waiting in the queue.

Maybe, Jade thought as she vacantly watched Joe French strut his tight blue denim jeans before his audience, maybe Oliver was finding her boring:

she hadn't been playing around as he'd expected, keeping him fuelled with tales of her own adventures. Was that it?

'Well?'

Jade's vision focused more accurately on Joe French. With a jolt she realised that everyone in the room had their attention fixed on her.

'I –' she began, having no idea of the question that had been put to her, let alone the answer. 'Er – pass,' she finished lamely amid a fresh wave of amusement.

'Highly unlikely that you will,' he replied.

He sought her out at the end of the lecture, planting himself in front of her in the corridor as she tried to squeeze past a fire extinguisher. 'You're never going to make it,' he told her, 'you haven't got what it takes.' He stood shaking his head at her, a cock-sure smile splitting his thin lips. His eyes flashed triumph through tortoise-shell glasses. He was as aware of her strong ambition as she was. Normally she was motivated and determined, often turning up late to be true, but never given to day-dreaming; always well on the ball. Today, though, she'd let herself down.

She said nothing; merely stepped back a little from his stale body-odour and let her gaze run down to his crotch. By the time her eyes returned to his, she had effectively castrated him.

Jade leaned over Oliver's sprawled body to plant a kiss on his lips but drew back with a little squeal.

She had found herself eye to eye with one of the chipmunks.

'Oh, Olly!' she reproached him with a gentle kick, bringing him fully awake, 'I do wish you wouldn't let them run loose all over the sitting room. It's bad enough having to put up with them at all, without having to wonder where they're going to pop up next.' She particularly objected to the way he handled them, treating them almost like babies. A bit weird really.

'Sorry,' Oliver mumbled, rubbing his eyes with a fist, 'I fell asleep.'

'I'm not surprised.' She held up the gin bottle.

'I had a hard day.' He yanked the bottle from her hand and put it on the sofa table, then gathered up the chipmunks and returned them to their cage. While closing the cage door he remembered, with a lurching beneath his ribs, his intention to sit Jade down the minute she came in and have a serious talk with her. Now he shied from the task. Some other time, he promised himself. Right this minute he was far too sleepy. It was late. There was an R in the month. Hell, he just didn't want to have to do it.

Jade glanced up with a rueful smile when he returned. 'You look a bit the worse for wear. Been celebrating something?' She crossed the room to where he stood.

Celebrating! Hardly. 'Uh-huh.' He tried to shake his head but she had reached up to smooth his hair, and when she had done that she tweaked each side of his face between finger and thumb, leaving him throbbing a bit and hoping to goodness he wasn't developing jowls. Slipping his arms round her waist he contemplated indulging in some serious fun and games, since she seemed that way inclined, but it turned out she was more keen to chat.

'So you've been drowning your sorrows, is that it? Has new bossy-wossy been giving Olly-wolly a hard time this afternoon too?'

'Now how did you guess that? As I told you over the phone, Benson had hardly put a foot in the door this morning before he started picking my brains apart. Hadn't even stuck his feet under the desk but wanted to know everything – and I mean everything – about the Bristol set-up. He's hardly let me pause for breath since.'

'Well, you can hardly blame him for that.' She drew him over to the sofa, swept crumbs away, clucking her tongue, and indicated that he should lie next to her with his head in her lap. 'He has to get to know what he's up against, doesn't he?'

'Talk about the Spanish Inquisition!' he moaned on. 'My head was spinning by lunch-time, I can tell you. And my throat felt like a sheet of sandpaper.'

Jade grinned as she began to soothe him again with cool slender fingers. 'So you simply had to introduce him to the local hostelry...'

'Did I heck?' His face darkening, Oliver launched into a detailed account of a problem that had cropped up just as he was about to die of thirst, and how he had begun to deal with it, when

Benson suddenly decided to stick in an oar. 'Him with his precious MBA!' Oliver concluded the saga with a snort of disgust. 'He knows absolutely nothing.'

Jade paid close attention as Oliver went on to tell her about the difference of opinions that the incident had revealed, the heated discussion that had followed, and the gradual fraying of his own temper. He had tried to be ingratiatingly polite, he assured Jade, but had finally stormed out of the room leaving the 'new boy' to find lunch for himself. 'Though in the normal course of events I would naturally have acted as chaperone.'

'Of course.' Jade stopped stroking his forehead and bit her lip. So that was how he had been able to phone her at lunch-time. She'd much rather he'd been holed up with Philip Benson.

Oh dear, it sounded as though he had made a hash of things. Certainly there seemed to be a clash of personalities, not to mention jealousy on Oliver's part.

Oliver had achieved his position the hard way, with little more to his credit than A-levels and an enormous amount of ambition. He could manage people well as a rule, being able to turn on the charm and the sweet-talk at will, but his lack of higher qualifications, plus a want of height, constantly bugged him. They were like two devils perched on his shoulders. Always with him. Always ready to hound him into trouble. No wonder Benson, with an MBA and the ability, by all accounts, to turn women's heads, had rubbed Oliver up the wrong way.

'Olly, you're your own worst enemy,' she told him. 'You mustn't let him needle you. I know it's going to be difficult. I know you expected to be given Benson's job. But your time will come one day – *if* you play your cards right. It won't, though, if you get on the wrong side of this man and cock up all your chances.'

Oliver closed his eyes. She was right of course. He'd behaved stupidly, even for him, and he couldn't think why Benson had affected him the way he had. But it didn't really help to be lectured by a woman.

'The guy just gets up my nose,' he grumbled. 'I'll remember to count to ten in future.'

'You do that, darling.' She bent her head to kiss him, her hair falling forwards to form a curtain round their private world.

'Bed?' he suggested when they parted for air.

'Only if you promise me something. Promise me you'll make it up with Philip Benson first thing tomorrow and invite him and his wife, if he has one, to dinner with us.'

'Dinner?' Oliver spluttered, making a pretence of falling off the sofa and rolling on to the floor. 'You really must be joking.'

'I'm not, I'm perfectly serious.' She planted a foot on his stomach. 'And you don't get up until you've promised.'

'I love it when you're mistressful.' He grinned.

'But I didn't really mean it the other day, you know, when I suggested you seduce the old geezer. Ouch!' He grabbed her foot and then her arm. 'Come here, you little minx!'

10

'Where would you like to eat?' Marjorie called out to Phil. 'The kitchen, the breakfast room, the dining room, the conservatory, or the terrace?'

'The terrace?' Phil threw down his jacket. He presumed she meant the ten slabs the builders had dumped outside the patio doors. They were hardly enough to wipe your feet on let alone set up table and chairs, and he was left in no doubt by her tone that somehow he was to blame. He was even to blame for having a choice of places to eat.

Marjorie managed to make everything sound like his fault these days. And he was trying hard. He'd arranged for her to join a sewing group, but somehow that had been wrong.

'I don't mind where we eat,' he told her. 'What are we having anyway?'

Knives and forks clattered on to a tray. 'Salad,' she told him a little tersely.

'Salad?' His gloom increased. He was already tired of salad but could see that the cooker still hadn't been touched. And as far as he could tell, no more unpacking had been done either. Boxes of stuff still stood in the same positions that they had when he'd left for work. What had Marjorie been doing with herself all day? It was time she snapped out of this negative attitude, but there was no way he could tell her that.

'Look,' he said over-brightly, finding himself still clutching a piece of paper, 'this was stuck in the letter box. Sounds just like your sort of thing.'

She barely spared it a glance. 'I'm amazed that anyone's come this far to deliver a leaflet. The milkman won't come, nor will the paper boy. And I don't think the postman knows we're here.' She snatched the bright yellow sheet from him. 'A coffee morning! Humph!' Treating him to the same look of incredulity that the sewing group incident had engendered she slapped it back in his hand.

'But this is for women on the estate over there –' he waved in the direction of the Red Sea '– and a lot of them will be wives of Spittal's employees. I think you ought to go. Especially as you need to make new friends. You have to make an effort, you know.'

She promptly changed the subject. 'Any news of Becky yet?'

'No, not a word.' He remembered, then, his good news. 'I saw a car for you today. There's a dealer near the office. I'm haggling about the price. You'll be a free agent then – can come and go to your heart's content. You could go and see Em at college for a while, and perhaps call on my sister, too. And you can go and see Tom and Beth, and Mum and

Dad, and . . . everyone. That'll be good, won't it?'

Even her smile was somehow disapproving.

'Oh, and another thing –' he sat down and reached for the salt-cellar '– we've been invited out to dinner.'

'Is that so?' For the first time she looked vaguely interested. 'Who can know us well enough to invite us out to dinner?'

'Well, it's my junior at the office, actually. Oliver Knox. And, of course, his whatever you call them these days. Partner I suppose. Not his wife; they're not married.'

'Good of them to invite us.' Sipping a mineral water she studied him over the glass. 'So what's the problem then? Do you feel he's trying to suck up to you, or something? That it wouldn't be wise to mix?'

'No, no, it's not that.' The idea of Oliver Knox sucking up to anyone! 'It's just that I feel we don't have a lot in common. They're younger than us and – well – modern. But I suppose we'll have to accept.'

'Yes, of course we'll have to accept.' She held his eye for a second longer. 'We *do* have to make an effort. Talking of which –' she forked up a piece of tomato and examined it '– I wondered whether you could do me a favour.'

Phil froze at the sound of her words. He knew at once that he wouldn't be able to. Something about the way she'd said it told him she was about to ask far more than he could possibly give. So why put him in this position? To put him in the wrong once again?

'Since you've dragged me down here away from the job your father gave me,' she went on, 'I was thinking that the least you can do is help me get another one.'

Phil gazed at her open-mouthed for a moment before glanced pointedly at the untouched packing cases. 'I should have thought there was enough for you to do around here,' he said, 'without looking further afield.'

Marjorie waved his words aside. 'You know very well what I mean: I need a proper job. Something on a par with what I've lost. Something that will give me some satisfaction. Working with your accountants, perhaps, or – oh, I don't know – you know Spittal's better than I do. *You* think of somewhere I'd fit in.'

Phil tried to keep his face impassive. Inside, he was panic-stricken. 'Marjie . . .'

'Oh, I know we wouldn't want to be on top of each other.'

'But–'

'And I wouldn't want you in charge of me.'

'I–'

'But there must be something I could do.'

'No. No, there isn't.'

'What?'

'I said no. I'm afraid there's nothing you could do.' He ran a hand through his hair. 'You see, you aren't even properly qualified.'

'I know that! Heavens, do you think I need to be told? I've nothing on paper and my age is against me, which is precisely why I have to come to you, cap in hand, and beg you to help me out. Oh!' She leaped up from the table. 'I might have known I'd be wasting my breath. You ruin my life, and cut me off from our family and yet you think you owe me nothing. Typical.'

She began to march from the room but stopped by the door to tell him: 'I know what your trouble is: you can't bear the thought that I might actually make a success of something, can you? You can't bear to think of me being in competition with you.'

Phil clutched his head when she had gone. Actually he'd seen her as a laughing-stock; seen her letting him down. How could she have got things so wrong?

11

Marjorie checked her appearance in the mirror. It made a change to be going out, and would be lovely to get away from this awful mausoleum of a house for a few hours, even if the couple they were dining with were so much younger than themselves, and complete strangers.

She peered at herself a little closer. Even with the glass tilted at an awkward angle, because Phil hadn't found time to screw it to the wall, her reflection didn't look half bad. She had managed to tame her hair reasonably well and her skin glowed from all the sunny weather they'd been having. A week of fruit and salads had improved her waistline a little too. For once she had no headache either. She even had some energy left, though it was early evening when she usually felt thoroughly whacked. Wonders would never cease.

Whatever her hormones were doing at the moment she wished they would stay that way and stop monkeying around. If you could have decent days like this, she put to herself, then the good hormones couldn't all be dead, could they? They were hiding around somewhere, waiting to creep out when the baddies had had their fun. So –

'Marjie!' Phil yelled from the bottom of the stairs. 'Taxi's here. Come on!'

She sighed, scooped up her handbag and ran down to find her husband jigging about in the hall with the front door wide open. A mini cab was revving up outside, and Phil began to gesticulate at her wildly.

She had hardly expected a compliment from him since they were barely on speaking terms lately, so she was not disappointed when none came. Certainly he spared a moment to look her up and down but whether he really saw her or not was another matter.

All he said was, 'Have you got your little doodah?' And of course she hadn't. She had left the bouquet that she'd bought for the girl with the unusual name – Jade – steeped in a bowl of water by the sink.

'You go and wait in the taxi.' Phil pushed her resignedly through the door. 'I'll go and fetch the flowers.'

But once they were on their way to Bath he calmed down enough to make stilted conversation with her, presumably for the benefit of the cab-driver's flapping ears.

'Is it my imagination,' he said, 'or have you been weeding out more of our clothes?'

'Well, I did take another load down to the charity shop, as it happens. It's easy now I have the car.

And by the way,' she added nonchalantly as the mini cab sped along, 'I'm going to be helping out there a couple of mornings a week.'

'Are you?' Phil turned back from the window, his eyes roving her face. 'Do you really want to?'

Marjorie took a deep breath. No, she didn't really much want to, but since all other avenues of occupation seemed to be closed to her, beggars could hardly be choosers.

'How many times do I have to tell you, Phil?' She could see that he'd already realised he'd said the wrong thing but continued to admonish him loudly. 'I'm used to having something to *do*. Helping your father was a full-time *job*. I need to fill up my *days*. And if you won't consider taking in lodgers or pulling strings for me where you know you could . . . well!' She folded her arms in a huff and turned to look out into the streets.

Bath seemed an interesting place, and Phil, checking his watch in grim embarrassment at her outburst, realised that they were going to arrive earlier than expected if they weren't careful. The invitation had been 'seven-thirty for eight', which in Phil's book meant seven-thirty on the dot. So he ordered the driver to take them on a quick tour of the city to fill up the time.

Marjorie tried to take in the sights as the driver swung them round corners and shot them down streets. She caught a tantalising glimpse of the abbey, a pristine, well-stocked park, and numerous Georgian properties, before the driver decided time was up and veered off in search of their destination.

Finally they turned into an impressive crescent of tall terraced houses with black iron railings along their fronts and boot scrapers beside their doors. The Georgian panelled doors were all painted white and had fan-lights over the tops.

Marjorie checked her dress. To her dismay the warmth of the car had produced a panel of creases across her lap. No doubt when she left the cab the back of her skirt would look like a scrunched up paper bag too. Somehow the state of her dress, and the distance that was forever widening between herself and Philip, managed to completely banish her earlier confident mood. The cab came to a halt, and as she climbed out into the warm dusk, her vision of enjoying a pleasant evening among new friends, melted into the shadows.

'Jade,' Oliver protested, 'I can't believe this! You've had the bathroom for over an hour and you're still not ready.'

Jade hobbled across the bedroom with her underskirt round her ankles. 'I beg your pardon, Oliver,' she shot back at him, 'but I have *not* been in the bathroom for very long. I've been doing things in the kitchen. Dinner parties don't put themselves together, you know. Here, will you do this up?' Sweeping her hair off her neck she tried to make herself shorter so that Oliver could reach her fastening.

He yanked at the tab. Did she have to make his

lack of height so obvious? And – he let go the zip as though scalded – wasn't this a new dress? True, she looked sensational in midnight blue, but even so . . .

'For God's sake, Jade, you didn't have to go to town for Philip Benson, you know. This thing must have cost a fortune. And you've dozens of dresses that would have done.'

'You're a fine one to complain!' She wriggled and tugged and pulled until the smooth sheath of shimmering silk fitted like a second skin. 'Especially as it's all for your benefit. For the furtherance of your career.'

'Oh, that's what it's in aid of, is it? I thought it was to make use of a previous extravagance of yours – some of that gourmet food. Not to mention an excuse to show yourself off.'

'Oliver!' Jade turned wide, puzzled eyes to him, clearly hurt.

Oliver guessed he was right about the food, but knew for certain he was wrong about the rest: a show-off Jade was not. She had had enough opportunity for that sort of thing in the past, prancing about on a cat walk, and hadn't aimed to turn heads even then. It was not her style and he knew it.

But he was in no mood to apologise. His problems were piling on top of him, particularly his shortage of money, and Jade wasn't exactly helping in that respect If only he could talk to her about it! Instead of which he could do nothing but nag and nag and hope she'd soon stop shopping.

There was this other thing, too, making him uneasy: this silly talk about seducing Benson. He wished he'd never started it.

He went over to the window and looked down into the crescent. 'You will behave yourself this evening, won't you?' he threw casually over his shoulder.

'*What?*' Jade stopped circling her lips with their final touch of gloss, turned and glared at his back.

'I mean, all that guff about you nobbling Benson . . . you do know I was only joking.'

'You were?' She sprayed on a light but exotic toilet water. 'I thought you were all for it . . . weren't you?' Finished with her preparations she left her seat in front of the mirror and sauntered up to Oliver with a gleam in her eye. For a moment he thought she was going to punch him.

'Just my little joke.' He manufactured a laugh. 'I didn't really mean it.'

'Well, now –' she folded her arms '– I thought it was for each of us to decide on who we have "on the side"? It's none of the other's business. We can come and go as we choose. Right?'

Only spluttering came from his lips. 'Yes, but,' he managed to say, 'Benson would *not* be a good idea. Believe me. In this situation . . . most unwise. It could be *my* career that went down the pan. And if – but you wouldn't. Because – well – would you?'

'Oliver, for pity's sake calm down. I do like mature men, as you know, but I've never had one

142

as old as that.' Pursing her lips she took on the appearance of one scanning a crowded past. 'Forty-two, forty-three's about my limit, I promise you.'

Oliver swallowed. Why forty-two, forty-three? What was the significance there? Did Jade actually mean she'd taken lovers of those particular ages? Sweat broke out along his hair line. Colour ebbed from his cheeks.

But a small commotion in the street forced him to put certain images from his mind. A taxi had arrived and he could see his boss, lean and handsome in smart grey trousers, a dark blazer and a blue shirt, helping a woman on to the pavement.

Jade was still wittering on about men. 'I can't even begin to imagine being with a man of fifty,' she said, wrinkling her nose and leaning across Oliver to see what had claimed his attention.

Then she saw Philip Benson.

Marjorie sat stiffly on the striped Knowle sofa, attempting to smooth her skirt without drawing attention to it. She stretched the cotton polyester over her knees, decided it was ridiculous like that and hitched it up again. Somehow it refused to look right.

Her handbag had become a nuisance too. It had somehow ended up in her lap when she first sat down; she had transferred it to the seat beside her for a second or two, but realising that Phil, or Oliver or Jade might sit on it, put it down by her feet. Now, thinking it would probably trip her up later on, she moved it to her other side. And all the time she was groping in her mind for something interesting to say.

She glanced up at Phil, who was still standing, hands in pockets, in conversation with the others. Normally she looked to him to oil the wheels of social situations like this. He was good at that sort of thing. But he appeared as thrown by his present surroundings as she was. Rather than leading the conversation, setting everyone at their ease, he was staring down at the magnificent Turkish rug on which the three of them were standing, nudging the pile with the toe of his shoe.

Marjorie wondered whether she should stand up again, since no one else had seated themselves, but at that point Oliver went off to make pre-dinner drinks and Jade excused herself to attend to things in the kitchen.

'Make yourselves at home,' she said, whisking out of the room with a light step, a dazzling smile, and a swing of her beautiful hair.

Marjorie and Philip exchanged glances when she'd gone, but neither uttered a word. There was plenty Marjorie would like to have said – about their beautiful hostess, about the spacious flat with its marvellously proportioned rooms, and how different she found everything from what she'd expected – but none of this was possible with their host and hostess within earshot. Their eyes parted and began to examine the room.

Marjorie's attention was soon taken by the high

ceiling with its thickly encrusted frieze. Someone, she realised, had gone to great lengths to pick out the many scrolls and fruits of the ornate moulding, in shades of blue and gold paint that toned perfectly with the sofa.

She went on to admire the marble fireplace, the gilt-framed mirrors, and the pastoral water colours on each of the walls. When she had relaxed a little more, she promised herself, she would take a closer look at the superb collection of antiques – in particular the blue and white porcelain dishes that had been artistically arranged behind the glass doors of an immense, glossy and highly decorative antique cabinet. She would love to see the rest of the flat too.

Of course, a place like this wouldn't have suited her and Phil because it had no garden. Being three floors above the ground, it couldn't have one. But if it had . . . Marjorie almost groaned her envy. This was precisely the kind of home to which she would like to have moved, given the choice. Just the right size for two. And in elegant, historic Bath! Why couldn't Phil have found them something like this?

Brightwells estate with its pathetic parade of shops, its swinging cranes, its baked mud and its tipper trucks – well, in no way could it compare.

Was Phil thinking the same? she wondered, turning back to him. Impossible to tell. He was staring hard at the back of the door through which Jade had disappeared.

'Here we are,' Jade said, suddenly returning

with a bone china plate on which she had set out delicious-looking canapés. Oliver bounded in behind her with a silver drinks tray, reminding Marjorie, because of the way he bustled about on his short legs, of a teddy bear TV puppet whose antics she'd enjoyed as a child. She hadn't expected to like the man, since Phil appeared not to, but thought she might take to him all the same.

'Excellent,' Marjorie murmured politely, popping a second ham and asparagus canapé into her mouth, although she suspected it owed nothing to the girl's culinary skills, having more than likely found its way from the food hall of a well-known store. 'I've just been admiring your room, Jade. I pity whoever it was that had the job of painting the coving. So finicky! And so high up!'

'Oh.' Jade smiled. 'That was me. Spent more than a week up a ladder, in odd moments. I like doing that kind of thing. In fact I painted most of the flat. It was a dump before I moved in with Olly. I wondered, at first, why he'd bothered to rent it. But clearly he saw its potential.'

'You did all this yourself? Well, Philip's father would just love you!' Seeing Jade's mystification she added, 'He runs a couple of DIY shops.'

'A chain of stores,' Phil amended, his eyes fixed on the contents of the cut-glass tumbler he'd been handed. 'He owns them, actually. I mean "it".'

'A chain?' Pretending to choke a little on her fino sherry Marjorie patted her chest. 'Well, I suppose you could call three back street stores a chain. As

146

for my father-in-law owning them: well, it's true, he does. But the way they're going lately, Phil reckons he'd be better off as a Lloyds' name.'

'I'm sure I never said that–'

'It's more or less what you said, dear.' She turned to smile at Jade. 'Not that Philip would know much about the business. He can't tell plumber's tape from Polyfilla.'

Phil sat down in a wing chair that protruded large clawed feet, and flicked imaginary fluff from his trousers. 'Well,' he bit back at his wife, 'we haven't *all* had your experience of life behind the shop counter.'

'But some of us could have done, couldn't they, if they hadn't been too proud?'

In the small, ensuing silence, Jade sought Oliver's eye. She was beginning to wish she'd never suggested inviting these people. Hadn't she endured enough years of her parents' bickering without taking on someone else's? She pressed on. 'So you worked in your father-in-law's shops, Mrs Benson? I'm sure that must have been interesting.'

'Marjorie, if you please. Well, yes, sometimes I did work *in* them. Mostly I ran the business side of things. Accounts and so on. I loved it. It's what I did before I had the children – worked for a firm of accountants.'

'And you had to leave it all behind to come down here? That must have been rather hard.'

'Well –' Marjorie warmed to the young woman

'– I must say I wasn't at all keen to move. It was really rather a wrench.'

'No sense of adventure, my wife. Likes things to stay as they are.' Phil leaned over the canapés and helped himself to one. 'She thought she would never make new friends, but it's proving less daunting than she thought. You've managed to make one already, haven't you, Marjie? Stella, I think you called her. You were telling me the other day.'

While Marjorie wondered how to respond to this blatantly patronising statement – it cut her to the level of a child being quizzed after its first day at school – Phil went on, 'And what do you do, Jade? What line of work are you in?'

'I'm a legal executive,' Jade answered quickly, eager to re-focus the conversation. 'At least, I'm studying to qualify as one; I shall be sitting for the Institute's exams later this year. But really I want to be a solicitor, preferably getting involved in court cases. So I intend to take it all a lot further if I can.'

'Phew!' Phil blew out his cheeks, as with one clearly impressed. He was about to express his admiration more fully when Marjorie butted in.

'Like a barrister, you mean? Good heavens. Now that's a job I could *not* do.'

'No, Marjorie, dear. Because you simply don't have the brain.'

Phil's unkind comment caused a ripple of amusement, albeit an awkward one, and Marjorie's

148

eyes glittered as she went on, 'What I meant was this . . .'

Ignoring Phil's forbidding expression – the one he wore whenever he suspected she was about to show her ignorance in company – she went on to explain that she couldn't see how anyone could possibly defend a person who was obviously guilty as sin, and perhaps even get them off a serious charge so that they were free to commit further crimes. 'I just couldn't do it,' she finished firmly. 'It really would be going against the grain.'

Oliver broke his silence. 'My sentiments precisely,' he said. 'Two-faced shysters most of these lawyers are. And Jade won't mind my saying this. She knows my views on the legal profession. They're –'

'He thinks,' Jade put in quickly, 'they're a bunch of –' She stopped, clearly unsure as to whether Oliver's opinion was at all repeatable in the older woman's company, thus awarding Marjorie the modesty – and no doubt the longevity – of Mother Teresa.

'Well, most of the ones I've come across rip you off something shocking.' Oliver clammed up again and took a gulp of his drink.

Jade smiled at the others and shrugged. 'He's only met one or two. Anyway, let me try to answer you, Marjorie.'

And Philip sat enthralled as the girl, radiant in her earnestness, put her case.

'You see, it's not for the defence advocate to take

on the whole responsibility of a case. I don't think so, anyway. Surely the prosecution has as much of a share in it too? Not to mention the judge in the manner of his summing up; *his* influence on a jury can be crucial. You see, I believe it's up to the prosecution to prepare its case properly and to cross-examine defendants effectively. If it fails in that duty and the defendant's acquitted, can the defence really be to blame?'

To Marjorie this sounded a cop-out, but she was too polite to say so. And far too sick by halves to trust herself to say anything more. This lovely young girl had everything: a superb home, a presentable young partner, a respectable career in the making – in fact the whole world at her feet. And that included Philip, sitting with his tongue hanging out.

'Well,' Philip said after a thoughtful pause, 'I must say I think it an excellent choice of career, Jade. At least *you'll* never be out of work. The way things are going these days, with everyone suing everyone else over the least little thing, we'll all be consulting our solicitors before daring to draw breath.'

They had risen from their seats as Philip spoke, on a signal from Oliver that they should begin their meal. Jade led them through a set of double doors into the dining room, where the mood of the party was lifted by the antics of Oliver's chipmunks in their cage.

'Jade's forbidden me to let them out this evening,' Oliver complained, but Phil looked relieved and Marjorie, unsure of the creatures, contented herself with cooing at them from a safe distance. It wasn't long, though, before something else took her attention.

At the far end of the room a pair of long, filmy curtains billowed by an open door and, enticed there by the warm scents of evening, Marjorie discovered that it led outside to a short flight of crazy-paved steps. Half-way up the steps sat a stone cat, and a little higher up an urn cascaded its abundant growth of variegated ivy.

'A garden?' she couldn't help asking, turning back to Jade. 'A garden right up here?'

'A roof garden. Come and see.' Smiling with secret pleasure, Jade glided ahead of her up the steps.

Marjorie let out a gasp when she reached the top. In the fading light she could see flagstones, raised brick flower beds, and patio containers by the dozen: squat wooden tubs, tall strawberry jars, terracotta pots and stone troughs.

The garden might have been tiny but was so attractive that it mattered not in the least. A wrought iron table allowed two or three people to eat in comfort, and an alcove of spotted laurels partly concealed a curved bench seat which was well-padded with bold check cushions in green. Most of the area was bordered and screened by flowering shrubs, but in places here and there stone balustrading could be seen, too beautiful to be covered up.

Urged on by curiosity, Marjorie put her hands on the cool, carved ledge and peered over. To her delight she found the city laid out at her feet, its lights beginning to sparkle as the evening deepened to night. She stood holding her breath, convinced she could hear the city itself, buzzing with human life.

'Oh, but this is lovely. Lovely,' she whispered. So much so that her vision blurred with tears and turned the lights into stars. Her skirt fluttered about her legs, caught on a current of air, reminding her of Spain; of balmy nights on a balcony, with the sea sighing unseen; of holding hands with Philip, and feeling young again.

A sadness overwhelmed her. A sorrow for things now lost.

'Do you know,' she said when Oliver had managed to usher them back to the dining table, 'do you know what Philip chose for us to live in?' She knew she shouldn't be saying what she was about to say but Oliver had been over-generous with the sherry decanter and she couldn't help herself. Resentment welled in her veins, drowning out all loyal thoughts. 'I don't know whether you know the Brightwells estate between Bristol and Bath?'

'Er – yes, we do know it,' Jade said carefully, lighting three blue tapered candles in a silver candelabra.

'Well,' Marjorie went on, 'enough said.' But she proceeded at once to say more. 'Our house is the one stuck all on its own in a sea of mud. And yesterday I went to a coffee morning –' she looked at Phil who knew nothing of this because she hadn't told him '– where, incidentally, I felt thoroughly out of place since the other women were all half my age with hordes of children in tow, and do you know what they said to me?'

'Marjie, I really don't think . . .'

'They said they'd nicknamed our house "Colditz". "Colditz" would you believe! Wanted to know what I'd done to be put there, and how had I managed to escape.'

That, she recalled, shaking out one of Jade's water-lily napkins with a firm flick of her wrist, was before they realised she was the sales director's wife. They'd hardly spoken to her after that.

'If you'd shown more interest in the move . . .' Phil ground out, but Jade cleared her throat more noisily than she needed and excused herself to fetch the starters.

Neither Marjorie nor Philip saw the look she gave Oliver as she sashayed from the room.

12

'Chipmunks!' Phil muttered to himself as he passed the door to Oliver's office next morning. Wagging his head he pushed open the door to his own. What a poser that man was! The jumped-up little ponce. For surely he kept the darned creatures purely for effect; to make himself more interesting; in the same way that he swanked with those wretched cigars.

And he was expected to trust a man like that?

Phil dumped his briefcase on the desk and scowled at it. He was damned if he was going to trust him with the Sinden fiasco. That needed careful handling. A potential market, such as Sinden had to offer, was far too big to lose, but he and his cronies were showing clear signs of looking elsewhere – probably in the direction of Spittal's biggest rival Foretec.

Foretec was run by an extremely astute entrepreneur by the name of Ericson – and Holy Joe would not be at all impressed if Phil let the market drop into his hands the minute he took over the reins. No, he certainly wouldn't. Well, that wasn't going to happen. He would scoot up to these Sinden people in Gloucester and jolly well sort them out.

Flipping open the briefcase he snatched up a sheaf of papers and put out a finger to buzz for his secretary. Then he changed his mind. He ought to see Oliver in person and repeat his thanks for last night; then he would tell him about the trip.

The spade bounced off the ground. Marjorie thrust it down more forcefully. Metal clanged on broken brick, pain jarred through fragile flesh, and Marjorie puffed with the unaccustomed effort. But all to no avail.

Leaning on the handle of the spade she surveyed her handiwork: a spade-width strip of lumpy soil a metre or so in length, and a growing mound of rubble. Not much to show for an hour's hard labour. And really two spits were her minimum requirements whereas she had barely achieved one half. The job would take her a hundred years at this rate. But what did that matter? She had nothing better to do. No fascinating career waiting in the wings for the likes of her.

She gazed about her. It was impossible not to compare what she had to contend with, with Jade and Oliver's miniature paradise. Lucky Jade! She had inherited her garden from the previous tenant; hadn't had to lift a finger. It simply wasn't fair.

'Gorgeous little garden,' Marjorie had said to Philip on the way home in the taxi. They had stopped bickering by then, having mellowed during the course of the evening with the help of a good deal of Oliver's alcohol, and she'd been sitting slumped like an over-stuffed pillow with her head resting on Phil's shoulder. 'Beautiful flat, too.'

'Mm,' he'd agreed sleepily, his voice growling close to her ear. 'A terrific meal, I thought. Food fit for a king.'

Marjorie lifted her head. This from a man who had always preferred good, plain home-cooking! 'Well –' she felt she had to put him wise '– I'm sure most of it was bought in. Pre-prepared, I mean.'

'So? Does that really matter?' He yawned, clicking his jaw. 'She's a lovely-looking girl.'

Marjorie had shifted to the corner of the seat then. 'Yes.' she'd said. 'Lovely.'

'Clever, too.'

Too beautiful and clever by half, Marjorie added now in her thoughts, parking herself on an old oil drum and wiping her beaded forehead. Phil had been right about that. As right as he'd been that morning on looking through the breakfast room window and seeing the beginnings of her trough: he'd told her she was wasting her time.

She had challenged him as to just when, precisely, the team of garden designers would arrive.

'You did say,' she reminded him, 'that we could have it done professionally.'

'Did I?' If he had ever made such a promise he'd obviously forgotten it – probably lost sight of it among the multitude of pledges he'd had to make to get her to move from London. 'Well, yes. Maybe I did. And we shall, one day. We shall.'

'One day? When? How soon?' Marjorie wanted action *now*.

'As soon as our finances have had time to recover.' He drained his big, breakfast-time mug and set it down on the table. 'We still have curtains to buy, haven't we? Blinds for the conservatory, too. And then there's the expense of your car. Anyway, it's hardly the weather for that kind of thing – planting and laying out lawns. Put anything in the ground at the moment and it'll shrivel to death within days.'

He had waved at the hazy sky, at the rapidly strengthening sun, both of which augured well for more hot weather to come, and Marjorie had pressed her lips together. She had already made up trays of seedlings and watered them with great care; soon they would need to be planted out. Just one small bed would have been something. Something to satisfy her soul. It seemed so little to ask.

But now, comparing the dug-over ground with the rest of the impossible plot, she had to admit defeat. At least for today, anyhow. Stella had invited her over for lunch.

Since moving to the Bristol site Phil had been vaguely aware of subtle differences between his office and Oliver's but had been too busy with more important matters to consider such things. It was only now, on stepping into Oliver's room and with the sun's full glare suddenly striking him, that the facts hit home: here there were windows on two of the walls whereas his own room had only one; it was lighter, brighter, and possibly even bigger. But that wasn't all. Oliver's desk had a useful extension on one end and a footstool underneath. There were two more pictures than Phil could lay claim to, and even a ceiling fan.

Sidling over to the nearest window he caught a glimpse of fields. Fields! Instead of a row of pylons and the car park! What was going on? His eyes circled the room once more as he made his speech of thanks for an enjoyable evening. He was *sure* this office should have been his. And he wouldn't have put it past young Knox to have swapped before he arrived.

'This Sinden business over in Gloucester,' he went on, the pleasantries quickly despatched, 'I'll be seeing to it all myself. Need to get my face known . . . that sort of thing. You know.'

'Oh, but –' Oliver froze in front of his coffee machine, his hand seemingly welded to the handle of the Pyrex jug '– that surely isn't possible?'

'What? Not – not possible? What do you mean by that?'

'Um –' Oliver cast about for an answer and miraculously found one '– well, Marjorie wouldn't be happy, for one thing. I mean, aren't you both waiting for a call? From the daughter expecting a baby?'

Phil accepted a cup of coffee and sipped the

bitter brew, recalling that Marjorie had mentioned the matter at the dinner, between mouthfuls of *gâteau Saint-Honoré*. Damn! He had promised her that nothing whatever should interfere with their plan to rush to Becky together, the minute they were called. He could hardly drop everything to fulfil that promise if he was in the middle of dealing with Sinden. It was going to be difficult enough as things stood, having to take leave at a moment's notice for domestic reasons; so soon after starting in the job too. He'd already squared that with H J, of course, but even so . . .

Phil sat down in Oliver's visitors' chair and toyed with a lacquered enamel fountain pen, turning it over and over on the desk top and making a tapping sound.

'I can handle Sinden OK,' Oliver tried to convince him, parading about the office with his chest thrown out. 'No problem. Just you leave him to me. He'll be eating out of my hand by the time I've finished with him.'

'Sure he won't bite it off?' Phil shook his head, scowling. 'I don't know . . .'

'I promise you, you won't regret leaving it to me.'

'Well . . .' Phil struggled to reason with himself. Oliver had a good track record, it couldn't be denied. He shouldn't let his dislike of the man colour his judgement.

So finally he conceded. There was nothing else he could do. Well, there was perhaps *something*: with Oliver out of the way for a while he could make one or two changes. Starting with moving offices.

Oliver cheered silently after Phil had slunk back to his desk. He punched the air with his fist. It had been touch and go for a while. His heart had leaped into his mouth when he realised Benson was trying to muscle in on his act, but it was all turning out fine. The visit to the expected grandchild would keep the boss from sniffing around Jade – oh, yes, he'd noticed how he'd ogled her! – while he, Oliver, went on the Sinden trip. And the Sinden trip would take him near to Sally and the kids for a last ditch attempt. He might be able to see the kids and sort out something with Sally, or with the solicitor he'd consulted in the past. She simply couldn't keep financially crippling him the way she was. Something had to be done.

Stella and her husband lived in a converted barn, high on the downs a few miles out of Bath. Marjorie, trying to familiarise herself with the controls of her new car and at the same time read a map spread out beside her, spared a moment to wonder why her friend chose to do her voluntary work so far from where she lived. But the question slipped her mind for the first half-hour of her visit; there were other matters to distract her.

Stella, she realised, arriving at the barn and locking the car door, must be worth a pretty penny. The barn rose up before her, larger than a chapel, its odd arrangement of doors and windows indicating dozens of rooms within. An impractical but snazzy sports car could be seen parked under cover to one side of the building, next to Stella's efficient run-about and a large four-by-four. Presumably there was yet another car that her husband used for work.

Stella appeared at the door while Marjorie was still coming to terms with her gracious surroundings.

'What a terrific view you have here,' Marjorie said, breathing in the cool dampness of a nearby shrubbery while scanning the valley below. She could see cows in a field, and farm buildings, and a railway tunnelling into a hill. On a patch of green sat a pretty church with a tiny, miniature graveyard, the tombstones protruding like teeth.

All around her was silence, save the faint swish of traffic on the distant trunk road: a more perfect position for a home would be difficult to find. But all Stella could say, turning her back on it, was a languid 'yes', which left Marjorie to assume that familiarity must indeed breed contempt.

She followed Stella to the sitting room – a large space at the centre of the barn, two stories high with a gallery half-way up and running along three sides. The wall without the gallery was entirely glazed and looked out on to a courtyard.

Fascinated by the ways in which other people lived. Marjorie longed to investigate the whole conversion, but it appeared not to occur to Stella that she might be interested. In fact Stella's attitude towards her everyday surroundings was so off-hand that Marjorie refrained from referring to them at all. She fixed her attention on her friend.

And now that she thought about it, Stella's other-worldliness showed in the way she did her hair – or rather, didn't do it, for it hung almost to her shoulders in a grown-out perm, badly needing a trim. And it showed in the things she wore. The clothes were of excellent quality and no doubt expensive, but they were dull and decidedly frumpy.

Today Marjorie sported a red linen-weave trouser suit and a knotted silk scarf, both of which might even have met with the approval of Becky and Em. The girls would probably have said something like 'nice suit, shame about the bum' and fallen about laughing, but never mind: half a compliment was better than none. Anyhow, Marjorie felt positively young and smartly dressed in comparison with Stella in her rigidly-pleated skirt, flat slip-ons, and primly-buttoned blouse – all of which were in shades of beige.

The food, when Stella brought it to the low coffee table at which they were sitting, showed little imagination either: wedges of Cheddar cheese lay on two white plates beside thickly-sliced granary bread, with short sticks of celery as an accompaniment. A choice of mineral water or orange juice was put to her.

'And you don't mind eating in here, do you?'

Stella stated rather than asked as she lowered her tray to the table.

'No, not at all,' Marjorie assured her, schooling herself not to look out into the courtyard where a wooden picnic table beckoned from the cool dappled shade of old trees.

As soon as Stella returned to the kitchen Marjorie loosened her scarf. In spite of the room's vast size it felt suffocating, the air unchanged in months. Not one part of the glass wall had been opened, she noticed, though a number of handles and hinges could be seen. By the time Stella returned with their drinks Marjorie had worked out that a large portion of the glazing could be slid back, making the room and the yard as one. And yet, on this glorious day, Stella chose to keep herself shut in. Perhaps she suffered from hay fever.

'You did say you wanted to lose weight,' Stella said, casting a dubious glance over the frugal meal as though seeing it for the first time, 'though heaven knows you don't need to. You look perfectly all right to me.'

Marjorie flushed and laughed. 'You're very kind, Stella. But try telling Philip that. He's always watching what I eat.'

'At least it sounds as if he cares.'

'Cares?' Marjorie doubted that, nowadays, and wondered at Stella's tone. Her words had sounded bitter. And as soon as they were out of her mouth she'd snapped on a celery stalk as though biting off someone's head.

It was then that, bewildered at finding her friend less mild and gentle than she'd thought on first acquaintance, and wondering whether perhaps her husband didn't care either, that Marjorie decided to change the subject and ask about her voluntary work. Why did she travel so far to do it?

'There must be something closer to home for you; though, for my sake, I'm glad you don't. You're the only friend I've managed to make so far.'

Marjorie couldn't see Phil and herself fraternising overmuch with Jade and Oliver. They would invite them back for dinner one day, of course, and they were a nice enough couple, but the differences in their ages and life-styles would allow for little else.

Stella was looking at her plate. 'Ian prefers it that way.'

'Sorry?'

'He doesn't really like me to work there. Thinks it's not good enough for me. But when Adam left home –' Adam was a son in New Zealand '– there was this great big gap in my life. I had to do something . . . and I've always had a fancy for running a shop or some such.' Stella's face became more animated than Marjorie had ever seen it. 'Do you know what I'd really like to do?'

'Tell me.'

'Well, I'd love to buy a canal boat and turn it into a restaurant.'

'A floating restaurant! Sounds great. Why don't you go ahead and do it?' Advising others to be adventurous was easy. Pity she couldn't come up with a similar plan for herself.

'Oh . . .' Stella shook her head. 'Anyway we argued, Ian and I, over my volunteering for the charity shop. But I held out –' she set her chin and straightened her shoulders as she'd probably done at the time '– and eventually he agreed; as long as I promised not to play in his back yard, so to speak – Bath being his back yard.'

Marjorie's eyebrows lifted.

'So,' Stella went on with a grim smile, 'I do my good works wherever I can be sure of not bumping into his business associates. Or their wives. Huh! As if any of them would walk into a charity shop. Them with their Porsches and Mercedes. I doubt whether they could walk anywhere if they wanted to. Lost the use of their legs.'

Stella's voice had risen a little higher with each condemnation. There were now two pink patches on her cheeks and, Marjorie thought, trying not to notice, big fat tears in her eyes. Poor Stella! Poor me! How do I handle this?

'I'm sorry.' Stella grabbed one of the pink paper napkins she'd provided with the meal and began to dab at her nose. 'I didn't mean to say any of that.'

'Oh, I didn't hear anything.' Marjorie waved a hand. 'Look, you're just having a low day. I get them too. Some mornings I wake up feeling absolutely lousy. Like I've got a hangover – you know? And I hardly ever drink! I'm afraid it's par for the course at our –'

'This is nothing to do with the menopause.' Stella shook her head.

'Well . . . whatever it is, would you like to talk about it? I mean, only if you want to. I wouldn't want to pry.'

'I wouldn't know where to start. I'm not used to talking about myself. No one to talk *to*. No one I feel I can trust, anyway.'

'Try. It might help. Just to get it off your chest.'

Stella, looking doubtful, pushed her food to one side. She took a breath. 'Ian and I were very close in the early days. We hadn't a penny to our name but we were happy. And Ian was going places; that much was clear. He's what's generally called a self-made man. Clever. Dedicated. He's hauled himself up by the boot straps.'

'He certainly has done well for himself.' Marjorie nodded at her surroundings.

'He owns his own company now. Manages it all himself. Loves it. Loves the challenge. I don't think he'll ever retire.'

'But I suppose it keeps him too busy. Is that what you're going to say? He leaves no time for you.'

'That's part of it, I suppose. I've always been secondary to the business. I complain about that, of course, and he tells me I shouldn't rely on him, I ought to mix more, but it's not as simple as that. The sort of people he has in mind for me to mix with, the circle in which we move – well, they aren't really our kind. Not my kind, anyway. I don't share their background. I don't like golf, and parties, and

– and all that sort of thing. It's not me, is it?'

Marjorie smiled her agreement. 'And money doesn't mean much to you, does it?'

'No.' Stella gave a small shudder. 'No. It was never what I wanted. But Ian did. And because he wanted money and success, and because I wanted him to be happy, I helped him all I could,'

Marjorie waited for her to continue, wondering what had gone wrong. Another woman, maybe?

Stella struggled for the right words. 'I used to be such a positive person,' she went on. 'Confident. When I look back –' she leaned forward with her elbows on her knees, digging her fingers into her hair '– I see myself as I was and I wonder where I've gone. Somewhere along the line I've lost my identity; become subsumed, somehow, into the marriage. Personally I haven't developed at all. I haven't lived *my* life. I've had no control over it. I handed that over to Ian all those years ago. I gave up my independence for his sake, for the business' sake. And now I'm left with what? Nothing. Nothing but regret. Bitter, bitter, regret.'

Marjorie floundered inwardly, not knowing what to say. Stella's words, frankly, frightened her. Even close friends seldom exposed their tortured souls in this way – and Stella was a virtual stranger. 'I'm sure Ian never intended –'

'Of course he didn't intend anything! I'm not accusing him. It isn't Ian I'm angry with.'

'No?'

'No! It's me!' She stabbed a finger at her chest.

'Me, for letting it happen. Why did I let it happen?'

'I suppose you didn't realise –'

'I didn't. That's true. I didn't.' She wrung her hands and fixed Marjorie with her eyes. 'Loss of self-esteem can happen so very gradually, you know. It's an insidious process; you don't see it happening. You put your trust in a man and little by little he puts you down . . .' Stella pressed two knuckles to her mouth. Perhaps she'd said too much. 'I'm sorry.' She forced the faintest of smiles. 'I hope I haven't scared you off.'

'Scared me?' Marjorie grimaced. 'Worried, is more the word I'd use.'

And later, as she drove home, having done her best to console Stella, her worry increased with each mile. It nagged at her and wouldn't leave her alone. It was only when Phil came home that she understood why Stella's outpourings so weighed upon her: couldn't much of what had been said apply to her too? Because hadn't she lost control of her own life – had it snatched away from her by Phil? And since then, what had he done to support her, to encourage her to start something new? Nothing. Rather, he'd pooh-poohed all her suggestions and made her feel quite useless. If she wasn't careful her self-esteem, like Stella's, would be whittled to nothing too.

13

The last person Jade wanted to bump into was The Beast from the basement. The Beast owned the building that she and Oliver lived in and let it out as three flats, occupying the 'below stairs' area himself. Whenever Jade came face to face with him every signal in her body switched to red alert. The gleam in his eye alone was enough to send her screaming in the opposite direction as fast as she could go.

This evening, willing herself to stand still, she waited as he hailed her across the vestibule, claiming he had something important to tell her.

'What is it?' Wide-eyed, she gripped the newel post at the foot of the stairs, wondering how nimble he might be on those big flat feet of his. Would she be able to reach the flat and slam the door behind her in an emergency? How fast could gorillas move? She scarcely took in what he was saying.

'Selling?' She picked up the salient word.

'That's right.' His grin showed tombstone teeth. 'You each have the option to buy. Or else you'll have to get out.'

Buy! Buy! Jade couldn't wait to tell Oliver. It had often passed through her mind that, after all the effort they had put into the place, at the end of the day it would never be theirs. But now it was a possibility. And she could tell Oliver right away because, having made her escape from The Beast, she could hear the phone ringing inside the flat.

But it wasn't Oliver; it was her sister.

'Oh. Selina,' she answered flatly, wedging the portable phone under her chin while pouring a glass of water. She kicked off her shoes, took the glass and the phone to the roof garden, and slumped down on the seat. Selina would be on the phone for ages, moaning about her boyfriends. She had three on the go at the moment, and Jade had little sympathy for the problems she brought on herself.

'Look, why don't you come round some time and we'll talk about it?' Jade told her as soon as she could squeeze in a word. 'Must go now. I can hear Olly. Come whenever you like.'

Oliver plodded up the steps to join Jade, stripping off his shirt as he went. 'You look too happy by far,' he told her morosely as she hurled herself into his arms. She was beaming with her news about buying the flat, but on seeing his glum expression her smile dimmed a little.

'What's the matter?' she asked.

'Benson. As usual. Need you ask?'

Jade swallowed. 'What is it this time?'

Oliver leaned against the balustrade, exposing

his bare back to the sun's dying heat. 'He's sending me over to Gloucester. I'll be away for several nights.'

'Well?' She leaned beside him. 'So what's so awful about that? What's different? You're always having to go away with the job.'

'I know. But I've been away a lot lately.' He stroked her hair. 'I want more time with you.'

'Darling.' She kissed him; a kiss that lengthened and lingered. How could she have thought he might have another woman? 'We'll just have to make more of the time we do have together,' she murmured. 'Won't we?'

'Now?' He smiled. 'Here?'

'I don't think anyone can see us. But first, let me tell you my good news. I'll bust if I don't tell you soon.'

'Go on, then. What is it?'

She explained how The Beast had waylaid her and how he was giving them the opportunity to buy the flat. But the more her face brightened at the prospect, the more his darkened and drooped.

'Jade,' he said, pushing her away from him, 'have you gone stark staring mad?'

'Oliver! Don't be horrid! What's the matter? I don't understand what's wrong.'

'No, you don't, do you. You haven't a bloody clue.'

'I beg your pardon?'

'About money. Not a bloody clue. How do you think you and I are going to buy this flat? Any flat.

Or even a cardboard box. I haven't the money. And you certainly haven't. You've been spending it all like water.'

Indignation flared. 'Most of what I've spent,' Jade began in a low voice, 'has gone on things for the flat. It was a dump when I moved in. Remember? Can you wonder I've so little left? But I haven't seen *you* making much of a contribution. Show me what *you've* bought. Go on. Show me!'

Oliver stood and stared at her. He couldn't point to one thing.

'Exactly,' she went on. 'So where's your salary gone? You earn heaps more than I do. Or is that a stupid question? Because you've spent it all on women, I suppose. That's why you're stony broke.'

'That's utterly ridiculous.'

'Is it? Is it really? A harem can't come cheap. And how about that blood-sucking wife of yours, not to mention the snotty-nosed kids?'

'Jade . . .'

'But this isn't about money, is it? It's really to do with commitment. Well I'm not asking for that; I wouldn't waste my breath. I know your views all too well. I've no intention of trying to tie you down, Oliver, the very minute you become free. I've merely made a practical suggestion. But it seems that even buying half a flat's too much of a commitment for you.'

She started down the steps, stopped by the urn and turned to him. 'If we don't buy this place we have to vacate it; find somewhere else. Perhaps you'll let me know what you want me to look for. A flat for one – or for two?'

'It's looking good, Marjie. Good.'

Standing at the door to the dining room Phil surveyed the table arrangement: best cutlery, pink napkins, and a centrepiece of bought rosebuds, just beginning to unfurl. Marjorie had done well.

It was their turn to entertain – not a return visit from Jade and Oliver but Marjorie's new friend and her husband.

Phil had breathed a sigh of relief when she'd told him about it. It meant she had made up her mind to overcome her fear of gas, and not before time, either. Oh, he could sympathise, of course, but to be honest he was tired of having to treat her with kid gloves; of having to tip-toe carefully in case he made matters worse and sent her over the edge again. He couldn't cope with another breakdown. Sometimes he wished . . . well, he wished she could be stronger, more go-ahead, more independent. Like young Jade, for example. Women these days were so different . . .

Well, anyway, at least Marjorie must have managed to make friends with the cooker, because she'd be pushed to produce a three-course meal of entirely cold ingredients, wouldn't she?

And, sure enough, he had arrived home from the office that evening and been hit by an unmistakable blast of garlic frying with onions.

'Pork medallions with mushrooms and cream,'

she told him happily – even a little smugly – as she unmoulded a salmon mousse ring. 'This mousse is for starters and there's my special lemon tart to finish. I've been in the kitchen all day.'

It was only when they were up in their bedroom, changing for the occasion, that Philip thought to ask her for some details about the expected couple. He knew they were in their own age group, which was all to the good. He also knew that Marjorie felt sorry for the woman she'd befriended, which was probably how she had put the gas business into perspective: she couldn't let her anxiety stand in the way of a friend's need.

He dropped a kiss on her head in passing; she was a good sort really. She might have been giving him a hard time lately, and maybe that was understandable; things hadn't been quite up to *his* expectations, if he was honest with himself, let alone hers. But now it looked as though she was making a real effort to settle into the new way of life, and he appreciated it.

'What was that for?' she asked, looking up from easing new tights over her toes.

'Just because.' He smiled at her fondly and began searching for his silver cuff-links. 'By the way, you'd better brief me a bit more about these folk. I don't want to go putting my foot in anything.'

'There isn't much more I can tell you. You know they live in a beautiful place called Top Barn; they have a son who lives in New Zealand; and they aren't short of a bob or two. He owns his own company, as I said –'

'And the woman's name is Stella.' Phil frowned with concentration, committing the facts to memory.

'Yes. And he's called Ian.'

'Surname?'

'Oh –' Marjorie shook her head '– I don't think Stella's ever said. Does it matter? Wait a minute. Yes. It's Ericson. Someone came to the shop and called her that. I remember it because of your father being an Eric and you Eric's son. Get it?'

'Ericson.' A switch clicked on in Phil's mind. Was it for the same reason as Marjorie's: that it echoed his father's name? Or was it for some other –

'*Christ all-bloody-mighty!*' He leaped off the bed as though his pants were on fire. Cuff-links skittered across the carpet and Marjorie drew lipstick on her chin.

'What ever's the matter, Phil?' She reached for a tissue with annoyance.

'Quick, give me some change.' He hauled up his trousers. 'No, don't bother. I've got a card for the phone. Somewhere in my wallet, I think. When are they going to connect us, I'd like to know? It's an absolute disgrace.'

'I don't know.' Marjorie shook her head at him as though he'd taken leave of his senses.

'I'm really sorry about this, Marjorie.' He looked at his watch, spun full circle, and checked the watch again. 'We're going to have to cancel. I only

177

hope to goodness I can get to the phone in time.'
He paused long enough to grab her arms. 'D'you
think they'll have started out yet?'

'*Cancel?*' she shrieked into his face. 'What do you
mean, cancel?'

'I'll tell them you've got a migraine. That won't
sound too feeble, will it? Yes, that'll do all right;
you're always getting headaches.'

'You're giving me one right now. And I'm *not*
going to find you their phone number. For heaven's
sake, Phil, what's got into you?'

He was flitting about the room like a fly trapped
in a jam jar.

'Foretec,' he snapped at her. 'I just hope they're
not ex-directory.'

'What –?'

'He runs bloody Foretec.'

'You've lost me.' She shrugged, spreading her
hands. 'And those are odd shoes you're putting on.'

'Sod the sodding shoes.' He carried on tying
laces. 'Foretec, you *must* know – I've talked about
them often enough – are one of our deadliest
enemies. Our rivals. Competitors. They make the
same stuff that we do. And Ericson runs the show.'

'So?'

'Sometimes I despair.' He threw her his best
what-kind-of-a-moron-have-I-married look. 'So we
can't have them over for dinner, can we?'

'Who says?' She ran after him down the stairs.
'We can have whoever we like.'

'Anyone but the Ericsons.'

178

'But that's being so silly. You don't have to talk about business. In fact I'm sure Stella and I would rather you didn't. We'll talk about other things.'

'That's hardly the point.'

They were out on the drive now, with Phil tugging open the door of his car and Marjorie pressing her hands down on the bonnet in a vain attempt to prevent him taking off. 'You can't do this, Phil. I won't let you. Think of all my cooking.'

He stuck his head through the window. 'Marjorie, I must. We can't have them here. Everyone knows that Spittal's have been cherry-picking on his patch. And the minute Ericson found out who I am there'd be salmon mousse on the ceiling.'

Philip returned from the phone box to find Marjorie standing in the middle of the kitchen staring forlornly at the salmon mousse in her hand. Garnished with twists of lemon and cucumber, and with a border of green-tinted mayonnaise, it looked most attractive. But there was only so much that two people could eat.

'Mission accomplished,' he said, throwing down his car keys and pulling out a chair.

'I should tip this over your head,' she told him. 'I think I'd enjoy doing that.'

He sat back with a wary eye on her. 'It isn't really my fault, is it? It's just one of those things. Unfortunate. And I'm sorry. Sorry about your friend.'

'What does cherry-picking mean, anyway?'

'Filching Ericson's best workers. Offering them

a better deal. Saves us training up staff, you see, and –'

'I think I get the picture.' She sighed. She would rather not get it, though. She didn't like to be reminded of the distasteful aspects of her husband's line of business. They made her feel uncomfortable about the roof over her head and the cars in the garage, not to mention the food on the table. And could she have run three shops without being equally ruthless? That was something she would never know now.

She slopped two generous portions of mousse on to their everyday plates, determined that none of it should go to waste. But she couldn't eat any herself; her stomach was churning with anger.

'And how,' she demanded, watching Phil prod his share with little enthusiasm, 'how am I supposed to face Stella in the morning? I'm on duty in the charity shop tomorrow and so is she. But I'll not be able to look her in the eye, will I? I'm hopeless at telling lies. I'll never be able to explain . . .'

Phil chewed over his answer for a long time. Finally he said, 'Actually, I think it would be better if you dropped her altogether. Find yourself another friend – couldn't you? It would make things so much easier if you did –'

'Oh, I'm sure it would make things easier! For *you*.'

14

Marjorie used the phone box every day to keep in touch with Becky. Was there any sign of the baby yet? The girl's reply was always of the wearied 'how-much-longer-can-this-take?' variety, for she was now several days overdue. So when next morning Marjorie received no answer at all she had no doubt as to the reason for it.

She immediately phoned Phil but he – most aggravatingly – was at an important meeting, which his secretary was loath to interrupt. Having then tried to contact her son-in-law, his parents, and Phil's parents, without success, Marjorie could do little else but return home, pack a bag, and wait. It would have been pointless to travel in separate cars.

She was on the verge of returning to the phone for the fifth time when Phil's car came hurtling across the Red Sea in a cloud of dust.

'So you finally got the news,' she snarled at him the minute he walked in to the house.

'Sorry –' he spread his hands.

'We'll never make it in time!'

And of course they didn't. When they finally reached Becky in hospital the initial flurries of excitement were over; Becky had had a post delivery nap and was sitting up in bed proudly clutching a cellular blanket containing her hours' old daughter.

'Charlotte Louise,' she announced, her face splitting wide with a grin.

Marjorie choked back tears and took her first grandchild into her arms, all disappointment forgotten. The baby was beautiful, safe and healthy; what more could anyone ask? Even the discovery that Steve's parents had kitted out the baby's cot and nursery with identical soft furnishings to those that Marjorie had brought, rendering her gift useless, was not enough to mar the occasion.

Philip was equally thrilled and couldn't stop talking about the new arrival, but after a few days, when Becky was allowed home, he began to show signs of restlessness. Marjorie attributed these to the fact that they were having to sleep in one of the spare rooms at his parents' house, but when she challenged him he said it was nothing to do with that.

'I just feel superfluous,' he complained, dodging Becky's husband Steve, who at the time was trying to erect the ironing board in the middle of the tiny kitchen while Marjorie boiled an egg for Becky's breakfast and Steve's mother brushed out baby bottles at the sink. He averted his eyes from the window sill above the sink where two nipple shields stood guard either side of a fiendish-looking breast pump.

'And anyway,' he excused himself, seeing that any minute now he would once more be demoted to 'chief folder-upper and consigner of laundry to the airing cupboard', 'Oliver Knox is out of the office for the next few days; I really ought to be there. It's all right –' he held up a hand to Marjorie '– you can stay as long as you like and keep the car. I'll go back on the train.'

'Suits me,' Marjorie grunted. Bristol and the Brightwells estate already seemed a long way off, not real somehow. She had slipped back into her old life with its familiar surroundings as though she had never been away.

Indeed, she even found herself again considering the possibility of taking over the shops. She could commute, perhaps; so could Phil. They could take it in turns to visit each other at weekends. Phil wouldn't miss her during the week, she was sure; and she would be too busy to miss him. They might appreciate each other more when they did meet up. Yes, this might just be the answer, the only difference being that she couldn't pop in and out of her old house.

She passed the house next day though, as she made her way to the local chemist on an errand for Becky, and stopped by the front gate. So, she thought, reading the loud blue and white sale board that reared up over the hedge, the relocation company hasn't yet found a buyer.

She scanned the garden. And discovered, as she had suspected, that their idea of looking after a property failed abysmally to match her own. Her mood, still on a high over baby Charlotte, sank several degrees.

For the first time in decades the front lawn bore a distressing patchy shagginess, and weeds exulted in being allowed to stretch their tendrils across the flower beds. Old leaves had sneaked from under the shrubbery to pile up along the doorstep, and whole flocks of birds had dared to disfigure the path. Marjorie glanced up and down the street wondering whether it would be wise to take a quick look at the back garden. Could she bear to see more?

Could she bear not to! Already she was at the side of the house peering through the wrought iron gate. The back lawn, she guessed, must have been mowed once since they'd left, but once was hardly enough. It needed regular clipping at this time of year, although she comforted herself with the thought that at least it was lush and green; a little neglect had allowed it to survive the current drought better than it might otherwise have done. And the rest of the garden had blossomed with the season's warmth. Putting her hand through to lift the latch she crept in, and spent many thoughtful moments wandering from bed to bed, meeting up with much-loved friends, wishing and wondering and itching to do a little tidying – until she remembered Becky's desperate need for anti-colic teats, sighed, and hurried away.

The print blurred and lost all meaning. Jade cupped her hands round her eyes, hunched lower over the book, and forced herself to concentrate. Fifteen seconds later she pushed the tome away. It was no good, she decided, stretching her arms to the ceiling: nothing was going in.

Altogether it had been a bad day, beginning with arriving later for work than usual. With Oliver away she had set three alarm clocks to go off at ten minute intervals but had stayed awake only long enough to switch them off one by one before snuggling back to sleep; and, as bad luck would have it, her tardiness had been witnessed, not by the kindly senior partner who usually turned a blind eye rather than confront her with her laxity, but by his briskly efficient son-in-law.

With old Godfrey Hart away on a fishing holiday, his deputy had taken the long-awaited opportunity to haul Jade over the coals; not only over her time-keeping but over a number of other matters that struck her as incredibly niggling and trivial and hardly worth his breath, while he clearly considered them to be mortal sins.

And now it looked as if trouble loomed at college too. Because if she couldn't get her head round all this legal stuff her career would never get off the ground. Not only that but Joe French, her least favourite lecturer, would have a field day over her failure.

Groaning at the picture this conjured in her mind

she laid her head down on her arms, from which comforting position she could see a patch of blue sky through the dining room window.

She had refrained from studying in the roof garden; for one thing the table wouldn't hold all her books and for another it was too distracting a place. Hours could be passed out there, simply by sitting and absorbing smells and sounds, or by leaning over the balustrade and letting one's mind wander where it willed . . .

Jade found herself leaning over the balustrade, her books abandoned, wondering what Oliver might be up to. They hadn't parted the best of friends. They had argued some more about money and she had flung at him, out of the blue and without even thinking about it, that she bet Philip Benson was never mean with his money. Which hadn't gone down too well. More like a red rag to a bull really. Oliver had barely spoken to her after that.

She sighed, rotated her head to ease her neck muscles, and suddenly craved some kind of relaxing diversion. A brisk walk, maybe. Perhaps as far as the shops. She might have a little look round.

No! She really must not go shopping again.

A swim, then, and perhaps a sauna? Yes, that was almost as inviting. She would take herself off to the country club before she changed her mind.

'And this is our aerobics studio,' the girl with the pony-tail announced in her best promotional tone.

Flattening herself against the door she allowed Philip Benson, her prospective client, to peer in.

But instead of appreciating the polished sprung floor and the airy ambience provided by a wall of full-length windows Phil found himself scanning the class-in-progress for a familiar figure. Disappointed at not finding it, and a little disgusted with the heavy odour of perspiration wafting towards him in waves, he drew back into the corridor, nodded at his guide and followed her to the next venue.

With time on his hands in the evenings Phil had soon grown tired of his own company and the house at Brightwells and, remembering a promise he'd made to Marjorie almost a week ago, had headed for the country club for a tour of its attractions with a view to taking up membership.

To be honest Marjorie had shown little enthusiasm for joining when he'd first suggested it; she knew Oliver and Jade were keen members because the subject had cropped up the night of the dinner party, but she'd said she couldn't see it as being a suitable place for a pair of old fogies like themselves. Actually, he recollected, she'd paused in her weeding and stone-sifting and looked up at him as though he'd gone gaga.

'It's fine for the young and fit,' she'd pointed out, 'but we're neither of those things. And you don't like Oliver anyway, so why run the risk of bumping into him socially?'

'I just thought –' he'd nudged a half-brick with

his toe '– it would be something for us to do together.' And he'd gone on to admit, a little shame-faced, that he felt bad about having to spoil her friendship with Stella. Joining the club was his way of making it up to her, he'd told her. 'We'll meet a lot of new people. And I'm sure it'll do us good.'

Yes, it must do them good, Phil assured himself, gazing now at the array of exercise machines lined up in the gym.

Not so good for the bank balance though. The guide rattled off a list of charges as she bounced ahead of him in her short skirt and spongy trainers. The final stretch of corridor led to the reception office where she turned and gazed hopefully up at him.

'Is there anything else I can show you, Mr Benson?'

Phil frowned as he took out his cheque book. Was he doing the right thing? A fool and his money . . . But within seconds the deed was done; too late to have second thoughts.

To celebrate his new membership – and to pass a little more time – he retraced his steps to the bar in the basement. The bar had been virtually empty only minutes earlier when the guide had led him through it; a solitary barman had been there installing a fresh barrel of beer. Now, however, the place was beginning to fill with noisy, exuberant club members, all so self-satisfied with their sporting successes and their sleek, toned bodies that Phil almost changed his mind about his intended solitary drink. It was only the sight of long blonde hair that arrested him.

'Jade!' he breathed, the name whispering past his lips. It could scarcely have been audible to anyone, yet its owner turned her head.

'So –' Jade tossed her hair over her shoulder and smiled up at Phil '– you decided to grace the club with your presence after all. I was under the impression that Marjorie wasn't keen.'

'Marjorie?' Phil echoed blankly. As though he could think of no one of that name. And how had he come to be standing next to Jade's stool at the bar? He had no recollection of crossing the room, or of whom he might have left flattened in his wake, or of what he'd said on greeting her. All he knew was that this slip of a young girl had the power to undo him in a way that no other female ever had. 'Well,' he said eventually, 'we decided it would be a good idea after all.'

Pushing aside all thought of Marjorie and her true feelings on the subject of joining, he commandeered a stool for himself. 'Mind if I join you for a drink? Can I get you another one of those?'

She tipped her glass of mineral water slightly as if to find out what it was. 'Oh, a small gin with double tonic please. By all means take a seat.'

And the conversation from then on ran in short spurts and long silences as each explained how they came to be at the club at that precise moment and why they hadn't brought their 'other halves' with them.

'Oh, but it's silly of me to explain to you where Oliver is.' Jade tinkled a little laugh. 'You're the big bad ogre that sent him away!'

Phil grinned and frowned simultaneously; an almost impossible feat that made him feel he'd developed a twitch. 'You're right about the first thing: yes, I know Oliver's in Gloucester, but I think it's most unfair of you to call me an ogre. Listening to you, anyone would think I'd sent him there against his will.'

'Well, you have . . . haven't you?' She cast him panicked look. Perhaps she'd put her foot in it. 'I mean, I'm sure Olly's keen as mustard to sort out the Sinden problem for you. And I know you can trust him to do it. It's just that – he doesn't like to be away from me for a single night, you see.'

'Now *that* I can well understand,' Phil said with more feeling than was wise, and this minor indiscretion had him running a finger round the back of his collar to let in air. Then he noticed that she was flushing too.

'God –' she slapped a hand to her forehead '– that must have sounded so . . . I didn't mean it the way it came out. I meant . . .' She sat looking at Phil with an anguished expression on her lovely young face, begging to be helped out.

But some devil seemed to have taken hold of Phil all of a sudden, making him a little *risqué*. 'What you really meant was not that he doesn't like to be lonely, but that he misses sex.'

'Exactly. No! Oh God!' If it hadn't been for the

190

twinkle in Phil's eye and his slow, spreading smile Jade would probably have downed her drink in one gulp and beat a hasty retreat. As it was she burst out laughing instead and soon had him rolling up too.

Other club members became aware of the two shaking bodies hunched over the bar and smiled at each other with empathy, but not without a few raised eyebrows to accompany the twisted grins. It was as if their owners were saying; 'Take a look at those two! And him old enough to be her father.'

Aware of this undercurrent behind him Phil sobered abruptly. 'I do hope I haven't embarrassed you.'

She sent him a sunny, reassuring smile. 'Well, I admit I felt a bit uncomfortable for a moment. It was only because your generation's not –' She stopped, alarmed all over again.

'Not accustomed to frank discussions of the unmentionable? And thank you, Jade, for bringing my attention to our vast differences in age.'

Jade decided it was time for a change of subject, rather than dig herself deeper into a hole. 'But you did send Olly to Gloucester, didn't you? I mean, he really did have to go?'

Sensing that something was bothering her he tried to read her eyes. But found himself lost in admiration of their clear healthy whites and sparkling blue-green depths. 'Actually,' he said, 'I wanted to go myself; but as Oliver pointed out, my daughter's baby was about to appear. So it wasn't really practical.'

He paused, wondering what it was she expected him to say. What did she *want* him to say? Whatever it was a lot seemed to hang on it. 'It wouldn't be a lie to say that, in the end, all things considered, it had to be him who went.'

'But it was initially his idea? That he should be the one to go?' The blue-green irises narrowed.

'Um –'

'In fact, you might even say he pressed for it?'

'I'd say . . . that would be overstating the case.'

'*I* wouldn't.' Jade was fuming now. 'I'd say I'd hit the nail right on the head. And oh what a fool I look, don't I? Here's me bleating on about how much Olly misses me and all the time he couldn't wait to get away.'

'I'm sure that's not the . . . Jade, what's wrong? What's the matter?'

'Oh, nothing. I don't want to talk about it. Sorry.' She slipped off her stool. 'Excuse me, but I really must go. I'm way behind with my studying. It's been lovely. Lovely bumping into you. And – and thank you for the drink. See you around sometime.'

'Yes. Of course. Sometime.'

He hoped it wouldn't be long.

15

Although a very busy man, Ian Ericson insisted on a full cooked breakfast every day, his favourite being large spicy pork sausages, preferably well-charred under the grill, cut up into half-inch slices and layered between two thick pieces of bread. If a fried egg was also incorporated, then so much the better, and to the whole he liked to add tomato sauce in thick red flowing streams and blobs of English mustard.

Biting into this concoction with his napkin tucked under his chin one sunny morning he still managed to ask Stella why she was not yet dressed. For some time now she had been sitting opposite him at their pine table with her chin in her hand, her eyes staring into space as though she was miles away in her thoughts, as indeed she was. Her hair had not been combed, and her old brown velvet dressing gown was wrapped around her thin body and tightly knotted to one side as if winter had arrived.

Ian, perspiring in a short-sleeved shirt that exposed his ham-like forearms, looked her over, vaguely concerned. 'Isn't it your day for the . . . you know?' he asked.

Stella roused herself to focus on him. Why could he never bring himself to say the words 'charity shop'?

'It is, yes. But . . .'

Ian chewed and waited for her to continue but she left the 'but' in the air, hoping he wouldn't press her further, and he seemed to be in two minds as to whether or not he should. He cleared his mouth of food, and drank half a glass of orange juice, but just when Stella thought he was about to pursue the question – perhaps ask her if she was unwell – he took another bite of his sandwich.

The smell of fried food that hung about the kitchen was enough to make her gag. She couldn't bear even to nibble at the square of toast on her plate. She felt thoroughly sick inside, but not ill in any way that Ian would understand. Nor did she understand herself, come to that. What *was* the matter with her? Did she have some sort of anti-personnel device clamped to her forehead? She must have, or why had her promising friendship with Marjorie Benson come a cropper already?

When the dinner party had come to nothing she was able to accept it, though it was a disappointment, but now that her new friend had failed to take her turn at the charity shop on two consecutive occasions, things were looking a bit suspicious. Marjorie hadn't even phoned to make excuses about not being able to do her stint, so what was

Stella to make of that? She surely couldn't still have a headache.

Apparently Marjorie's husband had phoned the night of the dinner party and spoken to Ian. Said something about his wife having a migraine. He'd been very apologetic about it, and neither she nor Ian had thought it anything but a genuine excuse at the time, only now . . .

And why invite her and Ian to dinner in the first place if she hadn't wanted to be friends? It didn't make sense.

Stella shook her head and noticed that Ian had finished eating. He had just thrown down his napkin, having wiped his mouth on it, leaving greasy red and yellow streaks criss-crossing the crisp blue linen.

'What's the problem?' he asked as he pushed back his chair and hauled himself to a standing position.

Clearly, Stella thought, it would have to be a very small problem, because he would soon be out of the door. 'Nothing,' she told him, managing to give him a faint smile. She knew what his advice would be, if she were to tell him what was worrying her: he would tell her to stop being so daft and phone the woman – ask her outright if her headache was over and when she'd be back on duty. But Stella couldn't do that. She didn't want to put Marjorie in the position of having to make more excuses, nor did she want to put herself in the position of having to face further rejection.

'Right,' Ian said. 'Good. That's all right then.'

He lumbered away, relieved that he didn't have to say or do anything, and Stella forced herself to think about the washing-up. How she hated all the mess and grease that splashed everywhere! The grill, the cooker hob, the work-tops. Day after day after day. She ought to get on with it, though, before it hardened any more. But she seemed unable to find a motive. Where was the point in anything?

She'd really thought Marjorie had understood her, in a way that few people ever had. For the few days since their first meeting, life had miraculously held a bit of promise. She'd had a feeling of things moving forward for once instead of stagnating or going backwards.

But perhaps she'd got it all wrong. Perhaps she'd scared Marjorie away. Why would Marjorie want anything to do with such a dreary specimen of humanity? What had she, Stella Ericson, to offer anyone? Not a single thing that she could think of. She might as well . . . well, she might as well not be here.

'Why are you doing *that*, Marje?'

Marjorie bristled at this particular shortening of her name – it made her sound like something hard, yellow and greasy – and turned from the kitchen sink to discover Steve's mother Elaine standing right behind her. The woman was breathing heavily with officiousness, her hands planted firmly on cushioned hips, and Marjorie found her, with her round, robust little body and calf muscles like those of an athlete, decidedly intimidating.

She struggled to meet the accusing eyes. 'I'm changing the solution,' she said, shaking the last drops from the baby bottle sterilising unit. She ran the tap. 'Then I'm going to round up all the dirty bottles and put them in it. And as soon as they're ready I'll make some feeds. Our young Charlotte's going through them like there might be no tomorrow, you know.'

'Yes, I do know. But there's no need.' Elaine flipped open the fridge to reveal a neat row of Winnie the Pooh bottles, filled to the two-ounce mark. 'I've done the feeds already. I'd also seen to the steriliser.'

'Oh.'

'I've peeled potatoes for tonight, put on a load of washing, and made a shopping list for Steve. Steve went back to work this morning but he'll shop for us on his way home.' She smoothed the giant cabbage roses on her sun dress with an air of satisfaction.

'Well.' Marjorie made a quick survey of the kitchen. Everything had been licked into order before she arrived, she now realised. Bleach fumes rose from the sink waste, the work tops were swept clear of clutter, and the floor had a freshly-mopped tacky feel underfoot. Within five days of Becky's return from hospital, and all the ensuing kerfuffle, life had returned to normal, it seemed.

'Well,' Marjorie said again, beginning to sidle

from the room, 'perhaps Becky has something for me to do upstairs.' It sounded like it, judging by the persistent *Nnyah! Nnyah! Nnyah!* coming through the ceiling.

But Becky waved her away. 'No, Mum, you mustn't help. Thanks all the same, but I have to do this on my own.' She was kneeling on the bathroom floor surrounded by disposable nappies and baby wipes, with the wailing infant on a changing mat in front of her. 'Of course you could help, ordinarily. But not right now.' She nodded towards the wind-up kitchen timer perched on top of the toilet cistern. 'I'm timing myself.'

'*Timing* yourself?' Marjorie raised her eyebrows at the impossibly-red plastic wind-up strawberry. Surely this was carrying Elaine's passion for lists, plans and timetables more than a tad too far? She must have been getting at Becky.

'I have to whittle down this whole operation to no more than fifteen minutes,' Becky went on, yanking the pink bath towel from under the baby and grabbing a doll-size vest. Then the tiny bottom – hardly enough to call it a bottom really, Marjorie thought – was rapidly basted with thick cream and a nappy velcroed in place.

'There!' Becky scooped up the baby, ran a brush over her downy cap and grinned at the pinging timer. 'Just made it. A good job it's too warm for lots of clothes; that's cut down the time a little. I'll get quicker, I'm sure, with practice. Oh no!'

Becky looked askance at her daughter. Charlotte

Louise had burped loudly, half her last feed flying out.

'But,' Marjorie ventured to enquire as Becky frantically set about cleaning the baby again, 'what are you getting so het up about?' Above the crescendo of protests from Charlotte she tried to explain that babies didn't understand time and motion. Nor did they care about efficiency. All they cared about was –

'Mum, I know all that.' Becky's voice wavered with suppressed tears. 'But I have to sort out some kind of routine, for heaven's sake. I simply won't have time in the mornings, will I?'

'Time?' Marjorie cast back in her memory to Becky's own infancy. There had been no time for anything, she recalled . . . and yet all the time in the world really. It simply hadn't mattered what the clock said. If you were still in your pyjamas at midday or the only person on earth snatching a bacon butty at three in the morning, then so what? Things sorted themselves out in the end.

'And I *can't* leave Elaine to do it *all*.'

'Elaine? What?' The name snapped Marjorie from her reverie.

'When I go back to work. And look at me!' Becky pulled at her stained T-shirt, glared at her wrinkled leggings and kicked out her bare feet. 'I haven't even started on *me* yet!'

'Back to . . . ? But that won't be for ages yet. Good heavens, it's years away. If you go back at all.'

'Don't be daft, Mum. I have to go back soon.

How do you think we can afford the mortgage?'

'But – but – you've got a baby now.'

'All the more reason to go back to work. Another mouth to feed. Clothes to buy. Things to get. Do you know what it costs these days to bring up a child until it's an adult? Fifty thousand at least. I read it in the paper. And what if Steve were to lose his job? He's a hundred per cent behind me in this, you know. We're both going to share the chores.'

Marjorie drew air into her lungs, a dozen arguments lining up. She supposed she should have foreseen all this; it was the modern way of going about things, after all. She didn't like it and couldn't agree with it, but who could blame Becky and Steve for following suit? Each generation seemed to get brain-washed into whatever line of thinking fitted in with the economic climate of the day, rather than what was really best for all concerned. Who could say one was wrong and the other right?

'What about this little mite?' Marjorie took the now cleanly-vested child into her arms and tried to console it. 'Who's going to look after Charlotte?' But she already knew the answer to that one. And it hurt not to be considered, even though she now lived miles away. Not that she would have wanted a full-time nannying job if she were close by; she still hankered after running the shops. But it would have been nice to have been asked.

'Elaine will look after the baby,' Becky said, not

looking in her mother's direction. She wound the timer to the ten-minute mark and turned the shower control. 'Now if you'll excuse me, Mum, it's my turn. Put Charlotte down in her crib.'

Two men in brown overalls reported to Philip's office as requested. The older one was slightly quicker on the uptake than the younger; even so, he needed time to think over the simple instructions.

'You mean,' he said with exaggerated movements of his hands, 'you want this lot put in that room, and that lot put in this?'

'Precisely. Pictures, rugs ... everything.' Phil made himself sound positive about his proposal but harboured sneaky feelings of guilt all the same. There was something demeaning about what he planned to do, when all was said and done. And he should never have sunk to this level; it was hardly characteristic of him. At least, he liked to think it wasn't. He'd been brought up better than that, hadn't he? Taught to play fair and square etc etc; not to resort to devious means? Trouble was, Oliver Knox did not bring out the best in him. Damn the man.

Yet why should he have the better office? Wasn't it enough that he had youth on his side, and a bright future ahead of him? Well, Phil argued, kicking his heels while the men began to drag filing cabinets into the corridor, it was hardly fair, was it? And he might not be able to recapture his youth, but at least he could – and should – have the larger room. It wasn't only fair, it was right.

Once installed in Oliver's old office he found himself at the window, taking a good look at the view. He nodded in satisfaction. The scene spread out before him was much more agreeable than the car park, if a little . . . dull.

He shifted position, crossed his other leg and leaned on the opposite shoulder. Actually, now he came to think about it, the car park had been quite interesting. At least there had always been something going on there: pretty girls flashing long legs as they manoeuvred themselves behind the wheels of their cars; people stopping to natter in groups; even the occasional prangs with all the commotion they entailed. The fields, though, were empty. And frankly already boring. Rather like his life at the moment, with Marjorie away.

A wave of loneliness suddenly hit him – almost a physical pain. Here he was, on the edge of Bristol, and he scarcely knew a soul. All his family and old friends were back in London. New ones had not yet materialised. In fact, at this moment in time there was only one person in the whole world that he could remotely call on as an acquaintance.

And she was Oliver's too.

From the window of the bedroom which had once been Phil's but which was now used for guests, Marjorie watched her father-in-law wend his way down the garden path between two neat waist-high box hedges, to an old and little-used greenhouse. At least, as far as Marjorie knew, the greenhouse hadn't been used for years, apart from housing junk, but recently Eric had taken to spending several hours a day in it.

Marjorie had expressed her surprise at this on the first full evening that she and Phil had spent with his parents in London. They had all been sitting round the oval dinner table – the one that Phil despised for its unnatural plasticky gloss – and were still elated over Becky's safe delivery. They were also a little merry on the champagne that Eric had produced to celebrate the arrival of his first great grandchild.

'I couldn't help noticing, Eric,' Marjorie said, fingering the deeply cut pattern of the crystal flute in front of her, 'that you were holed up in that tatty old greenhouse for a good part of the afternoon. What on earth were you doing there? You hate gardening. And why weren't you at one of the shops?'

She knew that he had delayed his retirement on account of the new manager he'd had to bring in; he couldn't 'go', he'd insisted, until he was sure the man was up to it. That meant he wouldn't take any leisure time at all, if she knew him as well as she thought she did. The most he'd ever allowed himself was one day a week – Sunday – and even then he rarely 'switched off'.

Eric sipped his champagne, stringing out the act so long that Marjorie wondered whether he'd heard her or not. 'I've taken up home-brewing,' he finally told her, but with little apparent enthusiasm.

'Yes,' Sheila put in brightly, while Phil and Marjorie stared at Eric as though he'd taken leave of his senses, 'he's found himself a hobby at last. A good idea, we thought, with retirement looming large.'

'Hobby?' Marjorie repeated. Work was the only pastime in which she'd ever known her father-in-law to indulge.

'Can't go on working for ever,' Eric grunted. 'Need something else to do.'

And as he coughed self-consciously, leaning forward on his forearms, Marjorie realised he looked different from when she'd last seen him. His grey-white hair was fluffed out round his ears in a more casual manner; he wore his shirt open at the neck without its customary tie. 'This new man we got in,' he hurried on, as if to direct attention away from himself, 'is damned good, you know, Marjorie. Damned good. Praise be where praise is due. I'll soon be able to leave him to it. Yes. I thank my lucky stars the day we found him.'

'His wife as well,' Sheila added. 'They came as a couple. Now there's a marvel, if ever there was one. Runs this house like clockwork, she does. I don't have to lift a finger. Not that I can do much now, anyway.' Shaking her head she looked down sadly at her degenerating limbs.

'Well –' Marjorie forced out in the small silence that followed '– how lovely for the pair of you.'

Though secretly their news had hurt her feelings. It was galling to find oneself so easily replaced; one's past services so quickly forgotten. And any half-formed notion she'd begun to harbour, of having been so badly missed that they'd beg her and Phil to return and take over received a severe knock on the head.

'So you see,' Sheila went on, 'Eric's beginning to have some time on his hands at last. Time to . . . do other things.'

Phil covered a smile with one hand. 'Like home-brewing, you mean.'

And Marjorie was hard-pressed not to smile too. Never in a million years would she have imagined such a hobby for Eric. Waiting for yeast to ferment. Watching until it had ceased. Where would he find the patience? It was only the brief but expressive 'careful what you say' expression she saw flit between her parents-in-law, that threw cold water on her mirth.

Later she had asked Phil if he'd noticed that look, and what did he think it meant? But being a man, of course he hadn't noticed a thing. And thought it mattered even less.

'Something's definitely afoot though,' Marjorie muttered to herself, drawing away from the bed-room window. Eric had reached the greenhouse now and disappeared inside, closing the door behind him.

She went over to the bed, intending to make it, but plonked herself down on it instead. Sheila's 'marvel' would make the bed. Indeed, she got a little huffy if denied the chore.

During the few days she had been in the house Marjorie had grown increasingly uncomfortable with the home help. She had only to put down a cup to find it at once carried off to the kitchen. And cushions were plumped up behind her as soon as her chair was vacated. She knew that the bed would be made by the time she reached the foot of the staircase; even her discarded underwear whisked away to be washed if she failed to take the precaution of tucking it out of sight. And for all this, they scarcely saw the woman.

Steve's mother was enough to live up to with her busy-body bustling efficiency, but this phantom cleaner was more than Marjorie could stand. In fact, so suffocating did she find the atmosphere in the house at the moment, what with the feeling of being watched and Sheila's pathetic gratitude towards her saviour, that Marjorie was soon prepared to face any diversion the outside world had to offer her. Even one she had been putting off.

Her mind made up, she was soon standing on the Indian rug in the hall carefully avoiding the polished wood block surround. She had changed out of her floral towelling slippers into strappy white low-heeled sandals and had a matching bag slung over her shoulder. No other alteration to her clothing had been necessary. Here in London the temperature seemed even higher than it had been in Bristol and a loose sun dress at all times was the only garment tolerable.

'You don't mind,' she asked Sheila, 'if I go and call on Tom and Beth?'

'Of course not, my dear. I wonder that you've not met up with your old friends already. You go and enjoy yourself.' Leaning on a stick with a duck's head carved for a handle, Sheila dismissed her daughter-in-law with a lethargic wave of her free hand. Perspiration oozed from pores along her upper lip; her over-powdered face looked paler than usual. The weather was taking its toll. 'I'm going up for my rest.'

'Hmm,' Marjorie grunted to herself, opening up Phil's car. In the normal course of events a get-together with Tom and Beth would have occurred as naturally as night follows day. She and Phil would have dropped in on them like a shot, long before he'd gone back to Bristol, if only Spittal's closure hadn't wrecked their easy friendship. Precisely why that had happened, Marjorie still had no idea. But, winding down all the windows and backing the car from the shade of an old chestnut tree, she determined to find out.

16

Beth's face displayed a mixture of emotions as she opened her front door to find that Marjorie had come visiting. Her old pleasure flared for a moment, but recent anguish surfaced too. She seemed not to know how to react. Even so, years of familiarity dictated that she should open the door a little further and stand to one side.

'How lovely to see you, Marjorie,' she said, recovering some of her composure if not her customary warmth. 'And many congratulations. Becky sent me a birth announcement card, and I couldn't be more pleased.'

'Oh, yes. Of course. Thank you.' Marjorie followed her old friend into the narrow passageway of the house, once again admiring and envying the natural wave of Beth's hair. For years it had neatly framed her rosy round childish face, needing little or no attention except an occasional trim. Not for her the hassle of perms gone wrong or of cuts that fell short of expectations. She had merely to let it be.

Raking her own untidy mop with one hand

Marjorie flopped on to the sun lounger in the garden to which Beth had led her, and eased off her shrinking sandals.

'Orange juice and Perrier?' Beth offered. 'With ice and slices of lime?'

'Sounds lovely.' Feigning the final stages of dehydration Marjorie squinted up at her with a grin. 'Can you believe this weather? Really! Who needs to go to Spain when the British summer's like this?'

'Spain? Well . . . no,' Beth agreed faintly, and with a small false-sounding titter, she scuttled away in her red thonged flip-flops to fetch the promised drink.

While she was gone Marjorie's thoughts flew hither and thither in a whirlwind of speculation. Were Tom and Beth planning to go to Spain this year? Had they already *been*? And if so with whom? Val and Ian, presumably.

Marjorie lay back so that most of her body was engulfed in the shade of a large sun umbrella with a straggly fringe. The more she thought about it the more she felt certain that Spain was very much on Beth's agenda this year. She bit the flesh inside her left cheek and tasted blood. Not that she'd expected to be included in any such plans in the way that she and Phil normally would have been: their house move would have put paid to that. But . . . no that wasn't true. What difference did a house move make? She *would* have expected to be included. Why not?

Hell, what had they done to be ostracised like this? What had caused this rift to open up between them? She really must find out.

'Oh, thanks Beth; that looks lovely.' She took the glass from Beth's tray and sipped gratefully, letting the cold citrus tang wash away the metallic taste of blood.

And then a horrible, long silence developed between them; one that was almost impossible to bridge. Neither of them seemed to know how to proceed. Finally, feeling it incumbent upon herself, as uninvited visitor, to get some sort of conversation under way, Marjorie broke the dead-lock by asking how Tom was getting along. 'Is he enjoying his early retirement?'

'Yes, he is! Thoroughly. He's getting along just fine.' Beth nodded in what Marjorie considered a grossly exaggerated manner. 'His time's taken up with wooden toys, would you believe? He and a friend are making them in the friend's workshop down the road. He's over there right now as a matter of fact. Spends every spare minute at it. He says there aren't enough hours in the day . . .' She tittered again. 'Well, it keeps him from under my feet! Of course, they hope to be able to sell them. The toys, I mean. Eventually. When they've got enough stock together.'

'Really? Well that's great.' Marjorie made a suitably broad smile, but in her heart couldn't see Tom being content with his new, diminished role in life, any more than her father-in-law appeared to be with his. A wave of pity swept over her: pity for all the poor souls around the globe who were condemned to pad out their days with home-brewing and making toys.

Or selling second-hand clothes.

'And you and Philip?' Beth ventured breath-lessly. 'How are you finding Bristol?'

'Well, we're not quite in the heart of Bristol, you know. Sort of mid-way between Bristol and Bath. Lots of fields all around, of course . . . and pretty villages. And we're settling in so well. You should see the house Phil found for us. It's ab-so-lute-ly gorgeous! You *must* come and stay. We've heaps of rooms – it's all new, did I tell you – and the bathrooms are a perfect dream.'

She washed out her mouth once more with a quick gulp of her drink and set the glass down on the lawn beside her. 'Phil seems to have taken on a new lease of life since we got away from London. He wants us to join the local country club. Well, of course it's a great idea, don't you think? We should have done something like that before. I understand they have a wonderful indoor swimming pool – an outdoor one as well. And the grounds around it are fabulous.'

'Oh, I'm so glad!' From the cushions of her lounger Beth had been watching this performance with increasingly animated relief. Now, struggling to a sitting position, she leaned forward to put her hand on Marjorie's arm. 'So glad, I mean, that you're happy there. So glad that your fears were all groundless. Because you *were* a little concerned at first, weren't you? And I was concerned for you, too. You didn't say much at the time – and naturally I didn't want to rub your nose in it, as it were – but I *guessed* you would rather have been in my shoes.'

'Really?' Marjorie frowned. 'Well . . . one was bound to have had reservations . . .'

'But Phil made the right choice after all!'

'Choice?'

'And now, of course, you've forgiven him. I kept telling Tom that you would.'

A breeze swirled into the garden, flapped at the sun shade and subsided. By the time it had died down Marjorie could see ninety-five per cent of the truth laid out in front of her. Even so, she couldn't accept it. For her to believe that Phil, who she had always totally trusted, had actually lied to her through his teeth, she needed to have it spoken out loud in words of not too many syllables. She needed to be told explicitly that he could have taken a lump sum redundancy payment if he had wanted to; that there had been no financial reason for him to take the Bristol job at all; that he could have stayed put and helped her run the family shops or looked around in London for another job. But Beth had said nothing of the sort in so many words and Marjorie knew better than to put too much reliance on idle remarks.

'One thing,' Beth was saying, 'that worried Tom and me a lot – and I must say it's made us feel very awkward with the pair of you – was how Phil could treat you like that. He should have told you about the redundancy money, *we* thought; not pretended it wasn't for him. But, heigh-ho; that's men for you. And it's all water under the bridge now. Isn't it?'

Marjorie closed her eyes. She had come to find out a few simple home truths, had been prepared to pin Beth down and drag them from her if necessary. But in the event no rack, branding iron, or pincers had been needed. And she'd learned far more than she'd bargained for.

When she opened her eyes again Beth appeared to be writhing in agony: something had told her she'd made an awful gaff. Marjorie was in no shape, though, to do anything for her. Excusing herself she swung her legs off the lounger and felt for her shoes. But she must have got up too quickly: a dizziness came over her, with Beth's voice floundering hollowly from far, far away. She forced herself to cling to consciousness until the grass at her feet, looking an impossible green, swirled back into focus, and Beth's shocking pink *Impatiens* shrieked at her from their pots.

'I think this heat's been too much for me,' she said, a hand straying up to her head.

Or perhaps it was the truth that had been too much.

17

The house echoed even more than it had before, with only Phil in it, and the thud of each kitchen cupboard door as he systematically searched for something to eat seemed to emphasise his aloneness. Or should that be loneliness? he wondered. Was there a difference? Whichever it was he didn't much like the experience. He frowned at a jelly mould he'd just unearthed. It was so big it might be useful for a children's street party but had no right to be cluttering up their new kitchen.

His frown deepened. He found dried spaghetti but nothing to go with it, and plenty of sugar that they'd mostly cut out. There was caster sugar in one cupboard, granulated in another, and half a packet of icing sugar in yet another. He sighed his exasperation. The cupboards were a total mess. Marjorie must have slung stuff in any old how as she unpacked the cardboard boxes, which wasn't like her at all. What was the matter with her lately?

And why had she gone off to North Wales to see Em without a word of warning? Without leaving ready-prepared meals? He'd long since exhausted the contents of the fridge. Yes, all right, he remembered telling her she could go visiting when they had two cars, and could hardly blame her taking him up on the idea. But why now?

He closed the last door with a report that shot through his nerves. Well, that was it. He'd never be able to put together a meal; he would have to go out to eat. And what better opportunity to try the food at the club? After a swim, of course. That was what the place was really for: keeping fit. He'd go and get his gear together. First though, he'd better check the timetable. It wouldn't do to turn up at a ladies-only session.

He found the club brochure still on his bedside table where he'd tossed it. And the pool was open for general use until ten, so that was fine.

His gaze slid down the page. *Advanced aerobics*, he read. Jade had said she did aerobics. But sometimes she did something called 'step'. What the blazes was 'step'? It was held on Monday, Wednesdays and Saturdays, whatever it was. Aerobics covered most of the week. And would Jade do the 'advanced' kind or the 'basic'? Sometimes she liked to swim. Or use the jogger in the gym.

He threw the brochure aside. What did he think he was doing? Trying to coincide his visit with that of a girl half his age who probably already thought him a bumbling old fool? Ridiculous. If he happened to bump into her again, well . . . And if he didn't . . . well again. It was up to fate to take a hand. Or not, as the case may be.

* * *

Phil wandered round the country club in his white shorts and navy T-shirt like a soul forever lost in limbo. Over the past three evenings spent combing each square metre of the premises he had become as familiar with its layout as he was with the hairs on his head. And if he did one more tour, he warned himself crossly, he would be in danger of gaining a reputation. '*There goes that eccentric old geezer with the skinny legs,*' people would soon be whispering. '*Never seems to make use of the club facilities; spends all his time here snooping about.*'

He sat on a wooden bench mid-way between the squash courts and the outdoor pool, pretending to enjoy the view spread out before him: smooth lawns running down to trees, and those trees gathering more trees until they filled the bottom of the valley with all the shades of green and blue imaginable. But the beauty of it was wasted on him.

I must stop this nonsense right now, he berated himself. I must stop looking for Jade. I'm not likely to bump into her 'accidentally' again, am I? I must accept the decision fate has sensibly made for me. It simply isn't meant to be.

He stood up. To hell with fate. To hell with common sense. Spinning on his heel he headed back to the changing rooms. If Jade hadn't been to the club for three consecutive evenings, he argued, then there must be something wrong. He threw off his shorts in the changing room and hurried into the showers. Jade could be desperately ill, lying in a coma, or . . . anything.

Supposing, he thought, lathering his armpits, her family hadn't dropped in on her lately? Supposing Oliver hadn't given her a call? Oliver was still taking an inordinate amount of time in Gloucester – and Phil would have a few words to say on that subject when he finally deigned to put in an appearance – meanwhile . . .

Phil snatched up a towel. The more he thought about it the more convinced he became that he really ought to go round to their flat and make sure Jade was OK. It was the decent thing to do under the circumstances. Something most people wouldn't hesitate over. And how would it look in Oliver's eyes if his boss had failed to go to Jade's rescue?

Smoothing his hair in the nearest mirror Phil caught his own quizzical expression. *Don't look at me like that*, he told himself silently. *I don't know what's got into me either.*

The street door to the flats where Jade and Oliver lived stood open to the summer evening when Phil arrived. Six flower tubs, which hadn't been there on the evening of the dinner party, now marched up the steps in pairs and the top step was further filled by the bulk of an ape-like man with a rag in his hand. He was busily polishing the brass knocker but stood aside to let Phil in.

'You must have been expecting me,' Phil joked

when Jade came miraculously to her door. 'But you forgot to roll out the red carpet.'

Jade covered her surprise at seeing who her visitor was and quickly caught his meaning. 'Oh,' she said, a wan little smile dying as soon as it was born, 'the owner thinks his efforts'll put at least ten thousand on the price, despite dry rot in his basement. He's selling up, you see.'

'Ah.' Phil waited to be invited in. But Jade seemed to expect an explanation for his being there, and it was only after he'd hesitantly told her how he'd been worried by her absence at the club that she opened the door a little wider.

'That was sweet of you,' she said soberly. 'You're a very kind man.' And a tear rolled down one cheek.

'Oh dear . . .'

'Don't mind me.' She dashed away the tear with the back of her hand and shook out her hair. 'You've caught me at a low ebb, I'm afraid. I'm simply wallowing in self-pity at the moment.'

Turning, and leaving the door open to its fullest extent so that her visitor was in no doubt that he should follow, she walked through the hallway with a slight limp. Over her shoulder she explained that she'd hurt her ankle on a kerb two days ago, in a rush to get to work, and hadn't been able to go to the club since.

In the lounge she indicated that he should make himself comfortable on the sofa and Phil sank to the bold striped cushions as one stunned: her outfit had temporarily mesmerised him. She was wearing a sort of Girl Friday thing in khaki, he decided, with a loose, fringed top and flappy shorts, also fringed, that frisked about the tops of her legs and were so brief that at times they displayed the lower swell of her buttocks too.

'Why the self-pity?' he managed to ask as she joined him on the sofa, propping her feet on a gigantic matching footstool and comparing the injured ankle with the sound one. 'Surely you have everything a woman could ask? Beautiful home, good looks, intelligence.'

She smiled. 'Not everything; I didn't have a guilt complex before you came.'

'Mm? Oh . . . sorry. I shouldn't have assumed, should I, that because everything appears fine to an outsider that it's necessarily so?'

'No, you shouldn't, should you. Can I get you a drink?'

'Actually, I only popped in . . .' But they finally agreed to share a can of well-chilled lager, and sipping gratefully he plucked up courage to ask her if she cared to talk about whatever was wrong. 'Is your ankle giving you gyp?'

She shook her head.

'Or are you missing Oliver?'

'Oliver?' She almost spat his name. 'He's not exactly helping the situation.'

Phil couldn't subdue the sudden lifting of his spirits elicited by this comment. It cheered him to think of Oliver being in Jade's bad books. He nodded gravely. 'He should be here when you need him, I know. But please don't blame me for this long absence. He ought to have done all I set him to do in two days. Three at most. He has no right to have stretched it out so long. He'd jolly well better be back for Holy Joe's big bash, that's all I can say.'

'Oh, yes. It's the annual barbecue soon, isn't it?' By her dismal tone it was clear that she was expected to accompany Oliver and wasn't looking forward to it. 'But don't kid yourself that Oliver's going about his master's business,' she scoffed. 'He probably did his Spittal's stuff in one day and is spending the rest looking up all his fancy women.'

'What?'

'Oh, don't look so astonished. He does have other women, you know.' She studied her fingernails. 'We have an open relationship, you see. Well, *he* does: *I* don't.' She looked at Phil. 'Sounds daft, doesn't it? I agreed to it, so I've only myself to blame, and don't ask me why; it would take too long to explain. I suppose I didn't think he'd really want anyone else . . .' She swallowed and looked back at her nails and Phil suspected she saw them through a veil of tears.

He cleared his throat. 'Jade, if Oliver's gone off with other women, or even just one other woman, then he must be out of his mind. I'm sure you're wrong, anyway. But – but this open relationship business: if you're not happy about it, and I can see you're not, then why on earth put up with it? You should leave him, Jade. Leave him!'

221

'I can't do that. I can't.' She put her glass on the table beside her and stood up. 'I know you must think I'm crazy,' she said looking down at Phil, 'but I happen to love the guy.' And he could see by her soft smile and expression as she limped about the room a little, that she really meant what she was saying.

Feeling much as a balloon looks three days after a party, he was about to drink up and make an excuse to leave when she suddenly dropped down beside him again.

'Oh, but Oliver's not even half of it!' She let out a long sigh. 'I'm in trouble with the boss at work. And I'm being harassed by my college lecturer.'

'Good lord. Not ... sexually?' Phil sat up straight, an eager prospective defender of a damsel in distress.

'Not now, no. There was a time when he pestered me in that way, but I soon put paid to that; since then he's been my deadliest enemy. Picks on me all the time at college and never misses a chance to make me look stupid or tell me I'll never make the grade.'

'Fine lecturer he is! He should be giving you encouragement, not saying things like that. He ought to be summarily dismissed. Why don't you report him?'

She shrugged. 'His word against mine. And anyway he's dead right. I'm *not* going to make it. I can't do it. I'm trying. God knows how hard I'm trying.' She paused to turn bleak brimming eyes on him. 'I don't know now why I ever thought I could do something in law. Huh!'

'But you can, Jade. Of course you can. You're just having a crisis of confidence at the moment, and we all get those from time to time. But you're bright and intelligent, you know you are. You can do whatever you want.'

Jade would not be convinced. 'I gave up a fantastic modelling career for nothing, don't you understand? And I feel such a fool. And when I think of all the money I'd saved . . . and all the money I could have earned since . . . I could have bought this flat virtually outright!'

Phil recalled her dry comment about the flower tubs; that the owner was selling up. 'You're having to get out?'

'Yes, since we can't scrape enough together to buy the place.'

'That's tough, after all you've done here.' He looked up at the painted frieze. 'And your superb little garden, too. But surely . . . I mean . . .'

'You think Oliver ought to be able to afford it?'

'Well, I wouldn't presume to speculate . . . but, yes, on his salary he surely ought to . . .' He stopped himself before he got in too deep; with an unmarried couple it was impossible to know how committed to each other they might or might not be. How did they arrange their finances? And where did Jade, on a low income, stand? The legalities were more complex than in a marriage.

Jade was shaking her head. 'I don't know what

Oliver does with his money, I really don't.' She darted a look at Phil and seemingly on an impulse added, 'We had a row about it before he left. The minute I told him the flats were up for sale he went all peculiar with me. Told me he had no money, and he's always telling me that. He's been getting meaner and meaner lately and it's obvious what it all means.'

'Well–'

'It means this is the beginning of the end, doesn't it? He doesn't love me any more.' She put the back of her hand to her mouth and sat very still, struggling to keep her sorrow reined in.

'Jade, Jade.' It was all Phil could do not to pull her into his arms – as he might have done with one of his daughters. But if he had, he knew that his comforting caresses would soon have broken the bounds of fatherly propriety. So he contented himself with laying his hand on her lightly tanned forearm and patting it.

She looked at his hand and a shuddering kind of sniff went through her. She jumped up. 'There's something else,' she told him.

18

Jade hurried into the bedroom. 'Come and have a look at this,' she called out to Phil, her tone brisk and determined. She was standing by the window when, his heart beating a little faster, he reached the door. He peered in and saw a large dimly-lit room, with its long, vertically slatted blinds keeping out the sun.

Jade pulled on a cord to admit a few dust-filled rays and marched round the bed to the wardrobes. She began flinging open doors, diving into the depths and dragging out dozens of carrier bags.

Apart from the clearly recognisable chain store plastic variety that began to form a heap on the carpet, there were maroon ones with gold lettering, matt blue ones edged in silver, glossy types with spots and stripes and several of the stiff white paper kind with smartly corded handles. All these bore up-market store names.

But Jade hadn't finished yet. Thrusting into the back of the cupboard she brought out arm-loads of hangers, from each of which a garment of some description dangled: dresses, tops and trousers; jackets, sweaters and bikinis.

'There!' she said at last and, seeing Phil hovering by the door, went over to pull him by the arm. 'Come here, please, and take a good close look. Please . . . look.'

Disturbed by the slightly wild expression in her eyes he silently obeyed. What was all this about? he wondered. Then he noticed all the price tags swinging from zipper tabs, buttons and labels, and experienced a sensation of falling backwards down an escalator. None of these things, he realised, had ever been worn. It looked very much as if Jade was one of those people who were thoroughly addicted to shopping for things they didn't really want. He'd heard about them, and felt sorry for them, while thanking his lucky stars that Marjorie had never been thus afflicted.

He turned to Jade who was staring at the heap of goods as though fully appreciating the extent of her problem for the first time. 'Does Oliver know about this?' he asked.

'I – I don't think he does. He's never said anything. I'm sure he wouldn't have kept quiet about it if he did.' She drew a long breath. 'It gets worse than this, actually. There's all sorts of stuff in the little loft space above the hall: nothing I really need. Duplicate kitchen things, mostly. Clocks. Table mats. Trays. You name it, you'll find it there.'

Phil smothered a ridiculous urge to laugh. This was really deadly serious, he told himself.

'I don't know why I do it!' She spread her hands. 'Well, I get a buzz out of getting the stuff, of course, but after that I feel awful. And sometimes the only thing that puts me right is another trip to the shops . . . And what do you think of this?' She had drawn a box from a shelf in the wardrobe, snapped back the lever and taken from it a sheaf of credit card statements. 'Go on, tell me what you think?' She sneered her self-contempt and her voice cracked on her words. '*Now* tell me what a clever girl I am!'

He watched her sit down on the bed and put her head between her clenched hands. Something told him she was about to break down; that during the past few days she had had time on her own to think and to brood, and hadn't liked what she'd come up with. Things had come to a head and piled on top of her.

He would like to have felt flattered that she'd brought her troubles to him, for him alone to solve; but he knew he happened to have walked in on her at precisely the right moment, and almost anyone would have done. Nevertheless, he was glad of the opportunity to help her.

'Right,' he said with all the authority he could muster, 'there's nothing here that can't be put right – or almost. Tomorrow you can start taking this stuff back to the shops.'

'I can't. Oh, I couldn't.' She looked up at him, her eyes wide and round.

'Yes, you can. And you will. I'll come with you if you like.'

'Will you? Would you really do that?'

'Of course. Now the other thing – is your purse in that handbag over there? Well, let me have it, please.'

She handed it to him, looking dazed.

'And I need a pair of scissors.'

Wordlessly she went to the kitchen and brought some scissors back, then watched with growing dismay as he cut up each of the credit cards he'd discovered in her purse. When he was about to slice through the last one she stopped him.

'No!' she gasped. 'Please, at least leave me with one of them! How can I live without a credit card?'

'How can you go on living *with* one? You can't, you know you can't. The problem would just go on.' He snapped the last card in two, gathered up the other pieces and threw them all into a waste bin. Then he took three twenty pound notes from his own wallet and squashed them into her hand. 'You can pay me back whenever you can. These will have to last you until Oliver's back, which can't be long now I'm sure, and then you'll have to tell him everything. I know it won't be easy, but you have no other choice. He may be more understanding than you think, you know. I'm sure he wouldn't want to lose you.'

She sank to the bed again, closing her eyes. 'Oh,' she said shakily, 'I do hope you're right. You know, now that those cards have gone I feel a kind of . . . relief, I suppose it is. A huge weight seems to be lifting from my shoulders.'

'Good.' He sat down beside her. 'We've broken that cycle, you see. Without them, hopefully, you'll soon shed the habit of spending.'

'I will. I'm sure I will.' She smiled sheepishly into his face. 'You've been so very helpful. You haven't told me I'm stupid, or wicked, or made a lot of fuss . . . And you really will help me take the stuff back to the shops? I don't think I could face doing that on my own. I bought some of the things a long time ago; the shop assistants are going to think it very odd. But with you and your air of authority perhaps they won't give us any grief.'

He gazed into her beautiful young face. Logistically, he didn't know quite how he was going to manage it but he wouldn't have backed down now for all the money in the world. 'I'll go with you, I promise.'

'It's strange but I feel better about everything now – even about my course. Thank you, Philip. You really are so sweet. Thank you so much for everything.' She leaned forward and kissed his cheek. Then she seemed to think that perhaps one small peck wasn't enough. She put a hand up behind his head, drew him closer still, and kissed him on the lips.

'Oh, Jade,' he sighed, 'Jade, darling. I'd do anything for you.'

Jade showered languidly, dried herself at snail's pace and slipped dreamily into a white silk dressing-gown. She couldn't believe what had happened that evening.

I've been to bed with Philip Benson, she told herself. *To bed with Olly's boss. Now, how did that come about?*

She wandered into the bedroom and began to tidy up. The whole place was a shambles, with all her purchases still dumped on the floor and the bedclothes a knotted heap. She stared at the scene of their love-making. She'd never intended anything of the sort to happen. No way. Certainly she found him attractive, and did more than ever now, but even so . . . Oliver's fifty-year-old boss. A married man with grown children – and he was even a grandparent now! Whatever could have possessed her?

When Oliver had first suggested this very thing she had thought it the height of folly. And it still was. Crazy. But something had sizzled between them when they'd been sitting on that bed together. She'd only meant to give him a thank-you kiss. But then she'd wanted to take things further. And it was obvious he had too.

Smiling at the memory she went to answer the door. 'Who is it?' she said into the intercom. Had Philip come back for more?

'It's me, Jade. Selina. Can I come in?'

'At this time of night?' Jade tutted. Her sister kept peculiar hours. But she had told the girl to come round sometime for a chat and had been taken at her word. 'Not out with the new boyfriend tonight?' she said, letting the girl into the flat. She smothered a yawn. She didn't know whether Selina even had a new boyfriend; it was difficult to keep up with her affairs.

Selina pouted, looking around. 'I was, but I had to ditch him. Nerd. Olly not back yet? Oh.' She'd spotted the mess in the bedroom, and slanted a knowing look at Jade. 'Looks like we've been having a grand reunion.'

Jade firmly closed the bedroom door. 'Actually, we haven't. Oliver isn't back yet. I don't know what's keeping him.' Then, suddenly weary of Selina's tales of love and lust she decided to head off yet another saga with one of her own.

Settling herself in a corner of the lounge sofa with her knees drawn up to her chin she proceeded to give Selina a blow by blow account of the hour of passion she'd just experienced with 'a guy she'd recently met'.

'Lucky you.' Selina sniffed. 'My bloke was really pathetic. No experience at all. Didn't know what it was for, I don't think.'

'You could hardly say that about Philip,' Jade murmured. You might say, she reflected privately, that he'd been a bit restrained at times – a bit tentative and kind of polite. He'd kept asking her if he could do this, that, or the other, before he did it, as though expecting to be refused. But a ham-fisted adolescent he was not!

She stood up, stretching her arms.

'Coffee, Sis? Or something stronger? You can have ten minutes to blab on about your men problems. After that I'm slinging you out.'

231

* * *

It was too beautiful a night to be wasted on sleep. Standing on his tiny patio with the house a slumbering beast behind him Phil lifted his binoculars to survey the heavens. Yes, there they all were: his old familiar friends. They never failed him. He soon located the Great Bear to the northwest and the Square of Pegasus in the east; then he picked out the summer triangle. But swinging round for a southerly aspect he trod on something soft. It was a clump of white lobelia, he soon realised, struggling hard for its survival. And he had flattened it. He had trodden right in the middle of Marjorie's flower patch and ruined the whole shebang.

Guiltily he propped the binoculars on the window sill, followed a strip of concrete path round the house to the outside tap and began to fill Marjorie's yellow watering can. It was probably too late, he decided, as the water thundered in. Too late to redeem the wretched plants. He had completely forgotten to tend them in her absence.

He humped the filled can back to the patch and spilled its contents out. Poor Marjorie, he thought, as the damp earthiness reached his nostrils. After all the work she'd put in. She deserved better than this, didn't she?

Marjorie! His wife! They'd been married for twenty-five years.

He put down the can and looked heavenward again. *What have I done?* he asked the stars. *What have I done? All I wanted was to live a little for once; to fly nearer to you.*

But for once they looked cold and distant. They failed to reassure.

19

When Marjorie returned to Brightwells she let herself into the house and began to wander from room to room, touching some things in wonder, staring at others as though they weren't real. The old familiar furniture in its new and unfamiliar setting looked as incongruous as she felt.

What am I doing here? she asked herself, gazing at a bright blue dishcloth that Phil had left draped over the kitchen mixer tap to dry. The house seemed even more alien to her than the day they'd moved in.

Philip, too, would be a stranger to her when he walked through the door. His body would be standing there, smiling a welcome, no doubt, and looking its usual, good-looking self, but what of the man inside? Where on earth had he gone? Who had she really married – a liar and a cheat?

She shrank from the coming confrontation, as if his deceit was something she should feel guilty about rather than Phil. How *would* she react when the time came? Could she even make her accusation? She wasn't at all sure she could. She might be hurt and seething inside, yet she hated dramatic scenes. And there was always the chance that Beth had been mistaken about the redundancy business . . .

She snatched up the blue cloth and threw it into the sink cupboard. Perhaps she would say nothing at the moment. She would wait a while and watch for further signs of Phil's guilt. And when she was sure she had a real grievance against him she would store it for a rainy day and come out with it when it could be used to maximum effect.

Right now she felt too drained by all the driving she'd done over the past few days to cope with anything more demanding than brewing tea. She was also depressed by her visits to Em at her college and Chrissie on her trout farm, neither trip having been an outstanding success.

Although loath to do precisely what Phil had suggested she do once she had a car of her own, visiting had seemed a good idea. Clearly she had outstayed her welcome in London, and certainly she'd been in no hurry to return to Philip or Brightwells, but at least Em would be pleased to see her, she had thought.

Em, however, had been wrapped up in a new boyfriend, a psychology student called Neil who appeared to be glued to her at the hip because, apart from when they were attending their different lectures, he went everywhere that she did, including, it transpired, to the same narrow bed in Em's room.

Marjorie, her mind on other things, had been slow to cotton on. With the three of them squeezed into the stuffy little room at the hall of residence and drinking tea from mugs that had rude slogans painted round the sides, she had been in the middle of showing Em the latest batch of photographs of Becky's baby when she caught a covert glance passing from Neil to her daughter. Her presence, it seemed, was causing a flutter of some concern.

At a loss, she looked about her. Apart from the standard bed, cupboard and desk, she could see a television, a hi-fi system, part of a drum kit, two pairs of walking boots in different sizes, a back pack complete with tent, a well-scorched ironing board, a drying rack, and a host of smaller items, many of which were patently not Em's.

The message hit home. Clearly, this put paid to any expectation she'd had of sleeping on Em's floor that night, even though it was strictly against college rules, or of confiding her troubles to Em in a heart to heart.

After an awkward meal together she'd made herself scarce and spent a lonely, uncomfortable night in a nearby hotel. And, taking her leave next morning she'd smiled into Em's fresh, untroubled young face with its familiar spattering of golden freckles, and wondered what she could have confided to her anyway. That her father was a selfish, lying bastard? That he was really nothing but a sham?

No, she thought, waving one hand from the

window of the car as she drove away, there are some things you can never tell your children.

But if you couldn't off-load on to your children, you certainly couldn't do it to a sister-in-law you rarely saw. And Chrissie had been so very busy.

Seeing her sister-in-law's face on answering the door to her two and a half hours later, Marjorie hadn't been sure that she was at all welcome, even though Chrissie and her husband Ray had constantly urged all and sundry to 'drop in whenever you're passing' – as though they lived in the centre of Birmingham and were on the way to just about everywhere instead of half-way up the Llantysillio mountain.

'Good heavens! Marjorie, dear!' Chrissie quickly suppressed her shock. 'What on earth are you doing here? Oh – er – dump your bag over there for a minute, won't you? I'll make you a cup of tea.'

Marjorie obediently placed her tapestry vanity bag by the dog's drinking bowl and stood awkwardly beside it. She had hoped to be putting the bag down for longer than a minute, and preferably beside a soft bed. But she soon learned that Chrissie had gone in for providing B & B for eight guests as well as running a tea room and helping Ray with the fish farm, so that night she found herself struggling with a lumpy put-u-up in the sitting room because all the bedrooms were booked.

Marjorie, watching Chrissie flying about the kitchen whisking cakes from a large shiny green oven and ironing her way through a stack of striped sheets, had begun to feel she was in the way within minutes of her arrival. Meaningful conversation was impossible; even gossip proved difficult. Whenever Marjorie opened her mouth to speak she was given a chore to do: baking tins to wash up, or a heap of white towels to fold neatly, and then the vacuum cleaner to be emptied.

She decided that enough was enough the following morning when an elderly gentleman in shorts, walking boots and an anorak, burst in on her while she was still untangling herself from the bed-clothes. Since she had been only half awake and he had been looking for the breakfast room, it was a toss-up as to who'd been the more surprised.

So visiting had not answered her problem at all; it seemed that no one had any time for her, nor had the brief spell away been long enough to begin to soothe her shattered nerves; she was still as con-fused and angry over Phil's behaviour as when she'd left Beth. The break had achieved nothing; merely put off for a few days her need to carve out a new role in life for herself. Now that need clamoured at her in the silence of the house: what now, then, Marjorie? What now?

Her eye fell upon a copy of the previous day's newspaper. It happened to be opened at the job advertisements. *Hard Bench Worker*, she read. *Target Recognition Instructor. Sork Z Op Temp, N17. Cellular Service and Logistics Specialists. Gas Sales Advisors.*

God!

She tossed the paper aside and let herself out

into the garden. Had Phil remembered to water her flower bed? Shielding her eyes from the glaring sun she inspected the modest patch. Not a bit of it. The plants were seriously flagging, and a cat must have been digging around. She sprayed on plenty of water and returned to the house to see to her indoor plants. Then, her most important tasks done, she put the kettle on for a cup of tea and checked the fridge.

There was a dribble of milk in a plastic container but nothing else except a rhubarb yoghurt that Phil, she knew, disliked. She sighed. Must she really go shopping? She picked up her handbag. To hell with it. And to hell with Phil. She would visit Stella instead.

It took Jade a restless night to realise that, far from Philip Benson relieving her of her problems, he had added to them. The knowledge, on top of the lack of sleep, made her even more sluggish than usual as she applied herself to her morning routine. She peered into the mirror for a long time and slowly examined her tongue.

Selina hadn't helped, either, she told her reflection. During their late night girl-talk she had referred to their menopausal mother. By all accounts she was having a hard time of it, Selina had said. Her confidence had taken a dive and she was depressed about losing her looks. And she had tried all manner of diets but couldn't shift any weight.

Jade hadn't been as close to her mother since giving up her modelling career, but she sympathised all the same. And as well as an image of their mother leaping into her mind, another had flashed – with alarm bells. Wasn't Philip's wife much the same age? Was she going through all that too?

Until then Jade had not spared the woman a single thought. Out of sight, out of mind, Marjorie Benson had been. In all her musings about 'openness', Jade suddenly realised to her surprise she had not once considered any other parties that were likely to be involved: the partners of those seduced by the unfaithful who, in a fit of pique, might go off and ruin some other relationship and . . . goodness, there seemed no end to it. But Selina had brought all this very much to mind in the slightly over-weight, over-the-hill form of Philip's wife. And once there, she was stuck fast and could not be ignored.

Jade hardly dared look in the bathroom mirror as she applied a light foundation, for fear of seeing an accusing face peering over her shoulder. *How can you do this to me at a time like this?* Marjorie Benson would be saying. And Jade felt one foot tall.

She patted on a dusting of powder.

And then, she recalled, flicking off the surplus with a large silky brush, when Selina had finally gone home leaving her to settle down in the king-size bed at last, Oliver had phoned.

'I'll be leaving Gloucester before lunch tomorrow,' he'd told her, his tone that of one wary as to the kind of reception he would be given; since their quarrel over the purchase of the flat, they had been circumspect in their dealings with each other. He'd cleared his throat and added, 'I'll be going straight to the office when I get back.'

'Don't forget,' she'd replied helpfully, 'that I have my evening class to go to. I won't be home until late.'

'OK,' had been his response and he'd smartly severed the connection, leaving Jade with nothing but a buzzing receiver on the pillow beside her.

Wide awake after that, she'd put the instrument back on its cradle and propped herself on one elbow. Oliver had sounded extremely subdued, she'd decided – not like his usual self at all. She had half-expected him to respond to her statement about being late with something sarcastic like: 'I won't hold my breath', or some such. Even in their present state of coolness that sort of thing was normal for him to come out with; a brief 'OK' was not. What was wrong?

She'd slipped back between the sheets again, suddenly pining for the old Oliver – the cocky, snappy one with the bluff, blunt manner. Few people ever saw the soft, sensitive side to his nature, but it was there. She knew it was there. And she loved him for it. It wasn't his fault, either, that he'd got so stroppy over money matters; the fault had been entirely her own. Oh, why had she gone with Philip Benson?

Her make-up completed, Jade turned abruptly

from the mirror and began to put on a short-sleeved two-piece in green. Her jaw was set and her face stern as she went mechanically through the motions. At four o'clock that morning she had made two resolutions: one of them had been to keep her little fling with Philip entirely secret from Oliver, because it would surely make things impossible between the two men, and anyway it seemed a good idea all round. And the second resolution was to put an end to the affair. Immediately.

She would phone Philip that very morning from the office, as soon as she could snatch a few private minutes, and tell him what a terrible mistake it had all been.

There could be few things more irritating than a broken watch strap, Oliver decided, finding that his patience had run out. He'd put up with doing without his watch for two days, but if he looked at his wrist once more and saw black hairs instead of the information he needed, he would explode. A quick trip into the centre of Gloucester was called for.

After a quick circuit of the shops nearest to where he'd parked, he chose the cheapest-looking jeweller's he could find, in the hope of not being charged too much for the repair of one small silver link, and sat down on an old bentwood chair at the assistant's suggestion while someone answering to the name of Jack set to work on the strap behind the scenes.

The shop had no other customers – time here seemed to have stood still – and Oliver silently drummed his fingers on the glass-topped counter while he waited with growing restlessness. He studied the walls, the ceiling, and the stock that glittered all around him – looking anywhere rather than be compelled to meet the eye of the elderly female assistant.

The woman had left Jack and the watch in the back of the shop behind a heavy velvet curtain, and was now sitting comfortably on the opposite side of the counter to Oliver, her arms clamped below her large bosom while her fingers worked frantically at a piece of white crochet.

Clearly she knew her pattern well; she was able to dart many a curious glance over her half-moon glasses at Oliver, much to his discomfort. He could almost feel each one of them pinging against his skin: tiny missiles in the shape of question marks radiating from her eyes. It could only be a matter of moments before she attempted conversation, he warned himself, and he willed Jack to get a move-on.

Jack dropped something in the back room and swore.

'Getting clumsy in his old age.' The woman smiled fondly. 'But he'll do you a right good job.'

Her complacency was a red rag to Oliver; it wasn't fair that she had nothing better to do than sit there fiddling with her useless bit of crochet while his whole world was upside down. For he was no further forward with his Sally problems than when he'd set out on this trip. If anything he was worse off. And now he was having to return to Bristol. Business-wise he'd already over-run on time. Take any longer and Philip Benson would think him inept.

He wished he was on the road to Bristol. Now that he was on the move he felt an urgent need to get back to Jade, though he couldn't think why. Surely nothing would have miraculously altered the coolness and tension between them. The old problems would still be there too . . . or would they? Perhaps – his eyes bulged at the memory of one of their last exchanges – perhaps Jade had left him – packed up her belongings and gone off to find a place of her own! His stomach performed a gurgle.

'Everything all right?' The assistant, fingers flying faster than ever with the crochet hook, felt compelled to enquire.

'Fine,' he snapped discouragingly. He was in no mood at all to exchange inane remarks. He wanted to be alone with his private thoughts and feelings. He stood up and wandered over to another showcase, one that allowed him to turn his back on the assistant without appearing rude. But it made no difference.

'Beautiful rings, aren't they?'

Oliver's flesh tightened. He hadn't noticed what was in the case, but now his eyes rested on a superb sapphire engagement ring, its price presumably so astonishing that the tag was turned face down to protect enquirers from heart attacks. He would have had to stand on his head to read it through the underside of the glass shelf. He didn't bother.

'Lovely sapphire, that.' The assistant chatted happily on. 'Whenever I look at it, do you know what I see?'

No, and I really don't want to.

'I see it on the finger of a beautiful tall blonde with the bluest of blue eyes. Slim, she is, and willowy, and she has the most perfect of smiles.'

Oliver swung round. But the woman was examining her crochet for the first time since he'd walked into the shop, so she was unaware of the effect of her words ... or so he thought. And anyway, Jade's eyes were blue-green, not 'the bluest of blue'. Still, blue was certainly her favourite colour and this ring would be perfect for her. In fact, if he scoured all the shopping centres in the world he doubted he would find something more suitable.

All at once he saw Jade standing beside him in a country church, or at a civil ceremony somewhere – he didn't care where, he wasn't fussy – and she was wearing a fabulous filmy white dress with this ring elegantly displayed on her right hand while he slipped a gold one on to her left ...

He drew a handkerchief from his pocket and wiped his face; the realisation of what he really wanted in life – commitment to Jade, marriage, wedding paraphernalia, the lot – having brought him out in a sweat. The fact that he'd done all that stuff with Sally didn't alter things at all. So why had he told Jade the complete opposite? And was it too late to put her wise now? Did he have the courage to tell her?

'Faint heart never won fair lady,' the woman said behind him. At least, that was what he thought she'd said. But as Oliver swung round, his jaw gaping a little at her words, Jack put in an appearance.

'Here y'are, lad,' he said holding out the watch and peering at Oliver over the top of glasses that were so similar to those of his assistant. In fact he looked so much like her all round, that the two simply had to be man and wife. 'It were only a little thing needed doing. I'll not be charging you owt.'

Oliver fumbled in his pocket for change, dropped it into a charity box on the counter, and gabbled his grateful thanks. It wasn't until he was half-way back to his car that he came out of his trance-like state. He looked back the distance he had come, rubbed a hand across his chin, and had a funny feeling that if he were to retrace his steps to the jeweller's shop, it simply wouldn't be there.

Jade's resolution began to dissolve as soon as she heard Phil's voice on the end of the line.

She had gone down to the basement of Hart, Bruce and Thomson in order to make the call, full of good intentions. Now she was sitting on a pile of old files, clutching an ancient phone to her chest.

247

She had hardly expected to find the heavy, dust-clogged piece of equipment in working order but thankfully it was.

While waiting to be connected she watched the feet of passers-by as they tramped along the pavement above eye-level in search of places to lunch. She shuddered; her own stomach felt too full with nerves, even to think of food.

'Philip? It's me. Jade Montgomery.'

'Jade . . .'

His voice held wonder, surprise and pleasure – but it was a knife-turn in her heart. Did she really have to send this man packing? Being with him for those few hours had been like – well – coming home. Like having Christmas just round the corner. Like wrapping up in a big hot towel on a cold winter's day. Like – oh, he made her feel so damned secure. What price independence, she wondered, looking round at the dingy walls of her workplace. Life with a man like that to protect you would be so . . . easy.

When she had hinted to Selina earlier on that her lover was not exactly a young man, Selina had muttered something about him obviously being a father-figure. The sort of father they both should have had but missed out on. Perhaps she was right. She would have loved to have had a father like Phil. But whatever the reasons for the attractiveness of the man, it was an attachment that could not flourish: he belonged to another woman.

'Philip, I –' she gripped the old braided flex and

twined it round her fingers '– I have something to say to you.'

'Fine. I'm glad to hear it.' He lowered his voice to an intimate level. 'And I've a few things I'd like to say to *you*, my dear.'

'No, I–'

'Will you meet me somewhere for lunch? We could drive out of town . . . somewhere quiet. No one would need to know.'

'No. No. Not lunch.'

'No? Oh, but of course! We've that other business to attend to, haven't we? You want to strike while the iron's hot and take some of your hoard back to the shops. Brave girl! So where would you like to meet up? The department store, or what?'

'Not . . . no!' Jade rubbed her forehead. The word 'hoard' had reminded her that she was supposed to have fed Oliver's chipmunks in his absence but had completely forgotten to do so. She hadn't even topped up their water bottle. They could possibly live on whatever food they had hoarded; but, dear God, how long could they go without water?

'It's very kind of you, Philip, but no. I don't want you to meet me. I'm perfectly capable of taking all that stuff back myself, I've decided. I'll not be troubling you.'

A pause spoke his disappointment for him. 'But it isn't any trouble. Really it isn't. Jade, why won't you let me help you?'

Jade swallowed and closed her eyes. 'What we . . . what happened yesterday, Phil . . . it must never happen again. It was a mistake. Foolish. And we shouldn't have . . . I'm sorry if –'

'Don't say that. Please. Darling! What happened yesterday was the most wonderful thing to happen to me in a long time. And – I thought it made you happy too. Didn't it?'

'That's not the point, Phil. You're a married man. And I've got Olly. And I love him dearly. And I like you very much. I do, truly. And if things were very different – but they're not. And –' She stopped biting her lip and shaking her head, her attention suddenly taken by a sound. Through the ear piece she'd heard a door open and close. Then Philip sucked in a breath.

'Oliver!' she heard him say from a distance. 'You're back!'

Philip's neck flamed red as he stared at Oliver across the desk. The heat spread to his ears. It was embarrassing enough to have the man walk in on him like this after changing offices behind his back, but to be caught in the middle of a clandestine phone call with his girlfriend – well! Not that Oliver could possibly know who was on the other end of the line.

'Warm enough for you?' Philip attempted levity. He ran a hand round his collar, and flapped at his shirt. 'It really is turning out to be an extraordinarily hot summer, isn't it?' Banal though the words were, they were at least true; temperatures were breaking records every day and there were constant pleas from the water companies for care and conservation.

Oliver's glance around the room ended with the ceiling fan. 'You've changed offices, I see.' His gaze returned to Philip.

'Er – yes,' Phil admitted, surprised by the indifference in Oliver's tone and the blankness of his expression. He could think of nothing to add by way of explanation. Only the truth would have sounded plausible, and he was not prepared to admit to petty feelings of jealousy.

Oliver dumped a bulging briefcase on the nearest chair and wandered over to the window. 'I often wondered whether you'd prefer the larger room. And it is yours, by rights, of course. Your predecessor – Platt – was allocated this room. But he asked me to swap with him. Said he preferred to look out on to the car park and keep tabs on the staff's comings and goings. Learned a lot that way, he always said.'

'Oh.' Phil breathed more easily. 'So that's all right then. Hm?' But he felt somehow wrong-footed. Had the implication been that he should be keeping tabs, too?

With his hands in his pockets, Oliver shrugged. 'Makes no difference to me.'

And Phil's eyes bulged slightly in wonder: this was not the reaction he'd expected. He'd imagined Oliver might have had some sort of snide comment to make, but quiet acceptance of the change and a faint half-smile of acknowledgement, were not

251

what he'd been prepared for at all. What was up? Oliver seemed to be only half the man he'd been before; half the man who had gone swaggering off to Gloucester claiming he would return forthwith bearing the Golden Fleece.

Phil found himself looking at the briefcase on the chair as though expecting to see scraps of lambs' wool poking through the join. Then a knot of apprehension looped itself round his intestines. Had Oliver made a cock-up over in Gloucester?

'Um . . . how did it go, then – with Sinden?' he ventured. 'Have you made sure he'll deal with us?'

'Sinden?' Oliver turned from his preoccupation with the open fields. Anyone would have thought he'd never heard of the name. 'Oh. Sinden. Yes. Of course.'

'Really? But that's great. Erm – well done, Oliver. Grand job.' He tried a warm smile, but felt so mean inside. First you nick his room and then you bed his woman, a voice inside him said. What a way to reward the man for his efforts.

Oliver merely nodded vaguely at Phil and excused himself, promising a detailed brief later on.

Phil's concern and perplexity increased. So there had been no cock-up with Sinden, he told himself, and Oliver didn't exactly look ill . . . and he couldn't possibly know anything about him and Jade . . . so what could be the problem? He went over to the window and paused where Oliver had stood, as if an aura of the man's thoughts might have been left behind for him to read. The old

Oliver had been bad enough, he decided; but this one was most unnerving.

Something stirred outside the window to distract Phil just then. His eyes narrowed. What the devil was going on out there?

Beneath the window stood a large yellow digging machine and a team of helmeted men. A vast area of land had already been roped round with orange tape. And amid shouts and bellowed instructions a long mobile hut was bedding down on to a suitable plateau. The signs were all too obvious: builders were moving in.

20

Marjorie rang the bell of Top Barn for the third time, a feeling of unease growing with each press of the button. She hated this. Hated ringing and waiting, ringing and waiting, because naturally it reminded her all too potently of the time when she had rung and waited at her parents' house.

She shuddered in spite of the heat of the day. What could Stella be doing? Then she tried to reason with herself, just as she had on that previous occasion: Stella's car's parked outside the garage, I can see it. She must be in. She must have the radio on and can't hear me. She's gone into the back garden for something. She's having a little nap. She's been taken out by someone, out with her husband Ian perhaps.

Yet those front curtains are drawn right across. And there's a feeling about the place. Supposing . . . ?

Marjorie strained to catch sounds coming from the house: the radio, perhaps, or a vacuum cleaner But all that reached her ears on that still, stifling summer afternoon, was the far distant clanking of a hammer as it rained blows on something metal. Clank, clank, clank it went, in time with her thumping heart as she left the shade of the thick vine that grew over the porch and ventured to look round the back of the house.

If Stella was in, she reasoned, and saw her peering in any uncovered window that she might find, then she could easily explain her presence. And if Stella really was out then no one would be any the wiser.

Even so, her first bold steps soon faltered as she scrunched along the gravel path that followed the walls of the house. She wished she hadn't to do this. Oh, how she wished Stella would pop up from behind the hydrangeas with a fork or a hoe in her hand! But nothing moved. Nothing. And then the picnic bench came into view, still waiting in its dappled shade with grass growing even longer round its feet than the last time she'd seen it. Did the Ericsons never eat alfresco?

Marjorie stopped. She knew she had reached the glazed wall that looked out on to the courtyard. And she recalled how Stella had complained about the impossibility of screening it successfully in any way; she felt like a goldfish in a bowl, she'd said, even though there was no one to see in.

Anyone attempting to see in would find it difficult, Marjorie decided; the slight tint of the glass and the angle of reflected light made it almost impossible. She would have to press her nose to the pane and cup her hands round her eyes.

Lord! What would Stella's reaction be if she was sitting three feet away with her stereo earphones clamped over her ears and a tea-cup in her hands? Marjorie shrank from the task. But why would Stella bother with earphones when she could listen to her Gilbert and Sullivan CDs at maximum volume without a soul anywhere near to protest?

She drew a breath and peered in. And knew at once that whatever Stella was doing, it was not drinking tea. Nor was she listening to music. Not like that. Not sprawled on the staircase with her feet splayed apart and one arm flung across her chest.

Philip stood on the corner of Queen Square in Bath, idly wondering which was the house that Jane Austen had once stayed in. He was also waiting for Jade to emerge from the offices of Hart, Bruce and Thomson. He hoped he hadn't missed her. She didn't know he'd be here because he hadn't been able to contact her again, and he badly wanted to continue their conversation of that morning – the one Oliver had interrupted.

Traffic thundered round the square, belching fumes into the sunlit air; people crowded the pavement. This was no place to stand and stare. But at last he spotted Jade tripping down the three steps from the solicitors' offices, her hair flying out behind her. She stopped in alarm when she saw him.

'Philip! You shouldn't be here.'

'I had to see you again.'

'You can't. I have my evening class soon. And anyway—'

'Forget the evening class, for once. Have dinner with me. Please? Just dinner. Where can the harm be in that?'

'No, Phil.' She tucked a piece of hair behind one ear, her eyes searching his face. 'You know this isn't right.'

But he could see her indecision. With his heart swelling inside him, he took her hand, put it to his lips, and led her back to his car.

Marjorie sat in a waiting-room at the hospital, shaking in every limb. She could not stop shaking no matter how hard she tried, even though a nurse was being very kind to her – just like they were in 'Casualty' – and had brought her a cup of tea.

Feeling the nurse's comforting arm slip round her shoulders she began to ramble on again about how she'd discovered Stella. The nurse had heard it all before but still she let Marjorie talk.

'L-luckily I found a side door open, or I don't know what I'd have done. I-I rushed in and she was alive. Alive, but unconscious, and I could hardly believe it was true. I just threw myself at her and started dr-dragging her, dragging her towards the fresh air.'

'I think you've been so brave,' the nurse said, 'especially after what you told me about your poor parents.'

'But it was a stupid thing to do! Wasn't it? Because half-way through the kitchen I realised that this was n-nothing like it had been with Mum and Dad; this time there was a glass and – and an empty paracetamol thing by the phone. So I shouldn't have moved her at all! She might fallen down the stairs and – and *broken* something.'

The nurse patted her shoulder. 'You did your very best. And you've saved your friend's life. You've been marvellous. And you've no reason whatsoever to castigate yourself like this. Now drink your tea – you'll feel better – before it gets too cold.'

But Marjorie was inconsolable. Ignoring the tea and covering her eyes with her hands she burst out again, 'I did the wrong thing! I got it wrong again!'

'Mrs Benson . . . please . . . from what you've told me it's perfectly clear that there was nothing you could have done about your parents.'

Marjorie dropped her hands to glare her scorn. 'I should have got there sooner,' she said, 'don't you understand?'

'But that's really rid–'

'I could have done. I could. If I hadn't stopped to chat to one of the neighbours . . . or stopped to run a comb through my hair . . . or to put bleach in the sink, or washing on the line . . . oh –' She hid in her hands again, overcome by her own words; words that she'd never been able to say before, not even to Phil because, like his parents and most other people at the time, he seemed to think that the least said about the whole sad business the sooner it would be mended. In those days there hadn't been the mania for soul-baring and counselling that existed now.

Marjorie assumed that everyone's silence meant they all privately blamed her as much as she blamed herself but were refraining from saying as much, out of kindness. Because she'd been punished enough, hadn't she? Pointless to keep going on about it

And then, of course, she'd had her 'nervous breakdown' which no one talked about either if they could help it. Mental illness was something else to brush under the carpet. And as time passed, the possibility of Marjorie putting her thoughts into words had grown ever more impossible. The last thing anyone wanted her to do was to rake it all up again.

'You've never said this to anyone before, have you? About feeling you were to blame?' The nurse, wise beyond her years and with a razor-sharp intuition, had seen straight to Marjorie's problem.

Marjorie gulped, shaking her head.

'That's a pity, it really is. You shouldn't have kept it all to yourself. Because now you've spoken out, you can see how illogical it all sounds, can't you? The fact is, you can no more be held responsible for reaching your parents too late than you can for getting to your friend in time. It was fate. Nothing more, nothing less. Just fate. No one's to blame for anything. Now, I'm sorry but I must be getting along. You think about it. Promise me you will? And do try to *talk* to someone.'

Marjorie watched the woman bustle away on squeaky shoes with a clipboard tucked under her arm, promising to return with news of Stella at the earliest opportunity. Left strangely alone in what was a sizeable waiting room she put her head back and rested it against the wall. Right now she was too exhausted to think about anything.

The clock on the wall directly opposite showed half-past five. While kneeling beside Stella in the garden, it had seemed an eternity until the ambulance had arrived but now she could see that the whole drama had been played out in less than three quarters of an hour.

Her head began to throb, the hands of the clock crept round, and she was beginning to wonder whether she could possibly sneak two of her own paracetamol from her handbag without it seeming to mock fate, when a large, full-chested man walked in.

Not one of Stella's doctors, surely? Marjorie asked herself. A butcher, maybe, in spite of his grey pin-striped office suit. He would have looked far more at home in white overalls and an apron, with a chopper in his hand, than in that suit. The jacket would never have buttoned if he'd ever made the attempt, and the sleeves showed too much cuff.

Taking a blue handkerchief from his breast pocket he mopped moisture from beneath a band of greasy curls and made straight for Marjorie.

'You must be Marjorie Benson. The nurse told me all about you. Ian Ericson.' A clammy hand swamped hers. 'How do you do?'

Ye Gods and little fishes, Marjorie thought. *Stella's husband?* A less likely pairing of man and woman she had never before witnessed. Could they ever have had anything in common?

'I've just seen –' he jerked his head in the direction of the door '– not Stella, they won't let me see her yet – but one of the doctors. He says they won't know for a while whether she's done herself any lasting damage – paracetamol's a tricky thing apparently – but at least they think she's going to pull through.' The last words came out in a sob. 'Thank heavens.' He surveyed her with bleak, harrowed eyes. 'And thank *you*. What might have happened if you hadn't arrived, well, it doesn't bear thinking about.'

'It was purely a stroke of luck, really . . .' Marjorie had stood up on his approach; now she sat down again and looked at her hands, surprised at what she'd just said about luck being involved. The nurse's words must have struck home.

The news about Stella naturally came as a tremendous relief, and yet other considerations had already begun to dull Marjorie's joy: why had Stella done this dreadful thing? What had driven her so far?

There was little doubt that it had been a deliberate act. It couldn't have been an accident. Stella must have wanted to end her life. But why?

And had – heaven help her – had Marjorie herself been part of the reason? Had Stella felt let down when their promising friendship had failed to take off? Maybe it had been the last straw.

Marjorie had still not been able to control the shaking of her limbs; now, with this new possibility of guilt being laid at her door she began to shudder even more violently.

'This has been as terrible a shock to you as it has to me,' Ian Ericson observed. He slumped on to the chair next to hers, put up hands that resembled bunches of bananas and rubbed them over his face. 'I must say I feel a bit like a jelly myself. God, why did she do it? Do *you* know? I've given her everything a woman can want. Everything. I'm at a loss to understand.'

Marjorie shook her head in a non-committal fashion. She could have hazarded a few guesses as to what Stella really wanted, as opposed to what her husband thought she did, but she kept them to herself.

'I don't know,' he went on, 'how am I ever going to thank you? How can I?' He appealed to her with those huge hands of his spread out.

'You don't have to thank me. Please don't. Because I feel I may be partly to blame. Perhaps if I'd been a better friend . . . well, I ought at least to have explained.' She made herself look into his greasy face and found it as grey with shock as her own felt. 'You do realise who I am, don't you? You were supposed to come to dinner with us the other day. But my husband phoned and put you off at the last minute. I've no idea what excuse he made in the end but it was probably completely transparent. I'm sure Stella was left thinking that something better must have cropped up.

'It wasn't true, of course, no way. I was bitterly disappointed not to go ahead. But my husband realised who you were, you see.'

She told him briefly about Philip's job, and clearly he had not made the connection at the time.

'I see.' His lower lip curled down in a wry smile. 'Your husband did have a point, I suppose. Conversation would have been a little – er – chilly perhaps; your dinner party ruined.'

'I suppose so. But the least I could have done was to tell Stella the real reason for my cooling off, instead of which I allowed Philip to talk me into dropping her completely, just like that, and giving up working with her in the charity shop. Goodness knows what must have gone through her mind.'

'Look, if anyone's to be blamed it's me for not realising something was terribly wrong with my wife. You deserve a medal for what you did this afternoon, for keeping a cool head. Especially –' he shifted awkwardly in his uncomfortable jacket '– well, one of the nurses was telling me about your parents. It must have been horrendously difficult for you . . .'

But while he shrugged out of the jacket, displaying dark circles under the arms of his shirt,

Marjorie continued silently to berate herself. Philip, to be honest, had never suggested that she shouldn't at least send Stella a written apology or an explanation. She could have done that much. But then Becky's news had broken and put everything else out of her mind. Oh, life seemed to be nothing but a winding path clogged with ifs and buts and maybes.

Ian had stood up to drape his jacket over the back of his chair; now he thumped back on to the seat, its legs protesting with a crack. 'I want you to know – I insist – that if there's ever anything I can do for you – *anything* – then all you have to do is ask. And I mean that. It's a promise. And I always keep my word.'

Marjorie rose to her feet to avoid the odour that steamed from his body. 'That's very kind of you, but really I'm just so pleased that Stella's OK. That's more than enough for me. Now I think I'll see if I can find the nurse. Maybe she can tell me if there's any point in my waiting around to see Stella this evening, or whether I should come back tomorrow. That is –' she looked doubtfully across the room '– if Stella wants to see *me* . . .'

'Hey, my little beauties!' Oliver went straight to the chipmunks' cage as soon as he got in from work that evening. 'Have you been a good boy and girl?' He flung open the cage and laughed as the animals hurled themselves at him in excitement, making their curious throaty churring sounds for all they were worth and searching frantically for the special tit-bits he always had ready for them.

He sat on the floor and leaned against the cage, feeding them sunflower seeds from time to time and letting them scamper over him. When they'd calmed down he pulled pieces of apple from his pocket and presented them with those.

'Poor babies,' he commiserated, looking at the state of their cage and noticing how low on water they were, 'has that naughty Jade neglected you? Never mind my little ones. Daddy's here now, and he loves you.' He held the smaller one and stroked its stripy coat. 'D-daddy's . . . h-here . . . n-now-ow-ow-ow.'

The chipmunk stopped wriggling from his grasp and peered up at him as he delved into his pocket for a handkerchief. It seemed to be saying to itself, 'What's *he* got to cry about?'

And when Oliver went to answer a ring at the door ten minutes later, he found Jade's sister Selina standing there with the same keen curiosity in her bright blue eyes. She made a quick appraisal of the old clothes he'd just changed into – and found them not very much to her taste, if her expression was anything to go by – then her gaze came back to his face.

'It's Jade's night for evening class,' he told her gruffly, beginning to close the door. He and Selina had little liking for each other and made no attempt at disguising it.

'Oh, sod. I'd forgotten that.' Selina stepped into

the gap. 'Will she be very late? I could come in and wait for her, couldn't I?'

For a moment or two they performed a sort of plodding, circling dance together in the tiny hall, with Oliver trying to fend her off and Selina trying to gain admittance.

'Please, Oliver, I won't be in your way. But I must talk to Jade about our mother again or I'll go stark staring bonkers.'

Oliver still wasn't sure whether Jade would be back at all, although none of her things appeared to be missing, but he couldn't admit as much to Selina. He gave up the struggle and let her take over the sofa in the lounge.

'What's the problem with your mother?' he grudgingly asked, slumping on to one of the armchairs. 'Is she ill?'

'No, not exactly.' Selina wrapped her arms round her knees. 'Well, she's got these frightful hot flushes and horrible floods and stuff – you know, that kind of thing?'

Oliver closed his eyes for four seconds and opened them again.

'But what worries me really is this obsession she's got with slimming. I told her, "Mum, you've got enough on your plate to cope with already; give the diet a rest." But will she listen? No. She keeps popping these pills like there's no tomorrow. Dozens and dozens of the things. I'm sure they can't be doing her any good.'

'But if the doctor prescribed them for her –'

'But he didn't. She's been getting them through the post.'

Oliver sighed.

'Do you realise you're eyes are all red and bleary?' Selina had been watching him since she'd arrived; now her curiosity got the better of her. 'I didn't know you wore contacts.'

'I don't. I happen to have perfect vision.'

'You would. Do you suffer from hay fever, then?'

'Not as far as I know.'

'Or have you been up all night, too?'

'Just because you spend all night clubbing –'

'Oh, I didn't mean me!' Selina tried to look coy. 'I meant you and – well, we all know what you and Jade get up to when you're apart.'

Oliver fixed her with a stare.

'Well, *you* get up to things. Jade told me. But Jade doesn't usually. She's not really that way inclined, you know. She only pretends to be open-minded for your –'

'What do you mean by *usually*?' Oliver had been sitting with his elbow on the arm of the chair and his head propped up by his hand, in the attitude of utmost boredom that he wished to convey to his visitor. Now he leaned forward, fully attentive, with such a fearsome look on his face that Selina shrank into the corner of the sofa.

'We-ell.' Selina spread her hands. 'What does usually usually mean? I mean, when you go off on your little sprees, Jade doesn't. As a rule. That's all.'

Muscles around Oliver's mouth made attempts

at producing speech for several moments before he could say, 'But this time . . . she did?'

'Did what?'

'Go with someone else. While I've been away, she's been with someone else.'

'So . . . what's wrong with that?' Selina's confusion increased. 'Isn't that what it's all about?'

A short silence followed while Selina attempted to think of something to say that would stop Oliver looking thunderous. She'd obviously put her foot in it. 'He was only an old fogey, you know,' she finally came up with. 'I expect she just felt sorry for –'

'Fogey? Fogey? How old?'

'Why don't you wait for her to tell you herself? When she comes in.' She slid off the sofa and ran behind it. 'I shouldn't have said anything, should I? I've spoiled your little game. I expect she wanted to surprise you, really, and now I've gone and spoilt it. Sorry.' She twiddled her fingers in a little wave and backed towards the door.

Oliver pounced across the carpet and grabbed her by the arm. 'How old was this fogey, Selina?'

'Ouch! Let go, you're hurting me!'

Oliver shoved his face up close to hers. 'How old was this man, Selina?'

'I don't know. I can't remember. Please let go of my arm.'

'Selina, I'm warning you, you silly little bitch.'

'Oliver! Stop! I don't think she ever said. All I can remember is that she called him Philip something-or-other. Just in passing, like. But why don't you ask her yourself? Aagh!' Suddenly finding herself released she rubbed her arm and fled the flat, all thoughts of her problematic mother banished from her mind.

She didn't stop running until she saw a bus waiting at a bus stop. With a leap as large as her skirt would allow she boarded it, though she had no idea as to its destination.

'Funny bloke,' she thought, smoothing herself down. 'What on earth's got into him?'

21

Philip took Jade to a pub that had at one time been used by quarrymen, and sat her down in a far corner of the dark interior while the other customers, almost without exception, flocked to the sun-drenched garden. She asked for wine and a pasta bake, and he ordered a beer and grilled gammon.

'So this is how it would be, is it?' she said, looking around at all the unoccupied tables.

'I don't understand what you mean.'

'Hiding me away in shady places like this. Afraid of who might find out.' Her solemn young face accused him; there was a glitter about her eyes.

He sat back as though she had hit him. 'I simply thought it would be more comfortable to eat in here. I'm sorry, I should have asked you. Would you rather we sat outside?'

But they both saw through his hasty excuse; his intention had been, as she had suspected, to conceal them from prying eyes.

She didn't bother to answer him but went on speaking her mind. 'You've two daughters almost as old as I am. And you've been married for years to your wife. What do you think you're playing at? I mean –' she put out her hands, palms upwards '– where's the future in all this? I presume you must have thought about that?'

It was the fact of his wife that most rankled with her. If he could do the dirty on Marjorie, she argued with herself, then was he such a great catch? At least Oliver, for all his talk, was really the faithful kind – well, he had been until this trip to Gloucester had cropped up, and what proof did she have that he'd been getting up to anything there? None whatever. But Phil? She knew exactly what he'd been getting up to behind his wife's back.

Yes, of course she loved to be with him: loved the way he drove the car with such skill, purpose and authority, for example, and the way he carried himself; she loved the way he cherished her, helping her into the car, fussing over her, and treating her like a lady. She loved so many things about him. But still she harboured doubts.

He hardened his mouth, not answering. What could he say in his defence? That yes, she was right, he was behaving abysmally to his wife? And that he refused to consider the consequences?

'Can you see yourself ever leaving Marjorie?' Jade put to him baldly.

He shot her an anxious glance.

'Or were you just planning an affair? I mean, am I to be something extra in your life? A bit of fun on the side?'

'Of course not!'

'Well, what then?'

He swallowed, looking wild-eyed. He seemed prepared to say almost anything, do whatever it took to keep her. 'Are you . . . asking me to leave her?'

'No. No, I'm not.' She sighed and leaned on her elbows. 'I'm trying to wind you up. To make you think of what you're doing. To make you see some sense.'

'But I don't *want* to see sense, Jade. I don't even want to think.'

'Now you're being silly.'

'I know.' He glared his defiance. 'And I don't give a damn. All my life I've been good old dependable Philip. Trustworthy to the end. And now I want to be something different. Any objections to that?'

'Yes, I have. Plenty. You can't do this, Phil, you know you can't. Because people are going to get hurt: Marjorie; your daughters; all your family – if we were to get too involved. Not to mention Oliver. But we need not get involved, need we? We can back out of this right now, without too much suffering on our part, and nobody need know that it happened. We've hardly got to know each other, after all. And that's the way it should stay. We'd be terribly selfish to prolong it, you know we would.' She waved a hand at him. 'Oh, this is an old, familiar story, Phil, and it's one that's best left untold.'

Philip glared at her again, his look saying that she had far too old a head on her young shoulders for his liking. And who was she, a member of a generation he'd always considered totally lacking in morals, to lecture to the likes of him?

'Well, if you're going to be like this . . .' He rose and strode over to the bar, had a short, heated exchange with the woman in charge of food orders, and jerked his head towards Jade.

She balked at the imperious gesture but had no desire to be left stranded in the countryside with no credit card and only one pound forty-eight pence in her purse, so she joined him.

He led her back to the car. 'Neither of us is hungry,' he declared, ducking under hanging baskets full of trailing pink geraniums. 'You've no objection to leaving, I suppose?'

'I think it's a good idea.' She gave a small sigh of relief. Her words must have found their target, thank heavens. He was seeing sense after all. He would take her back to her flat and that would be an end to it. They would part for ever more. It was all that they could do. The simplest way and the best.

As they hurtled out of the car park she gripped the inside door handle. Philip seemed in a hell of a mood with her. But she'd only said what had had to be said. And it hadn't been easy. Heaven knew how she yearned for him to touch her, to hold her just once more. But one of them had had to keep their heads in all this, and it certainly hadn't looked like being him.

She watched in dismay as he swung the car, very suddenly, down a dusty, narrow lane. He braked hard and she threw him a stony look. What now, she thought, her heart pattering, as his hand switched off the engine.

Her eyes met his. Silly question. His intention was perfectly clear.

Since Marjorie had described her new home in such detail at Jade and Oliver's dinner party, Oliver had no difficulty in finding it. Spotting it in the distance, he propelled his car across the Red Sea, intent on doing murder. Philip Benson was not going to get away with what he'd done. Oh, no. There'd be hell to pay for this.

The cloud of dust he'd stirred up was still hanging in the late evening sunlight when Marjorie came to the door.

'Oh,' Oliver said, taken aback: he hadn't expected Marjorie to be home. She hadn't figured at all in his imaginary interview with his outrageous boss. 'I was expecting to find only Philip,' he said. 'I thought you were still away.'

Marjorie had been staring vacantly at Oliver's attire. In his hurry to get at Phil's throat he'd not stopped to change out of the old sleeveless cotton vest, check shorts and casual canvas shoes that Selina had disapproved of. She stopped her perusal of his unusually hairy legs to look blankly into his face. 'I'm back.'

'Yes,' he said. Did she even remember who he

was? She looked so remote and pale that he wondered whether she was ill. 'Is . . . Philip home?' he asked, now a little concerned.

'Philip? Why, what time is it?'

He had no idea either. He held out his wrist, now reunited with its watch, so they could both see the clear white dial. 'It's almost nine o'clock.'

'Well, where is he then?' she queried in a waspish sort of way.

Oliver snorted. 'If he's not here, need you ask? I can see by your face that you know what's been going on. Evening classes, my foot! Who's been teaching what to whom, I wonder?' His eyes narrowed. 'How did you find out, by the way?'

'Sorry? Um . . . look, won't you come in? I'm not sure I understand. *You* don't know Stella, do you?'

'Stella?' He followed her into the house.

'A friend of mine.' Her eyes were wide with disbelief. 'She nearly died today. But if you don't know her . . .'

'Christ. Nearly *died*?' So *that* explained her strange manner. 'But she – she's all right, is she, now?'

'She will be all right, they hope. I g-got there just in t-time. She was lying on the floor and I found her and – and – she'd taken . . .' Marjorie groped for a chair, evidently still thoroughly shocked.

'Grief. So that's why you were looking so . . . Oh Lord. I thought it was because –'

She sat very still and tense for a while, her mind ticking over what he'd just said, albeit rather

276

slowly. 'You thought I knew something else?' Her eyes sought his but he looked away, pretending to plump a cushion. 'Phil's not . . . no! It can't be, can it, that he's had an accident, or you wouldn't be here looking for him. What, then? What is it that I don't know?'

'Would you mind if I smoked in here? A cigar? Bit overpowering, I'm afraid, but I really could do with one right now. Dreadful habit of course. Jade –'

'I like the smell of cigars. They always remind me of Christmas. My father used to –' Her face crumpled.

Oliver dragged on his cigar, wishing he hadn't walked in on all this – this misery. Especially when all he could deliver was more of the same. But he couldn't possibly tell her about Philip and Jade. Much though he would love to unburden himself, to talk to *someone*, he couldn't off-load this on to Marjorie in her present state of mind. Could he ever? It wasn't what he'd come for anyway.

'I'd better go,' he said, swiftly rising.

'No! No, please stay. Would you? I really could do with the company. I feel so . . . You need not make polite conversation. Just sit here. Philip must be home soon. Where is he? I'll put the television on if you like. And I'll get you a drink. Scotch? Beer? I'm sorry, I can't quite remember what you like.'

Oliver groaned silently. He felt her desperate need and could see no way of extricating himself.

Damn Philip for not being here when his wife needed him.

He allowed her to make him a gin and tonic; but the first sip told him that she'd been over-generous with the gin. It was almost triple strength. Compensation for his giving her his time, perhaps.

He grimaced. 'Great stuff this, but I do have to drive home sometime.'

'Sorry. I didn't think. I – I'm not quite my usual self.'

An understatement if ever there was one, he thought.

She looked at the television but didn't switch it on. Then she suddenly confronted him. 'Don't tell me they've been having an affair. Your Jade and my . . . oh, please don't tell me that!' Her contorted face was watching his and there was no way he could mask the truth. 'They have, haven't they? Good God.' She closed her eyes and sat quite still. 'Good God.'

She had made herself a drink as well, but she didn't turn to it. She seemed unaware of her surroundings, seeing only with an inner eye.

'I'm sorry,' he muttered helplessly. 'This is very hard for you. Must be a dreadful shock.'

It was a while before she answered.

'Funnily enough, it isn't. Not so much of a shock as you might expect. You see, I've already found Phil out in one lie – quite recently in fact. He lied to me about having to move because of his job. Said he had to, he had no choice. And all the time he could have taken redundancy and helped his parents. We need never have moved here, you see? It was the last thing I wanted to do.'

'Heavens.' Oliver also wished the Bensons hadn't moved.

'Oh, I suppose it may not seem much to you.'

'Yes, it –'

'But it does to me. You see, it makes me view our whole marriage in an entirely different light. I've been living with someone I trusted, someone I thought I knew; but now I don't know him at all. Do you understand? And now this! But somehow it doesn't seem so incredible, if you think about it. If he's capable of one deception, he's capable of goodness knows how many.'

She stopped and let out a gasp. 'Oh, how awful of me, I was forgetting. This affects you just as much! Though at least you two aren't married. Can it be as painful if you aren't married? Forgive me if this is a stupid question.'

'Huh!' Oliver sent a puff of smoke down his nostrils. 'I *am* married, as a matter of fact. Technically, at least. I know precisely how painful all this can be. But believe me, it hurts as much if you're not legally married as if you are.'

'Married?' Marjorie's head whipped round. 'You and Jade? I thought –'

'Not me and Jade. No. I'm married to a girl called Sally . . . until the divorce is made final. She's the mother of my two small children.'

'*Children?*' Marjorie sounded as if she'd reached

overload: further information was almost more than she could take in.

'Yes. Two.' His face softened. 'A boy and a girl. But I hardly ever see them. So I suppose you could say that puts me even lower in your estimation than Philip currently is. At least your husband seems to have been a good father to his children.'

Marjorie groped for her glass and lifted it to her lips. Maybe she was listening to him; maybe she wasn't. It didn't really matter. Sitting there amid a hotchpotch of furniture that he only vaguely noticed as being fit for the council dump he continued to unburden himself, to tell her all the things he normally kept to himself because he found it so difficult to talk to Jade and there wasn't anyone else he could confide in.

'You know I went over to Gloucester? Well, that's where Sally and the kids are. So I thought, if I try just once more to talk some sense into her she might agree to cut down on her demands. She's crippling me financially, you see, and causing problems between me and Jade. And when I got there she appeared fairly reasonable for once: rational, more mature. And there didn't seem to be a bloke around either. I sensed that no one else was living in the house. You can feel these things, I think, can't you?

'Anyway, I made a fuss of the kids, though I don't think they know who the hell I am any more. They're both so very young. Only tots. But the cutest little . . . And then I sat Sally down and showed her on paper what my outgoings to her will be, now that I've been given no choice, and what they are for myself. And then I added them up and put them beside my salary and the result was pretty obvious: the one nowhere near covered the other, did it?'

Oliver settled further in his chair and put one leg over the other. ' "Tell me the answer to this one, Sally," I said. So she studies the figures, or pretends to, and then shoots me this odd expression. "There *is* an answer to this," she said. "You can move back in with me. I made a bad mistake, Oliver. I shouldn't have gone with someone else. You're a good man, really, and you didn't deserve to be treated the way I treated you. I'm sorry, honestly I am. But I'm prepared to try again, if you are." Or words to that effect.'

He'd forgotten the drink at his elbow now, and a long ash had eaten into the cigar before he continued the tale.

'Now, if she'd only said all that months ago . . . But too much water's gone under the bridge. I looked at her and I knew: there was no way I could go back to her. I wanted to because of the children. You've no idea, Marjorie, how much I yearn to have those children back. And they almost persuaded me. I had only to look at Billy and Melissa – my darling little Missy – and I very nearly agreed. I wanted so much to be their father. But how could I go back to Sally? I don't love her any more. I did once, of course, but –'

Oliver paused to take stock of Marjorie, but even

if she was listening he was sure she wouldn't judge him. And he so wanted to say it to someone.

'Sally,' he went on quietly, 'killed all the love I had for her stone dead, the day I found her with another man.' He cleared his throat. 'And now I've got Jade who's worth a dozen Sallys.'

He blinked hard, realised that Marjorie's carpet was in grave danger and knocked his ash into a tray.

'Did I say "I've got Jade?" Correction: I had. Now I'm left with nothing. No wife. No Jade. And no kids.' His lips trembled. 'Have you any idea how it feels to walk out on two beautiful children, knowing that you must never see them again? Because you know you can't give them what they need and that by butting in and out of their lives you're doing them more harm than good?'

Marjorie had a hand over her eyes, her head turned away.

He rubbed his nose. 'I'm not doing any good here, either.' He jabbed the cigar into the ashtray and stood up. 'I'm sorry. I didn't mean to say any of this. All I came here for was to kill your wretched husband. I'll go now. I'll . . . go.'

Some time after Oliver had gone, Marjorie tipped the remains of the cigar into the kitchen bin and poured away their drinks. She wiped her face on a cool flannel in the cloakroom and slipped into the darkened garden. She badly needed fresh air. She couldn't pull herself together at all; couldn't begin to think straight. The day had passed like a dream.

282

Or rather, like a nightmare. First that business with Stella, and then that news from Oliver. It was all too much to take in. Phil . . . and that beautiful girl?

On reaching her bed of annuals she looked down. Yes, they'd all perked up all right. Looked quite healthy now. But what the hell was the point?

She kicked at the nearest lobelia. Then kicked to the end of the row. Then she kicked and kicked in a fury, until every plant lay in shreds.

22

Philip put a flowered china mug on the bedside table.

'Tea,' he said, touching Marjorie's exposed arm. The arm had been flung across her face, the back of her hand resting on her forehead. It was a sign he knew all too well. 'Headache?' he asked, smitten by a ton of guilt.

'Mm. Terrible,' she murmured.

'Poor thing,' he said, pulling a sad face. Somehow, seeing her looking as bad as she was obviously feeling, made his attraction to Jade seem even more of a sin than it was. 'I'll go and get you some pills.'

Last night, the realisation that Marjorie was back home had given him quite a shock. He had stolen into the darkened house hoping she would be asleep so that he wouldn't have to face her immediately. An evening spent with Jade had made him feel a different man; wouldn't he therefore *look* different? And if Marjorie were to wake up wouldn't she notice? He had undressed in the bathroom like a bashful bride, and shoe-horned himself into bed as though it contained an unexploded bomb.

Once lying stiffly beside her in a state of acute alertness the enormity of what he had done had begun to dawn on him. Marjorie's physical, deep-breathing presence gave substance to the dreamy, dazzling craziness of the past few days. Marjorie was real; Jade was real. And he, Philip Benson – four weeks from his fiftieth birthday – had been cheating on his wife.

He had even resorted to doing that cheating in the back of a car that evening – something he'd not done for many a long year, but where else could they have gone? And some of Jade's words had come back to him as he lay next to Marjorie in the darkness: what *did* he think he was up to?

The words came to him again as he scrabbled about in the bathroom cabinet looking for the headache pills. He'd never been much of an actor and he was already finding it difficult to appear normal. His conscience was playing tricks on him too: when he'd gone down to put the kettle on he was sure he could smell Oliver's cigars wafting about in the air, somewhere around the lounge door.

He went back into the bedroom with the flat carton of pills and a glass of water. 'You were fast asleep when I came home last night. I had to go out for a meal. There was nothing at all in the house. And the service was dreadfully slow. It was quite late by the time I got there; I'd been working all hours on Knox's debrief. Then old Hemmingway-Judd kept me nattering about this, that, and the other, and –' he paused; was he going OTT on the excuses? 'Well, you know how it is, Marjie, don't you?'

Marjorie dragged herself to a sitting position. 'Oh yes, Phil, I know all about it. I know *exactly* how it is.'

He shot her a narrow-eyed glance. 'Of course, I would have phoned if I'd known you were back; the cable's been put in at last. You – er – didn't try to phone me at work?'

'I had other things on my mind.' Her hand groped for the bubble pack of pills and she held them up. 'See these? Well, Stella took loads of them yesterday afternoon. Fortunately I found her in time. They think she'll be OK.'

'Er – Stella?' Where had he heard the name before?

Marjorie gulped down two of the pills and fixed him with a bleary glare. 'My friend from the charity shop.'

He'd been climbing back into his own side of the bed; now he stopped, half in and half out. 'Oh – 'he said carefully '– her. But my poor dear! How absolutely awful for you! No wonder you've got one of your bad heads.'

She flopped back into the pillows, turning away from him.

'Look,' he said, trying to visualise his office diary. He had heaps to do, but at least it would keep

287

him from having to face Oliver. 'Would you like me to stay home today? I –'

'No! No, please don't. I'll be perfectly all right on my own.'

'But Marjorie, are you sure?' He eyed her more closely now. He'd only just fully realised the implications of what had happened. This hoo-hah over Stella couldn't have happened to a less suitable Samaritan than Marjorie. It must have seemed to her like a ghastly re-run of the past. What if it upset her so much that it tipped her over the edge and brought on another breakdown? It hardly bore thinking about.

No, that was the last thing he wanted right now. The only advantage, he thought, reaching for his mug of tea – and heaven forgive him for seeing any good in such a thing – was that it might serve as a distraction. Marjorie would perhaps be too pre-occupied with it all to notice anything amiss with him.

'I really do think I should keep an eye on you, you know,' he persisted when she made no reply.

But much to his surprise she suddenly threw off the thin cover which was all they'd been able to tolerate that summer, and began to shuffle towards the bathroom.

'No,' she argued vehemently, 'I'm going to *have* to get rid of this headache. I'm not going to lie here and give in to it. I should be visiting Stella at the hospital this morning and I don't want to let her down.'

Philip stared after her for a while, then shrugged. Perhaps he had underestimated her. Perhaps she wasn't about to throw a wobbly after all. To the accompaniment of rushing water sounds he slowly sipped his tea before following her into the bathroom, where he found her lying in deep foamy suds with a hot flannel draped over her face. Sometimes heat seemed to help her headaches; sometimes she preferred something cold.

'Marjie,' he said looking down at the mound of wallowing pink flesh and trying not to make a comparison, 'there's something I've been meaning to tell you.'

Marjorie went very still. 'What?' she managed to say in a thin, reluctant voice.

'It's about the MD's annual barbecue. It's this coming Saturday evening, so I hope you'll be recovered by then. It's absolutely compulsory, of course. You know the sort of thing: you *will* all come and be sociable; you *will* all bring your partners; you *will* look as though you're enjoying yourselves, even though it's a crashing bore.'

He half hoped she might plead to be let off; it would make things a whole lot easier if she were not to come. With Jade there – well, it was going to be bad enough trying to keep up a front with Oliver, but with Marjie there too he wasn't sure he could cope.

Marjorie pulled down her flannel. 'Well, of course I'll be better by then. And don't make it sound like a duty; it might be quite good for a laugh. Huh! When did we last have one of those? Anyway, at least we'll know someone there.' She looked Phil straight in the eye. 'Oliver Knox and Thingy – his girlfriend. What was her name? I've forgotten.'

Thingy, indeed! But he couldn't trust himself to say Jade's name in front of her. He picked up his shaving gel, squirted it into his palm, and began to scrape at his chin.

Marjorie suddenly came out with 'Jade!'

Phil reached for a piece of toilet roll and stuck it on a blob of blood. 'By the way,' he said, a little tersely, 'I'm afraid I've got bad news.'

When his words brought no reaction he glanced at Marjorie again and found she'd gone so still this time that the water had ceased to swirl. Her breasts made the only movement visible as they boldly bobbed about above the bubbles. 'Well?' she finally croaked at him.

'Well, I did water your plants while you were away, honestly I did, but when I glanced out of the window a minute ago it seemed as though every cat in the neighbourhood came into the garden last night. They've dug every one of them up.'

'Marjorie?'

The voice had a disembodied quality to it against a background of busy rumbling, and she guessed its owner was using a car phone. She also guessed it was Oliver.

'Yes, Oliver, what is it?' she asked briskly, leaning

forward to check her face in the hall mirror; she'd been about to set out for the hospital and could have done without the interruption. She smiled sourly at herself. Her first call on the new phone, and already she was regretting that it had at long last been installed.

'Look. About last night,' Oliver was saying. D'you think we could just forget it? I mean, like, maybe I was a little hasty, you know? Telling you the things that I did? I may have been jumping to silly conclusions, you see. In fact I'm sure I have.'

Marjorie frowned. For a second or two it sounded as though Oliver was driving his car through a hail storm, a tornado and a scrapyard, all at once, and she feared for his life. How could he concentrate on a telephone conversation and still safely negotiate traffic hazards?

'You mean, all that stuff you told me about my husband?' she queried. 'My husband seeing your Jade?'

'Precisely.' He forced a laugh down the line. 'I can be a bit of a hothead at times, you know. Act before I even think. And . . . I've got it dreadfully wrong this time. I've made one hell of a monumental boob.'

'You really thinks so, do you?'

'Oh, yes! I really do. It was all because of something her sister told me. That was all I had to go on. And she's an empty-headed little . . . well, her tongue does tend to run away with her, you know, and she gets hold of the wrong end of the

291

stick. So I shouldn't have set too much store by what she came out with, shouldn't have gone off at half-cock the way I did. It was really utterly stupid of me. Utterly, utterly crass.'

A pause.

'I'm so sorry if I've upset you, Marjorie. And all for nothing, I'm sure.'

'Sure,' Marjorie said flatly.

'Well . . . am I to be forgiven?'

'There's nothing at all to forgive.'

Marjorie tramped along miles of hospital corridor trying to track down her friend. Her footsteps beat a rhythm on the tiles: don't get mad, get even; don't get mad, get even. But it was so hard not to get mad. How had she managed to stay so calm this morning with Phil? How had she managed to lie in bed, feigning the first headache that she'd ever feigned in her life and pretending nothing had happened?

She had amazed herself with her act. Every part of her being had been telling her to lash out at him with her fists, tear him limb from limb, scratch his wicked wandering eyes out of their damn stupid sockets. That's what scorned women did, didn't they? Yet she'd not even hinted that she knew.

How dare he do this to her? After all these devoted years? To lie to her and drag her miles from where she belonged, to a place where she'd felt so hopelessly alone with her dreary moods and her wretched headaches, and so horribly middle-aged

– and to dump her? He'd all but ruined her whole life.

As for Oliver deciding to give Jade and Phil the benefit of the doubt and pretend nothing had happened – well, he might be able to fool himself but nobody could fool her. She'd crashed the phone down as soon as he'd rung off and let out a great whoop of derision.

Don't get mad, get –. A patient rolled by on a trolley, making her break her step. But I *am* mad, she thought. Deep down I'm boiling, roiling, bloody, ruddy MAD.

She was so mad, that her rage and indignation seemed to have dulled the shock of Stella's attempt on her life. And she had done a lot of thinking in the night, before Philip crawled into bed beside her, especially about the advice the nurse had given her.

The woman had made so much sense. It *was* fate, wasn't it – her parents' death? Nobody could be blamed for it, unless you lined up everyone at the water-heater factory and pointed a finger at them for their shoddy workmanship. No, she hadn't been permanently knocked sideways by this horrific reminder, as Phil obviously expected her to be. Rather, it was as though a weight had lifted from her shoulders and a positive strength had poured into her, made even more powerful by her burning wrath.

But underlying her anger with Philip she realised how inevitable an affair with another woman had been. Somehow she'd known that something in their marriage had died, way back, when all this moving business started and he had behaved so uncharacteristically pig-headedly. Learning about the redundancy offer had strengthened her misgivings, and his infidelity had solidified them.

Or could she go back even further than that, to the months when she'd worked for his father without his knowledge? What kind of a marriage did you have if you felt you had to keep anything secret? Especially something so trivial. She'd never analysed her reason for secrecy before, but now she saw that she had tried to appear as Phil wanted her to be – the devoted 'girl-next-door' he thought he'd chosen for a wife – rather than be her real self.

She sighed as she turned a corner where thin old men were waiting in washed-out pyjamas for heaven only knew what. No, she wasn't so very surprised at what had happened, especially with a girl like Jade by way of temptation. The way his eyes had followed her around, that night of the dinner party had certainly not gone unnoticed.

Ian Ericson had had his wife installed in a private room at the hospital, but when Marjorie eventually found Stella she thought she must have wandered into a florist's shop by mistake.

'They're nearly all from Ian,' Stella told her, raising a languid hand in greeting and waving at all the bouquets. 'Typical Ian, this is. Throw enough money at a problem and it's solved, according to his way of thinking. They're supposed to cheer me up, of course, and all they're succeeding in doing is – ' She turned her head away, too upset to continue.

Marjorie placed her puny offering of yellow roses on the window sill and sat on the bedside chair. 'He really does care for you, you know,' she tried to assure her friend, though privately she thought Ian's message could have been more sensitively expressed.

'So where is he?' was Stella's scornful retort.

'I'm sure he'll be along soon.'

'I suppose so,' Stella grudgingly conceded. 'It is Saturday after all; even he doesn't work on a Saturday, though he might be out playing golf.' She made a show of smoothing the top edge of the sheet that covered her. 'He – er – told me I had you to thank for finding me yesterday. You reached me just in time . . .'

'I found you, yes.' Marjorie smiled at the pale, exhausted-looking woman. 'Whether or not you can genuinely thank me for doing so is another matter. I have a feeling that perhaps you'd rather I hadn't.'

Stella attempted a sneering laugh but succeeded only in a slight jerking of her body. 'I don't know what I want any more. I wonder whether I ever have. Did I mean to put an end to everything, I ask myself, or was it a cry for help? That's what everyone always wants to know on these occasions, isn't it? Well, even I don't know the answer to that one.'

'If it's help you want, then – then I'm here.'

Marjorie twisted her wedding-ring round. 'I won't desert you again, Stella.' She went on to explain about the dinner party and precisely why it had been cancelled.

Tears glistened in Stella's eyes as she listened, and she felt under her pillow for a man-size tissue, seemingly too full to speak, so that Marjorie was left in little doubt that that unfortunate episode had been partly responsible for her desperate act. Other factors beyond Marjorie's control must have contributed too, of course, but an apparent withdrawal of friendship might well have pushed her beyond the limit.

Marjorie felt her finger-nails digging into her palms. *This is all Phil's fault!* she screamed silently. None of it would have happened if he'd had the guts to face up to Ian Ericson at the meal. As if he hadn't already done enough, now he had nearly killed her friend!

'Heavens,' she said, filling an awkward silence, 'I need you, Stella, even if you don't need me. Right now I . . . but that's another story.' Much though she would like to tell someone of her marital problems, now was hardly the time, nor Stella the most suitable listener.

Not that Stella seemed to be hearing Marjorie any longer. She had closed her eyes and appeared to have succumbed once more to sleep.

'I'll call again tomorrow,' Marjorie whispered, touching her lightly on the shoulder, 'when you're feeling a little better.'

She crept out on the balls of her feet, but on closing the door with the gentlest of clicks became aware of a presence looming beside her. It was Ian, looking ill at ease in beige slacks and a lurid green shirt with sun glasses tucked in the breast pocket. His arms were loaded with yet more flowers for Stella, plus half a ton of black grapes.

'She seems to be having a nap,' Marjorie told him, a finger to her lips. Then she drew in a sudden breath. She had barely given serious consideration to what she was about to ask, but it must have been brewing in her mind subconsciously and now she plunged straight in: 'I wonder . . . do you think I could have a word?'

Ian's face went blank for a moment, showing only the haggard remnants of a sleepless night. Then he registered surprise and a faint touch of alarm; perhaps he was recalling his rash promise of the previous day. 'Yes, of course,' he said, indicating a row of tubular metal chairs pushed up against the corridor wall.

Marjorie sat down slowly, marvelling at her own temerity. A few hours ago – could it really be only that long? – when Ian had offered her some kind of reward for saving Stella's life, she had had no intention of ever taking him up on it. But her whole life had turned upside down since then.

She cast him a side-long glance. Did fairy god-mothers – or godfathers – really expect to be called upon to grant a promised wish? And didn't most of the old fables warn against cashing one in?

She searched her memory as she crossed her legs and smoothed the knees of her white summer jeans. She could recall that it was foolish to use a wish for wishing all future wishes to be granted; that could lead to disaster. No, she wouldn't make that mistake. But to use her one wish wisely . . . surely there was no harm in that?

The temptation to spend it was overwhelming. It had begun to burn a hole in her pocket. And Ian Ericson was struggling to conceal his impatience. She must speak now or he would get up and walk away.

23

'A *job*?' The irises of Ian Ericson's eyes became momentarily surrounded by white.

'That's right.' Marjorie pulled herself up straight, though her legs felt weak. 'I'm sorry to have to trouble you when you've such a lot on your plate, but I'm desperate. I need a proper job. In your company – Foretec. And I don't mean brewing tea.'

'But–'

'Something in your financial department would be just right for me, I'm sure. I wouldn't let you down. Oh, I know I may not have qualifications on paper, but I'm really good with figures. You see, I was doing that kind of thing up in London, before my husband was transferred to Bristol . . .'

'Your husband, ah yes, now what of him? I'm glad you brought that matter up. Because, of course, he needs to be considered in all this, before we go any further.'

'Who, Phil? Oh, no he doesn't! This is nothing to do with him.'

Ian's brows crawled up his forehead and hid amongst his greasy curls. 'But I rather think that we must. You see, your husband works for a rival company, as we both know all too well. It's already made things difficult between us and it would make things awkward all round.'

'I –'

'Did I say it would make things awkward?' He rubbed the back of his head. 'A bit of an understatement, I think. It'll make things nigh on impossible. You can see why I say that, can't you? How would I know, for example, that you weren't passing him information: stuff that might help him in his job? Facts that could prove detrimental to *my* business, and make me look a stupid old fool?'

Now it was Marjorie's turn to look wide-eyed, 'But I wouldn't dream of doing such a thing! It never would have entered my head!'

Ian stopped rubbing his head to give her a lop-sided smile. 'No, I can see it wouldn't. Of course. Silly of me. But that sort of thing does go on, you know. And even if it didn't happen with you, it wouldn't look too good, would it, if I were to employ someone in your position?'

Marjorie bit her bottom lip and chewed on it for a moment or two. Then she said, 'There's something I think you should know. You see, there's simply no question of my feeding Philip information that would be beneficial to him, even if I was that way inclined – for the simple reason that he and I, well, we're not getting along very well. In fact, I believe he's having an affair.' She forced herself to meet Ian's not wholly unsympathetic gaze. 'I really do need a job, you know, for a number of personal reasons, not least as some kind of insurance. If Philip and I –' she swallowed '– well, if it ever came to it, I wouldn't want to be left alone with nothing at all in the world. I don't mean he'd see me penniless; I mean I'd need something for myself. Something I could hold on to – if you see what I'm getting at . . .'

Ian fell silent for a while. 'Fair enough. That's understandable And if I *were* to give you a job I can see that you wouldn't jeopardise your position by passing my secrets to an enemy . . .'

'No, I wouldn't.' Her face brightened in expectation.

'But perhaps –' he smiled faintly '– you might be willing to find things out for *me*? Or to assist in a spot of *dis*information?' He looked away into the middle distance. 'I'd give my right arm to know why Sinden's gone cold on me. I thought he was in the bag. But someone, it seems, has lured him away.'

He looked back at Marjorie, his face an unreadable blank, and she blinked vacantly back at him. She'd heard all about Sinden from Philip. Had Ian really meant what she thought he meant? And if he had was he being serious? 'Does that mean you're going to take me on?' she parried, breaking that line of thought.

'Ah, hey there now, wait a minute.' He put up a massive hand, and inclined his head a little. 'I'm thinking more in terms of a trial run. Wouldn't that

301

make much more sense? How about you coming along to the office one day, and we'll try you out on a thing or two?'

'Yes! Oh, yes. Yes, please. That sounds a wonderful idea. When would you like me to start? Tomorrow? The next day? Or the one after?' Just let her get a foot in that door!

'Well, really, there isn't any hurry. And no doubt you'd like a while to get over this business with Stella. I saw how dreadfully shocked you were yesterday, and–'

'But I really don't need any time. I mean, I'd rather not be left to sit around at home thinking about things. Heavens, no. The best thing I can do is to plunge myself into something absorbing and keep myself as busy as I possibly can. So I'd like to get started straight away, Ian, if that's all right by you.'

'So how was Gloucester?' Jade asked coolly, when Oliver came home from work.

They'd barely spoken to each other that morning, having both overslept by half an hour, which had suited Jade fine because she'd hardly been able to look Oliver in the eye, let alone converse with him; and it had suited Oliver too for similar reasons to Jade's. But they couldn't avoid talking for ever.

Oliver caught the fake feather duster she'd just tossed at him and eyed her warily. Her tone had suggested to him that she suspected something;

that she knew he'd been to see Sally, though he'd never whispered a word.

'Do we have to do this tonight?' he said, referring to the housework on which she'd begun. She organised cleaning binges once a week, and at the moment was flitting about the lounge spraying furniture polish that reeked of pine; his job was always to flick over the ornaments in the display cabinet, clean the shower and hand-basin in the bathroom – but not the WC which he refused to touch, even with thick rubber gloves – and to empty their three rubbish bins.

Jade stopped spraying and buffing to brush her brow with the back of her hand. 'Yes, we do have to do this this evening. And you didn't give me an answer.'

'I presume I'm allowed to get changed?' He picked a pink feather from his suit sleeve. 'And Gloucester went very well, as a matter of fact. "Sir" actually seemed quite pleased with me.'

'Oh. So it was worth all the hassle, in the end?'

'That depends how you look at it.'

Jade rubbed hard at a table top. 'You were gone an awfully long time.'

'I know but it couldn't be helped. Did you miss me after all – penny-pinching bastard that I am?'

'Did *you* miss *me*, more to the point?'

They studied each other's faces across the room, both with plenty to say but neither knowing how to let it out. Jade was full of remorse about going with Philip but wanted reassurance that Oliver hadn't had a fling. And Oliver wanted to talk about Sally and their money problems, but not if what Selina had said was true.

Both were waiting for a sign, a clue as to how to proceed. When the phone range suddenly, neither made a move to pick it up.

When the phone had rung twelve times Philip gave up. He slipped the new office mobile in his pocket and strolled slowly back into the house. He thought his discreet movements over the past ten minutes had gone unnoticed by Marjorie – she'd been polishing her best court shoes when he'd left her – but when he stepped back into the conservatory she was there, standing behind a large parlour palm and watching him.

'I think it's got some kind of bug,' she said, putting out a hand to touch a frond. 'Nothing seems to get rid of it.'

'A pity if it has to be slung out.'

'Yes,' she said shortly, walking off, but not before eyeing his trouser pocket.

Phil put a hand on the phone when she'd gone, and let out a troubled little sigh. Now that Marjorie was back home, it was impossible even to have a word with Jade. Even in so large a house, complete privacy was difficult to come by. Had Marjorie seen him out by the fence, he wondered, his elbow propped on a post while making the call, in an attempt to disguise the deed? He hoped not. The fact that she'd not said anything outright was nothing to go by; she had a habit of not saying things at the time you most expected them but coming out with them at awkward moments. Or was she still in a stew about her friend?

He'd rushed home early, intent on cosseting her and supporting her all he could, but strangely she'd flapped him away.

'I'm all right!' she'd practically shouted at him. 'Don't treat me like Dresden china.' And she'd flounced across to the ironing board and started banging the iron about, intent on murdering a white blouse.

He'd eaten the pasta and sauce she'd put out for him, wondering whether he should be worried. Was this abnormal behaviour towards him due to the shock she'd had over Stella? Or was she genuinely annoyed over his concern for her because she really was OK? He had no idea what to think, much less what he should do. That's why he'd so badly wanted to talk to Jade. Being a woman, and an extremely intelligent one, she'd surely have some idea. He wanted to talk to her anyway. He wanted . . . her.

24

Either Dermot Dodds was an abysmal teacher or Marjorie was slow to catch on, and as her second morning at Foretec dragged by, she began to fear that the latter must be the case. Perspiring inside her white blouse she glared obediently at the computer screen and forced herself to think. It couldn't be that difficult, after all. Little kids could handle these things, so why shouldn't she? Yet so far it was so much gobbledegook, and she wished with all her being that she was miles from the Ian Ericson establishment. And to think that only forty-eight hours ago she'd been so eager to work in this place!

'I think I have a problem here,' she was finally compelled to admit. She turned to the young man at her side, a sheepish smile on her face. 'I seem to have lost my little arrow.'

Dermot flicked back his hair and leaned forward. 'Roll the mouse,' he ordered peremptorily.

'But I am,' Marjorie shot back at him. 'And I tell you, the arrow's done a bunk.'

Dermot pursed his lips in a silent whistle – he'd

been doing a lot of that since Ian put him in charge of Marjorie – and took control of the mouse. A few quick movements on the mousepad and the arrow miraculously appeared.

Marjorie blinked, confused. Where had it been when she wanted it? But she wasn't given time to dwell on the mystery; Dermot wanted to move on.

'Perhaps you'd like to check on the e-mail again,' was his next weary suggestion.

Would she like to check on the e-mail? She looked at the keyboard and frowned. She'd already forgotten what to do. Her powers of concentration were set at zero these days. What a time to take on a new job. Well, how was she supposed to get to grips with all this new-fangled technology, with the antics of an errant husband clogging her brain?

And she was convinced, now, of Phil's deceit. She'd been watching him closely for clues these past couple of days, unwilling to rely solely on Oliver's testimony, or even on her own suspicions, and she'd found that he was not only making sneaky phone calls and wandering about the house looking like he was 'on something', he had also, last evening, resorted to a dubiously late meeting at the office.

Her finger hovered above the right part of the keyboard – as far as she could recall. 'Um . . .'

Dermot reached over with another sigh, tapped at the keys so quickly she couldn't tell what he'd touched, and went back to his silent whistling. But since there was nothing of interest in the e-mail he suggested that perhaps it might be a convenient time to take her on a tour of the premises.

For the next half hour she tottered along in her smartest shoes, trying to keep up with Dermot's long strides. Racing from one work area to another and trying hard not to pant, she wondered once again whether it had been such a wise move to corner Ian into giving her this opportunity. Could she really see herself working here? She felt so hopelessly out of touch. But having made such a fuss about needing work she could hardly go running to Ian with her doubts after only two days. It would make her look such a fool.

Feeling even more sorry for herself than she did for the faces wilting in the sun's unusual heat behind too many acres of glass, she pounded along walk-ways and corridors. So far she hadn't seen anyone remotely her age, apart from Ian himself. What did they do with the older workers?

She cast Dermot a sidelong glance. His face was tanned but unlined, his hair a rich brown with no grey. And all the women she'd so far seen were bright, pretty young girls; they had shapely legs, skimpy skirts and neat little wasp-like waists. It was like watching a science fiction film, in which no one ever need age; they were injected with a wonderful youth drug and lived for a thousand years.

Dermot took her to the observation window of a special pollution-free room, where workers wearing white garments from head to toe carried out finicky work on long benches. Watching the identical, sexless forms, she wondered whether this was where the old folk were put to work – where their seniority could give no offence. These people could be quite ancient, she thought. But somehow she didn't believe it.

Returning to the office with swollen feet, her relief at being able to sit down again was not to last for long; the dreaded computer was still there, tirelessly ready to torment her. Why hadn't she realised she'd be expected to use one of these things? Talk about stupid and naïve. And, oh, how she wished she'd taken more notice of Phil's laptop, then she need not have appeared quite so ignorant.

She had looked at Phil's neat little machine from time to time, peering over his shoulder to witness the clever things he'd done on it, but none of it had made much sense to her. And quite often, when she passed him by unnoticed, he seemed to have nothing but an amusing cartoon puppy romping about on the screen. 'For relaxation,' he'd told her glibly, whenever she'd caught him out.

'Shall I show you how to organise the files, then?' Dermot was asking her now. He sounded as though he hadn't much hope of her getting to grips with those either. But she brightened at the suggestion; this sounded more up her street. Anyone could understand a filing system, couldn't they?

She was already half out of her seat, and looking about for the filing cabinets . . . until she understood that he hadn't meant files as she knew them. He'd meant data files stored on diskettes.

If Philip was aware that Marjorie's routine had changed considerably over the past few days he didn't remark on it once. Perhaps he hadn't even noticed, she decided as she slung her work shoes to the back of the cupboard in the hall. She had easily made it home each evening before he put in an appearance. And in the mornings he hadn't spotted the fact that she had half her clothes on under her long-length dressing-gown.

As soon as he'd left for work she'd slung off the dressing-gown and rushed round the house to finish getting ready and was away across the Red Sea herself within minutes of his going. She hadn't yet figured out why she was keeping it all a secret. She could have told him she'd found an office job without going into details. She need not have mentioned Eric at all. But she didn't feel inclined to talk about anything with Phil these days – any more than he seemed to want to talk to her. Secrets were becoming a habit.

Phil dumped his briefcase on the dining table and followed it up with an extra pile of paperwork tied round with off-white tape. 'I'm going to have to work at home some evenings this week,' he said. 'Things have got a bit on top of me.'

It was on Marjorie's lips to say she wasn't surprised. If he was spending all his time on an affair, what else could he expect? But she said nothing. And tried hard to dismiss a vision of Jade on top of her husband.

'These are Oliver's reports on the Sinden job,' he went on, muttering mostly to himself. 'I told you about that, didn't I? I really must study them in detail, in case Holy Joe asks questions at the barbecue.'

Marjorie stopped winding their silver carriage clock. The barbecue was this coming Saturday. 'Why would he wait until then?'

'Well, thankfully he's away at a conference at the moment, so he can't be breathing down my neck.'

'I'd forgotten all about that barbecue.'

Phil pulled an end of the off-white tape and coiled it round one hand. 'Well, you don't have to go to it, if you don't want to. If you're not really feeling up to things.'

'I told you I'm perfectly OK,' she snapped. When would he see that she didn't need his molly-coddling? But at the same time she tensed at the thought of the ordeal. She would have to face Jade and Oliver in Phil's presence, and wasn't at all sure she could cope. It would be dreadfully awkward for all of them.

'How are you getting on with Oliver now? You seemed not to like him at first.'

'Oh –' he shuffled the Sinden reports around '– I've been lumbered with a lot of meetings lately. Haven't seen him that much.'

Probably more by design than accident, Marjorie

thought, watching Phil sifting through the reports with little enthusiasm. Then she became transfixed by the name of Sinden in bold black and white type at the top of a page. That name kept cropping up.

'I think I'll make myself a drink,' Phil suddenly decided, straightening up from the work. 'Shall I get you one too?'

'Mm? No thanks. I don't want one.' That name, she was thinking. That name . . .

But, absorbed though she was in trying to recall where else she'd heard it, she was fully aware that Phil hadn't gone straight to making his drink. He had stepped out into the garden again, and she knew precisely why he'd done that.

Fortunately the answer she wanted flashed into her mind before anger had a chance to blot it out. Sinden was the name Ian had mentioned! Ian had said – what was it? – that he'd give his right arm to know why he was losing Sinden, and who was luring him away . . .

Marjorie looked down at the paperwork. Ian had made some other remarks at the time, remarks that were vague and obscure. Had he really meant what it had sounded like – that he wanted her to act as a spy? Not that she would dream of doing such a thing . . .

She glanced out of the window, her rising anger with Phil making her shake. How dare he go and make that phone call, right here under her very nose? The cheek of it! The brass nerve! Before she realised what she'd done, she'd picked out the

313

sheets covered in figure-work and concealed them in her apron's front pouch.

She met Phil in the hallway with his drink.

'I think I'll go down to the library,' she told him. She knew there was a photocopier there.

'Fine, if you think it's still open.'

'Late night,' she told him, hurrying past.

25

The only normal thing about Oliver's Saturday was Jade's announcement that she had to go shopping. She had propelled herself from the bed before he even woke up – a 'first' if ever there was one – and had scrambled into white stretch cycling shorts and a strappy striped top that had more holes of the intentional kind than it had threads to hold them together. A somewhat unsuitable outfit, he considered, considering her destination, but she was out of the door before he could say a word.

Not that he had any words for her. They had been avoiding each other all week, a comparatively easy thing to do since they were busy most of the time, but how they would manage all weekend was another matter. At the moment she seemed to be on the other side of a chasm, entirely unapproachable, but how could he begin to bridge the gap? How could he challenge her about her going with Philip Benson when he had always advocated such behaviour? As for this shopping and spending business, well that problem was all tied up with telling her about his financial problems with Sally.

And was he ever going to be able to come clean about how he and Sally had split up?

Jade probably no longer cared what had happened, one way or the other, and if he did manage to tell her she'd no doubt say something along the lines that she wasn't at all surprised Sally had ditched him; he was nothing but a loser, wasn't he, and she was thinking of doing the same herself.

He mooched about the flat for a while, dreading her laden return from the shops. More stuff to moulder away in the bottom of the cupboard, he grumbled to himself, while he was virtually broke.

In the event, however, she came back to the flat twenty minutes later carrying only a long French stick and a quarter of breaded gammon, which she proceeded to split into two snacks. Leaving one in the fridge for him and taking the other into the dining room, she told him she must get down to work for the rest of the day.

His face must have revealed his thoughts. Usually on Saturday mornings they made love, cooked a huge breakfast, and caught up on each other's gossip.

'Sorry,' she added shortly, as he slunk away to the roof garden to dwell on times past, 'but I don't want to be disturbed until it's time to get ready for that wretched barbecue.'

She remained closeted with her books until he put his head round the door towards evening to tell her she had half an hour left before they must go.

'Are you *wearing* that?' Philip asked Marjorie with a stricken face. They were about to get into the car and head for the Hemmingway-Judds' barbecue but he had apparently only just looked at her properly for the first time that day.

At one time, and not so long ago, that sort of remark would have sent Marjorie flying back to her wardrobe for a major re-think; now she merely looked down at herself, pinched her well-padded thighs and said, 'Yes, I'm sure this is me inside.' And, lifting her head high, she flung open the passenger door.

The offending outfit consisted of a loudly floral-printed tunic top and matching baggy trousers – a definite mistake. It had been an impulse purchase made on one of their Spanish holidays. Out there on holiday amid the sun and sangria it had been just about acceptable attire for one of her age and dimensions; back home it had been quickly con-signed to the back of the wardrobe. More recently it had found its way into one of the plastic sacks destined for the charity shop, but Marjorie had raided the bag that morning with a determined gleam in her eye. She would look awful, certainly, and create quite the wrong impression, and Philip would curl his toes in horror. Good. Serve him jolly well right.

Philip sat speechlessly beside her. He'd had a haircut that morning, had doused himself in an expensive-smelling after-shave that she'd not known him use before, and was looking sleekly groomed in impeccable cream chinos and a navy open-necked shirt. She could almost have fallen in love with him again, had it not been for the twitch of distaste around his nostrils, and all the recent goings-on.

He couldn't help but have noticed how her feet bulged out of gold stiletto sandals, which he would consider 'tarty', and that she had varnished her toenails red. He hated large hoop ear-rings too. But what could he say? He surely wouldn't have the nerve to criticise her, under the circumstances, would he?

He hadn't. He merely turned on the ignition and set them on their way.

Mike Oldfield's 'Portsmouth' was screeching across the back lawn of the Hemmingway-Judds' spacious and gracious country home when Oliver and Jade arrived. Set in a village to the south of Bristol the house stood almost alone among green fields. The spire of a church and the outline of barns could be seen half a mile away, but otherwise the catchy tune coming from two large speakers disturbed only the converted farmhouse and the clutch of workers' cottages strung out along the approaching lane.

Oliver's gloom increased as he slammed the car door and stood looking up at the old leaded windows and attractive thatched roof; he hadn't forgotten Mrs Hemmingway-Judd's fondness for all kinds of old-fashioned dancing, nor how determined she could be that no guest should fail to enjoy it either. At best he had hoped to have a bit of a laugh with Jade, who had not yet experienced one of these crazy sessions, but that was out of the question now. Weighed down by all his problems, his heart simply wasn't in it, even though Jade stood tall and proud beside him in a stunning white strapless sun dress, and her hair like a cape of gleaming gold.

The weather could only aggravate his mood; throughout the day the sun, which everyone had long been taking for granted after so many weeks of it, had gradually faded away, casting a sickly yellow dullness over everything and bringing a sticky warmth to the air.

And the last person Oliver wanted to see was Benson. Yet the Bensons must have arrived only seconds earlier; they were still hovering round their host receiving their welcoming chat when he and Jade walked in.

A distant roll of thunder accompanied their progress across the lawn and everyone looked skyward, exclaiming sudden concern.

'Ah! Oliver!' H J declared on seeing him. He clapped him on the shoulder. 'This is our young Oliver who's worked such wonders for us with Sinden,' he enthused. 'Have you met him yet, Marjorie? And Oliver, have you met Philip's charming wife? Good. Good. That's right. But I've yet to meet your delightful lady here.' His glasses flashed over Jade and his eyes boggled so hungrily behind the rimless lenses that Mrs Hemmingway-Judd had to nudge him in the back.

'*Lovely* of you all to come,' she told them in a cut and polished accent that made Oliver squirm. 'Now you will all help yourselves to punch, won't you?' She waved an arm so smooth and dimpled that it resembled a chubby infant's. 'You'll find it over there between the *Kalmia latifolia* which has been an absolute delight this summer, I must say, and the *Leycesteria formosa* which I've no doubt soon will be.'

In the past Oliver would have exchanged solemn but amused glances with Jade at this, but now he wouldn't have been able to catch her eye if he'd wanted to; her attention was fixed on Philip. Instead he met Marjorie's watchful gaze.

'Marjorie!' he found himself saying. 'You're looking bright and cheerful, I must say. Who needs the sun with you around? Come on now, you simply must have a dance.' And although not a soul had yet ventured into the circle of cleared grass he grabbed her hands and swept her to the centre of it.

The record had changed to something he vaguely remembered being forced to dance to at school: 'The Dashing White Sergeant', or some such. What he couldn't remember at all were the steps. But that didn't stop him; he couldn't have cared two hoots. He began to jig and jump, and twirl the laughing, protesting Marjorie round in such a glorious abandoned frolic that his reckless mood instantly fired hers.

Normally she would have shrunk from making any kind of exhibition of herself, but in her current frame of mind she needed little encouragement. She too threw caution to the wind and joined in with a whoop of laughter.

'Stop!' she giggled hysterically, pausing only to tug off her shoes. She kicked them into the astonished onlookers, now gathering to watch the spectacle, and they landed at Philip's feet.

'For God's sake,' he muttered, hardly daring to watch his matronly wife galumphing about the lawn with his dwarf-like junior. How could she make such a fool of herself? And in front of the MD of all people. 'Jade –' he groped for her hand '– please help me out with this.'

Thinking to draw attention away from the cavorting couple Philip took Jade into the arena, where he attempted to steer her into a more decorous form of polka. It was his hope that other couples would soon follow. But they didn't; the entertainment was too good.

If Marjorie and Oliver made the audience laugh, then Philip and Jade caused them to gasp; the two made such a fine, graceful couple as they skimmed across the grass in the eerie evening light. They swayed and swirled in exact time with the music, their eyes locked together and their feet moving as one, so that before long they had succeeded in drawing attention from the others only to find it transferred to themselves. Even Marjorie and Oliver stopped eventually, sensing that some sort of spell had fallen over the company. And, seeing the lover-like performance, they, too, were soon transfixed.

'Bravo! Bravo! Thank you all so much.' Mrs Hemmingway-Judd bustled into the arena as soon as the music ceased, clapping her hands in delight; this barbecue, she obviously thought, had all the promise of being a success for once if people were going to volunteer like this. Weather always permitting, of course. 'Now everybody, 'The Gay Gordons' next, I think.' She began to urge people into a circle, forming pairs.

'Drink this,' Oliver ordered Marjorie, bringing her a glass of punch. 'I found it between the whatsifolia japonica and the thingummium, but it won't give you much of a kick, I'm afraid. If I remember from last year's effort it'll be one part alcohol to a hundred of watered-down juice.'

'Oh, Oliver,' she groaned, dragging her eyes away from the groups of guests mingling aimlessly on the terrace. The terrace stretched across the back of the house, and she could see Philip's head, earnestly bent towards Jade's beside a white wire frame that trailed red roses. They appeared to be deep in conversation.

'I know.' Oliver turned his back on the scene. 'They've got it badly, haven't they? Silly of me to try to pretend . . .'

'I had hoped you were right about all this: you

322

know, believing you'd jumped to conclusions? I think part of me's been giving them the benefit of the doubt, while all along it was patently clear. And now, seeing them together just now . . . oh, what are we going to do about it? Whatever *can* we do?' With her face twisted in anguish she forced herself to look away, fixing her gaze in the direction of the barbecue instead, where billows of black smoke signalled bad tidings for their evening meal.

Oliver shook his head. If only he had an answer.

Marjorie fumed in silence. How dare Philip flaunt his love in front of all these people? For surely there couldn't be a soul at this party who hadn't understood the situation by now? She couldn't be imagining all the glances that had been directed at her over the past few minutes, or the way folk nodded and nudged and huddled together.

Oh, how humiliating it all was! Sending those photocopies to Ian by first class post was nowhere near enough of a revenge. As for Oliver, standing there with one hand in his pocket and a lost look on his face, what a spineless individual he was turning out to be! Well, she wasn't going to take this lying down, even if he was.

She drained her glass, thrust it at Oliver, and without thinking what she was going to do, charged across the grass in her bare feet, like a bull setting its sights on a cow. And she might have been a bull, considering the way a path cleared before her. She soon found herself confronting Philip and

Jade, with H J at the latter's elbow and an audience of interested onlookers on the fringes of her awareness. Oliver, she sensed, had tagged along behind her but at a cautious pace.

'Ah, Mrs Benson!' H J greeted her with a nervous tweak of his glasses. 'We were just discussing careers. Young Jade here, as you probably know, is hoping to go into law.'

Marjorie glared her contempt of the girl. 'So I understand.'

'I – er – 'he tried again to get the conversation under way '– I'm afraid I don't recall what it is you do, exactly, my dear. I'm not sure Philip's ever said.'

'No?' Marjorie jumped in before Phil could make excuses for her; she noticed he'd already opened his mouth to tell the world she did nothing at all to earn her keep. 'Well, that's because he wouldn't want you to know about it. As it happens I've just secured a good position, working for the accountant of a firm in Bath. Very interesting, it is too. Especially as they're your rivals. Heard of the name Ericson at all? Owns a place called Foretec? Yes, I thought it might ring a bell.'

'Marjie!' Phil could stay silent no longer. His face long with astonishment, he turned and appealed to H J. 'But this simply isn't true, Jocelyn. She doesn't work for Ericson. She doesn't work at all. I'm dreadfully sorry, really I am. She's not been at all herself lately . . .' He shook his head at Marjorie, denying her as his wife.

H J looked from one to the other.

'You *used* to work for an accountant,' Jade put in gently. She stepped a little closer to Marjorie as if to corner an imbecile who'd escaped from a mental home. 'I remember you telling us so . . .'

Marjorie looked daggers at her. How dare this young bitch stand there treating at her as though she'd gone off her trolley?

'It's true, I tell you, it's true!' She scowled at them one by one, coming back to Jade. 'And what do you think *you* know about it, might I ask? What do you know about anything except stealing other people's husbands? You simpering little whore! You've already got one married man; what do you want with another one? What *is* it with you and married men? Do you find them easier to walk out on?'

'I –'

'And have you no decent feelings? Is it not enough for poor Oliver here, that he's already been dumped once? Apparently not. You go gaily on to the next one and clearly don't give a toss. Well, you're perfectly welcome to *my* husband, and jolly good riddance, I say.'

'*Marjorie –!*'

But she was too wound up to call a halt. 'I've no further use for the smooth-tongued cheating bastard. Take him! He'll lie through his teeth and wangle his own way, just like he did to get me to move down here. Then he'll just up and leave you one day. One day when you're old and grey. And then you'll know how it feels.' She shot a glance at Phil. 'But what can you expect from such selfish low-down scum, such cow manure, such – such stinking, putrid –'

'Don't mince your words, Mrs Benson,' some wag dropped into the sudden silence. 'Give him a piece of your mind!'

But no one saw fit to laugh.

26

'Well –' H J pressed his hands together in a helpless gesture. Used to thinking on his feet he might be, but this situation was beyond him.

'Jade!' Oliver stepped into the breach. 'Our hostess expressly wants you to help with the next dance. You're so good at it,' he added with a trace of sarcasm so light that only Jade would pick up on it. Leading Jade away from the group he cast a baleful look at Marjorie, who was also being led away, but in the opposite direction, by Phil.

Marjorie looked back too, her horrified expression communicating to him that she hadn't meant to make him look like a pathetic wimp in front of everyone; she'd only wanted to hit out at Jade and Phil. Oliver waved to show that he understood, that it was all right, that she'd done them all a favour by bringing everything out into the open, and about time too. He doubted whether she got the message, though; there was only so much that could be conveyed without words.

'I don't understand how she knew.' Jade looked dazed as she followed Oliver from the scene, and her face was unusually pale – even under the faint tan that she'd allowed herself to acquire that summer though she knew she'd regret the sun's destruction in later years.

'About you carrying on with her husband?' Oliver grunted. 'She wasn't born yesterday, you know.'

'And you knew, too, didn't you?' She gazed at him with wondering eyes as he guided her, not towards the dancers as he'd suggested, but to a gate at the end of the garden. Not caring how it might look to those watching, he unbolted it as if he owned the whole property and ushered her through into the adjoining copse.

'Yes, I knew about you and Philip,' he said, letting the gate clatter closed behind them. He breathed in the cooler air and looked up at the darkening sky.

'But how did you know? And what? I mean, there's not really anything to know. I've seen him so very little. We've hardly – And anyway, what did she mean?'

'Who . . . Marjorie?'

'Yes, about –' Jade looked at him curiously '– about you being dumped before. Why on earth should she say something like that?'

Oliver sat down on a log he'd spotted. So he was finally going to have to come clean. 'Sit down, Jade.' He moved along the log to make room for her.

'No. I can't. I'm too bloody mad with that

woman to keep still. You weren't the only one she slagged off. How dare she say all those horrible things about me?'

'*You're* mad with Marjorie Benson? I don't believe I'm hearing this. And how do you think *she's* feeling?'

'Well –'. She shrugged belligerently but looked guilty nevertheless. 'OK, so I haven't done her any favours. She hasn't got a lot going for her, has she? But it wasn't really my fault. Philip made all the running you know. I didn't want any of it to happen.'

'No, neither did I,' Oliver said with feeling. 'Now sit down, Jade. Sit down. We've got a lot of talking to do.'

Philip steered Marjorie to their car. 'Wait here,' he snarled through his teeth.

As if she could drive off like this, she thought, brushing dirt and grass off her bare feet. She assumed he'd gone back to the Hemmingway-Judds to excuse them both from further festivities, because he soon returned carrying her shoes and handbag. He flung them into her lap, but instead of walking round the car and getting in the driver's seat he trod the ground outside her window, in the manner of one crushing grapes.

She wondered what he'd said to H J. 'Sorry about the wife, H J, but you know what women are like at their time of life, nudge-nudge, wink-wink? Say the most stupid things. Not a word of truth in any of it, of course. Jade and I carrying on? Well, I ask you, does it seem likely?'

Anything to preserve his reputation.

After a while he leaned into the car. 'If you go back there *now*, it wouldn't be too late.'

She forced herself to look at him. 'Go back . . . where?'

'Back in there.' He jerked his head in the direction of the music. 'You can say you haven't been well – that you didn't mean what you were saying; you've had too much sun, or something, and you jumped to the wrong conclusion.'

Marjorie turned from him in disbelief and stared blankly at the windscreen. The tax disc, she noticed, had begun to bubble and become unstuck.

'Wrong conclusion?' she echoed stupidly, knowing how it irritated him whenever she did this. 'I don't understand what you mean.'

'You know perfectly well what I mean.'

'Do I? Oh, I see. You mean about you having it away with Jade Montgomery.'

His eyes snapped to hers, looking wild in his desperation. 'And about your working for Ericson. Say you made that bit up, too, on the spur of the moment. Tell H J you –'

'But it isn't the wrong conclusion.'

'– that you're very sorry; you know you've made a fool of yourself and –'

Her voice rose a few decibels. 'I said, it isn't the wrong conclusion. Is it, Phil? *Is* it?'

'Please –'

'It's the truth!' She was shouting now. She didn't care if everyone at the barbecue could hear her. 'And anyone with half an eye can see it's the truth. You can't imagine that any of that crowd back there are in any doubt, do you?'

'– just go and –'

'You expect me to perjure myself –?'

'– at least try to limit the damage you've done.'

'*I've* done? You creep! How can you stand there saying that? What about the damage *you've* done? You've wrecked our marriage and you've ruined my life. Not to mention the hurt you've caused. Don't you feel remotely ashamed of yourself? How you've got the nerve to stand there expecting me to cover up for you – well, it truly beggars belief.'

'Marjorie –'

'Tell me you haven't been seeing her.'

'What?'

'Go on. Tell me!'

'I – listen, I –'

'Well, of course you can't. You had it all planned out, didn't you? It was your idea I went visiting. You could hardly wait to get me out of the way.'

'But I'd never even met Jade then!'

'Only it didn't quite work out. I came back and spoiled your fun. I suppose I shouldn't be here either, really. I'm cramping your style again. What a pity!' She clamped a hand over her mouth in an attempt to dam her emotions. If Phil couldn't see what he'd done, there was no point in wasting more words.

331

Philip leant against the car with his eyes closed, and stayed that way for some time. Finally, realising that Marjorie was never going to leap from the car to do his bidding, and that he couldn't force her no matter how much he would like to, he hurled himself into the driver's seat and drove them home in silence.

'I suppose you realise you've ruined me,' he said, once they were back at their house. 'If that was the intention of that dreadful scene in front of Jocelyn and his wife, then you've succeeded admirably. My career's completely finished now. It's curtains.'

'Oh stop being so damned dramatic. People have affairs all the time. H J may not like the idea very much, but it's hardly grounds for dismissal.'

'H J has very high principles, I'll have you know. But I wasn't referring to that. The fact is that he won't have taken too kindly to having a cloud put over his wife's big do. It's the highlight of her year, by all accounts, and your spoiling it alone's enough to put me in his bad books. Thinks very highly of his wife, does H J.'

'Which is more than can be said of some of us,' she snapped. 'And would it be asking too much for you to accept that it was your actions that prompted the whole scene in the first place?'

But he pretended he hadn't heard. 'Either I or Knox are going to have to leave our jobs now; we can't work together after this. And Knox seems to be the blue-eyed boy at the moment so something tells me it'll be me.'

He'd begun pacing the lounge since they'd walked into it. Now he stopped and glared at her.

'I'll have no income then. I suppose you didn't even think of that. How the hell are we going to manage without money, I'd like to know?'

'We?' She sneered. Did he mean him and Jade? Probably. Why let twenty-five years of marriage stand in his way?

She dropped her shoes and made straight for the old bureau next to the fire place where they kept a couple of decanters. She never drank brandy but now she poured out half a balloon of it and took a generous sip.

The glass shook in her hand; still not a word from Phil about *his* appalling behaviour, of what he'd been doing behind her back! Not a word of apology, of regret. All he could think of was himself. Well, if this was the real Philip Benson she was seeing, then frankly he was no great loss. All those things she'd said at the barbecue were true. How could she have been so blind as not to see it all these years?

'I don't care what you do,' she told him wearily. Her anger had suddenly blown itself out; he no longer seemed worth getting worked up over. 'Your problems are no business of mine any longer. And don't try to lay blame at my door. You started it all, remember, when you decided to "play away." You should have thought of the consequences long ago, and not start bleating when things blow up in your face. What was it you were always telling the girls?

"Our actions always have consequences"? Huh! Pity you didn't remember that yourself.'

She continued to sip the brandy, wandering about the room as though viewing its contents with purchase in mind, while Philip darkly looked on.

'I'll take half the house and my car,' she finally announced, as though they'd been on offer, 'and any savings we have left. I think you owe me that much. More, probably.'

His eyes rounded. 'You don't mean that.' He actually looked quite shocked at her words, as though until that moment he had taken it for granted that his marriage would remain intact; that his relationship with Marjorie would be unaffected while he did whatever he wanted with Jade. As for what Jade wanted or expected, he probably hadn't thought about that either.

'I can assure you I'm perfectly serious,' she told him. 'I'd like to buy myself a flat or something. With a bit of money behind me, and the salary I shall be getting at Foretec, I should be able to cope.' Although it occurred to her as she spoke that she need no longer be tied to Foretec or to that particular part of the country at all. She could go anywhere.

Philip now stood open-mouthed as well as wide-eyed, and appeared to be thinking with difficulty. 'You don't mean to tell me it was true?' he said eventually, his face long with disbelief. 'You're not really working for Ian Ericson?'

'Started four days ago.' She turned her back on

him, smiling. Triumph tasted so sweet – and the prospect of freedom even better!

'How the blazes did you manage that, then?'

'None of your ruddy business.'

'But what in hell's teeth did you think you were doing? You must have known what an impossible situation you would have put me in.'

She rounded on him. 'Do you really think I cared? I was hardly going to come crawling to you for permission. You'd have put a damper on it straight away.'

'I certainly would. I can't understand why you're so dead set on getting work anyway.'

'No, you can't understand anything, can you? I could talk to you until I was blue in the face.'

'Hmph!' He wasn't listening to her, even now. 'You'll never be able to hold down a job, you know. Well, I ask you, what can you do? You're not even *au fait* with modern practices.' He barked a contemptuous laugh. 'Last time you worked in an office they were using abacuses, I should imagine. Quill pens, and sand for blotting paper.'

She buried her nose in the brandy glass. Little did he realise how close to the truth he'd come. She was about as sure of making a go of it as she was of sprouting new teeth. And heavens, she'd just remembered the wretched photocopies again! What was Ian Ericson going to make of those? She sucked in a mouthful of brandy and felt it burning a pathway to her stomach.

'Thank you for your kind vote of confidence,

Phil, but so far I'm managing fine.' And she *would* make a success of things, she *would*. Phil would be forced to eat his words . . . one day. 'Anyway, why you should be at all concerned with what I'm doing I can't imagine. You ceased to care about me long ago. If you ever did.'

'Marjie . . .' he sighed, and for a moment she thought he was softening towards her, that he was about to tell her what a stupid mistake he'd made and that he still loved her and didn't want any of this to be happening. Soon he might fall on his knees and beg to be forgiven. So how would she react if he did?

But he didn't.

'I can see you're in no mood to listen to anything I have to say at the moment,' was all he said. 'Look, I'll go and stay at a hotel somewhere – give you a chance to calm down. You're angry, I suppose, understandably so. Maybe you have a right to be.' He flapped his arms aimlessly against his sides, and left.

Maybe she had a right to be angry? And could he really believe she didn't know precisely where he had gone – and into whose arms he'd be falling? She looked at the last of her brandy and didn't know whether to laugh or cry.

To the accompaniment of 'Come, lasses and lads; get leave of your dads', Oliver explained to Jade, mumbling the words out of the side of his mouth, that he had lied to her about leaving Sally.

336

'Actually it was the other way around, just as Marjorie said.'

Jade had been sitting beside him on the log, with her elbows on her knees and her chin in her hands. Now she dropped her hands and turned to him in astonishment.

'It was really Sally who left you? But why didn't you say so before?'

Oliver was flummoxed at her matter-of-fact tone. The least he'd expected was a scornful little snort. '*Say* so?' He looked horrified. 'But . . . I didn't want you to know.'

'Obviously, you didn't. And why not, I ask myself?' She nudged his arm. 'Don't tell me you were really ashamed of it, ashamed of being left.'

It took him a while to explain that that was precisely how he'd felt. It had been an insult to his masculine pride. Surely she could see that?

Jade fell silent for a while. 'Oh, Olly, you men are so silly. Such idiots with those egos of yours. It would have made no difference to me whatsoever. In fact you would have gone up several notches in my estimation. To think of you left with those children . . .' She shook her head. 'You don't know much about women, do you? Well I'll tell you something: I could have accepted the fact that your last partner left you, much more easily than I could your going with other women! But I suppose you thought that made you look real cool, letting me think that you played around? I . . . well, I know I let you believe I accepted that way of living and

337

wanted the same for myself, but actually I never did.'

'You didn't?' He face lit up at that – until he remembered Philip Benson.

'No,' she went on, 'and I never did it myself – go with other men I mean. I've never even looked at anyone else. Not until – until I thought you were seeing someone in Gloucester. I guessed that all your other conquests were simply talk, you see, but this one seemed – well – genuine. So I . . . I retaliated.'

He couldn't bear to look at her; the thought of just how she had retaliated was like a knife twisting in his heart.

'I went to Gloucester on business,' he said. 'That was all above board. But I also wanted to see Sally about things. She's bleeding me dry of my money . . . which brings me to something else.' He looked straight at her now, but decided enough was enough. There seemed no point in bringing it up now.

'Oh, forget it, it doesn't matter,' he said wearily. 'You don't want me any more, do you? You want Philip Benson. You may have gone to him in the beginning to get your own back on me, as you say, but now you've fallen in love. Any fool could have seen that this evening.'

'Oh, Olly, I –'

'I can't say I really blame you. He's a bit long in the tooth for you, I would say, but at least he must have a bob or two. Which is more than I have. I'm having to give most of mine to Sally.'

Jade screwed up her face. 'People don't fall in love with *money* . . .'

'Oh yes, I'm afraid they do. Especially women. I do know *some*thing about women. It's a power thing with them. Status. You know what I'm talking about; don't pretend you don't. And Philip Benson's got it in spades. What's more, he'll be able to keep you in the manner to which you were once accustomed, won't he? You'll be able to shop till you drop without a care in the whole wide world. And I hope it makes you happy.'

'Oh, Olly, I –' She shook her head, too appalled at his view of things to speak. And if he knew about her shopaholic tendencies why had he not spoken out? If only he'd tried to stop her, instead of Philip Benson . . .

He was scrambling to his feet.

'Come on, let's get out of here. I can't stand another minute of that jolly jiggety music.' He jerked his head in the direction of the barbecue party where Mrs Hemmingway-Judd could still be heard clapping her hands to the beat.

'That's right, everybody,' the clipped accent rang out over the hedgerow. 'All change partners *now!*'

Jade needed to go to the bathroom as soon as she and Oliver returned to the flat. When she came out she found him standing in front of the chipmunk's cage as though carved in stone. He managed to turn horrified eyes to her when she joined him and her stomach performed a sickening lurch; if they'd gone and died on him it was mighty bad timing on their part. He'd had enough trauma lately. But no, she could hear at least one of them scurrying about on their climbing branch.

'What is it?' she asked, coming up warily behind him.

'I can't believe it.' He'd gone pink with indignation. 'Take a look at this!'

'What? Where?' She hooked her hair behind her ear and peered more closely, then drew back with a shudder of disgust. 'Ugh, the ugly little things! Babies! With no fur. But I didn't know they were expecting any.'

'Neither did I.' He was still in shock, staring at the new parents as though they'd committed a crime. 'The naughty little beggars!'

Jade giggled at his reaction. 'What's naughty about having babies, Olly? It is what animals do.'

'Yes, but only adult ones. These two are only –'

'Babies? But they're not really, are they? They must be full-grown now. It's only that you still treat them that way.' She looked at him for a moment then something seemed to click in her mind.

'Olly,' she said quietly, recalling how he'd always fondled and fussed over the animals ever since he'd brought them into the flat, how much he loved and cared for them, how he attended to their every need. They were his substitute children, and the realisation gave her a funny feeling inside. 'Olly,' she began again, 'you miss your children, don't you? Young Billy and cute little Melissa?'

He'd only once shown her a photograph of them, which he'd quickly stuffed back in his wallet. It was as though once out of sight they were out of mind. But they'd always been at the back of *her* mind – and his, she now guessed, too.

'And I always thought you didn't care.' Now that the truth had dawned on her she found it hard to take it in. 'Because you never talked about them, I thought you didn't care!'

'Of course I care! I love them. I never wanted to hand them over to Sally. I didn't think she was a fit person. So I tried to look after them myself but, well, somehow I couldn't cope.'

Jade listened as it all came tumbling out of him, the words painful for him to utter, the emotions impossible for him to suppress. She watched in a kind of daze as the bumptious, presumptuous little 'macho' man crumbled before her eyes and metamorphosed into a crying, caring 'nineties' one, the likes of whom had been reported as gradually increasing in numbers throughout the land, but who was still considered by many to be a complete and utter myth.

And such was the well of pity he'd touched in her that she was almost on the verge of tears herself, when the phone began to ring.

She picked it up in the lobby.

'I'm not sure,' she said into the receiver, running a finger round the edge of the Moorcroft vase. She was aware of Oliver wiping his eyes and watching

341

her from the dining room, so her words were few and unrevealing. 'I don't know, it's all a bit difficult. Well, yes, all right. Yes. I will. Oh, fairly soon, I should think.'

'That was him, wasn't it?' Oliver sniffed loudly, burying his handkerchief in his trouser pocket.

Jade inspected her nail polish. 'Yes.'

'Well, what are you waiting for?' He shrugged in a 'don't care' fashion, the old Olly reasserting himself. 'Go!'

He shooed her away with his hand. 'Go on, go to him, go.'

She shook her head. 'I don't want to leave you like this.'

'Oh, don't you worry about me.' He looked up at the ceiling. 'I'll pick up the pieces, I expect. You know me. Can't keep me down for long.'

Jade collected her handbag from one of the dining chairs where she had left it. She could walk to the hotel Philip had mentioned; it wasn't very far. But would Olly really be all right? Yesterday she wouldn't have doubted it. Today she was far from sure.

Half-way out of the flat she stopped and looked back at him, but before he could glance round to witness her hesitation, she pressed on. And closed the door gently behind her.

Jade didn't go straight to the hotel. She stopped by the weir at Pulteney Bridge and stood looking down into the rushing water.

'Money, love and power,' she murmured to herself. They could all blind you to the truth. And she couldn't see *that* clearly even now.

She'd genuinely fallen for Philip, and as Oliver had been quick to point out, he seemed to have plenty of money. And she was honest enough with herself to admit that money was an extra attraction. Coming from a family that had constantly had to look out for the next penny, it was bound to figure large in her life. But what would happen to Phil's supply if he divorced Marjorie as he had led her to believe he would? If there was one thing she'd learned from Oliver it was that ex-wives came expensive.

Power could be very seductive too, but only if used in the right way. Sometimes, she had already noticed, Phil wanted too much control. She hated it when he drew her away from her law studies, not giving it half the importance that she did. In that respect he'd become almost as discouraging as her tutor. He'd even said he wanted to look after her and she need not worry about a career. Oh, he'd certainly changed his tune! Could she live with a control freak who only had his own interests at heart? Heavens, she could end up as another Marjorie, without a life of her own!

Then there was penniless Oliver, who truly loved her to bits. He came with a barrow-load of problems and was a financial nightmare, but at least with him she'd feel free. She loved him for his vulnerability, and for so many other things. Oh dear. Which was the right man for her? The decision had to be made.

She remained for some time in thought, only stirring herself when a group of rowdy youths who had already passed her once, looked likely to pass her again. They appeared to have been having a bet between them as to who would dare chat her up. But none of them was given the chance. Feeling vulnerable at that late hour she ran off to the hotel, not pausing for breath until she reached room thirty-four.

Phil greeted her ecstatically.

'You've been absolutely ages. What kept you?' He drew her over the threshold and took her into his arms.

'I came as soon as I could,' she said, the moment her lips were free. She went past him into the room, looking vaguely around her and taking in very little.

'It was the best I could get in a hurry.' He looked apologetic. 'And the most I reckoned I could afford. I'm afraid I'm going to have to cut down a bit. I think I've had it with H J. I'll be out of a job for sure.'

'Nonsense.' She smiled him her encouragement. 'Not for long anyway, even if it came to that. A man with your expertise?'

'A man of almost fifty?' he countered. He shrugged and went to the window, rubbing the back of his neck in an embarrassed kind of way. 'Look, I'm sorry about this evening – the scene at

344

the barbecue. It was truly bloody, wasn't it? I've no idea how Marjorie found out about us.' He smiled. 'But I'm rather glad she did. I couldn't imagine having to tell her myself.'

Jade sat down on the nearest chair. It looked the kind that was sure to be replicated throughout the entire hotel and would be found in exactly the same position in each bedroom, between the dressing-table and the luggage rack.

'You haven't left Marjorie, have you?' She looked up at him, wide-eyed.

'Mm? Well, of course I have. Why wouldn't I? Don't sit there, my darling, come over here with me.' He patted the bed that he'd just sat on, but she failed to respond to the invitation. She sat staring at the pattern of shapeless blobs in the carpet, not seeming to hear what he said.

'Where are your things?' he suddenly demanded. 'Didn't you stop to pack a bag?'

'No. No, I didn't.' She raised her head, breathed in, and looked into his eyes. 'I haven't come to stay with you, Philip. I've come to say good-bye.'

27

Marjorie slammed down the phone. 'This I can do without,' she muttered. Now what the hell was she to do? She looked at her watch. Eight forty-five, and a Monday morning. What a great way to start the week. She should be on her way over to Foretec. She *had* to go to Foretec and put Ian right about those wretched photocopies, explain how they'd been a stupid mistake. And then she would tell him about her father-in-law . . .

Half an hour later she was standing over Ian's desk.

'Good morning, Marjorie, how goes it?' Ian leaned back in his chair. 'Isn't it great to see Stella improving?' He looked immensely relieved, but also decidedly strained. The worry of his wife would forever be a burden on him now.

'Yes, oh yes, it's wonderful.' Marjorie had spent an hour the previous afternoon at the hospital with Stella and they'd had a good long chat. She had found herself telling Stella practically everything: about how things had been going downhill between her and Phil, how he had got himself involved with his junior's partner; and naturally they discussed her job.

Stella listened attentively as Marjorie tried to explain her desperation for some sort of role in life.

'Now that I can well understand,' Stella said, 'but are you sure this is really you?' She seemed incapable of understanding why anyone would volunteer themselves to work for her husband.

Marjorie, of course, was as doubtful about the job as Stella. The more she thought about it the more doubts she had. It wasn't only that she was struggling with modern work methods and feared she might never make the grade, it was the manner of acquiring the post that troubled her. She had tried to ignore what she'd done but the episode had left her with an unsatisfactory feeling of obtaining something under false pretences. She was a fraud, even a blackmailer – and latterly an industrial spy! As for how she would be forever viewed by her work colleagues for sneaking through the back door, well, it wouldn't be in a way that she would want to be, that was for sure.

Oh yes, she had doubts about it all, she thought, looking up to find Ian's eyes on her and wondering what she was doing here in his office. Then she remembered; how could she have forgotten?

'Look, Ian, there's something I really must tell you.'

'Ah. I thought that might be the case.' Pulling out a drawer in the region of his right knee he cast her a wry little smile. Seconds later her sheaf of photocopies was smacked down on the desk. 'I found these most entertaining, I must say. I – er – presume they were sent by you?'

'Well, actually . . . yes, they were. But I'm afraid it was a terrible mistake.'

'Dear me, now, was it really? You mean they weren't meant to come to me?'

Marjorie's heart had been sinking at the tone of his words, and his face had gone very straight. She'd been crazy to think he'd give them back. And even if he did, he'd obviously seen all the figures . . . and could use them to his advantage. The trouble was, he could undo all Oliver's good work in no time, and Olly didn't deserve that to happen. It was Phil she'd wanted to land in the mire, not Oliver. Oh, she wished she hadn't got into all this.

Eric must have been reading her thoughts. Placing his big hand on top of the heap, he said, 'I could do a lot of damage with these, you know. Could really set the cat among the pigeons.'

'Yes, I do realise that. A-and is that what you intend to do?' What price would she have to pay to stop him? It hardly bore thinking about.

'No,' he said, suddenly grinning. He threw them to her side of the desk. 'I think I must want my head tested, and Stella would never believe this, but I'm going to pretend I never even saw them. It'll cost me a king's ransom, to boot. When I think what I'm turning away . . .' He shrugged his big square shoulders. 'But there you go,

Marjorie, my dear. Life's a funny old thing.'

Marjorie's mouth fell open. 'But . . . why? Why are you –'

'Why am I not putting the kybosh on Spittal's deal and getting back what I lost? Well, I could undercut these prices –' he waved a hand over the tables of figure '– no problem there at all, but is that really what you want? Somehow I don't think it is.'

'Does what I want count?'

'But of course it does. It always will. I shall never forget that you saved Stella. What kind of man do you think I am?'

He heaved himself out of his chair and came round the desk to join her. 'Look, you know you could have landed your husband in a lot of bother with this, don't you? That was obviously your motive. Oh yes, Stella told me about your problems. And how does the saying go? Hell hath no fury like a woman scorned?

'But didn't it occur to you that you'd have been the prime suspect? Then everyone would have known what had happened. And it wouldn't have looked too good – not for you, me or the whole company. No one would have wanted anything to do with Foretec from then on – *or* with Spittal's, come to that.

'No, if you intend going in for this kind of thing, Marjorie, you have to be a lot more devious than you've been. And besides, do you really want to hurt Philip that much?'

Tears leaped into her eyes. 'Yes,' she managed to

blurt out. 'And I couldn't even get that right could I? I've made a mess of this and upset everyone at the barbecue, and even Stella looks at me as though I've gone doolally.' She shuddered a drawn-out sniff and wailed, 'What's the matter with me?'

Ian looked most uncomfortable. Comforting weepy women wasn't his forte at all. He was wringing his big podgy hands while shaking his head. 'Nothing's the matter with you,' he ventured. 'It's your Phil who's gone off the rails. And he's been making enough of a fool of himself, don't you think, without you needing to stick in the knife. Look, I know he must have hurt you badly, but how about giving him another chance? You've been together a long time, haven't you, so he can't be a bad old stick . . .'

'He doesn't *want* another chance!' she snapped, stepping away from the arm that was about to go awkwardly round her. 'All he wants is that girl! He's absolutely besotted with her. He –'

Oh, she didn't want to be talking about this, any more than Ian did. She blew her nose and made an enormous effort at normality. 'Forget about my problems; there was something else I wanted to talk about. I'm afraid Philip's father is ill; he's had to go into hospital. And his mother's never well either. I – I really ought to go to them. So I was wondering, could I have some time off? I –'

'Yes, yes, of course. Take all the time you want.'

'Really?' She'd thought he might be awkward about it. Instead he sounded . . . relieved.

* * *

She was loading the back of her car with a hastily-packed hold-all and various oddments from the fridge, when Phil's car pulled up on the drive.

'Good heavens, how did you hear about it?' she demanded as soon as he'd half climbed out. 'I've been trying for ages to track you down.'

His office had been the only point of contact that she could think of, but none of the secretaries in Phil's department appeared to know anything of his whereabouts, or of Oliver's. At least that's what they'd pretended. Some of them had sounded nervous to find her on the other end of the line – nervous, cagey, and anxious to end the conversation. Marjorie was left with the impression that the minute they put down the phone they burst into hysterical laughter. News of the scene at the barbecue must have travelled fast.

'Hear about what?' Phil asked frostily, slamming his car door. There was a tired sagginess to his face, she noticed, but didn't like to speculate as to what had brought that about. 'And what are you doing here at home? Been given the sack already?'

Suddenly she understood why *he* had come to the house: he'd been hoping to sneak back for more of his things while she was out at work.

She refused to be drawn by his snide remark. 'Your father's been taken ill,' she told him baldly. 'I had a phone call, first thing, from Becky, but I didn't know where you were. He's had to go into hospital.'

Phil dropped his off-hand demeanour immediately. 'Oh no! What for? Is he bad? Is that where you're going, then – to London?

'Of course I'm going to London. They're still my in-laws after all.' She rummaged briskly through her baggage, wondering where she could have put the car keys. Annoyingly they had gone missing just when she wanted to convey an impression of competence, practicality, and control.

'Apparently, would you believe it, Eric's had a *second* stroke. Not a word to us about the first! Your mother said she hadn't liked to bother us at the time. It happened shortly after we moved here, you see. They didn't even let on to Becky because of the baby. It was a mild stroke, as it happens, and they thought they could cope on their own.'

'But . . . what about your job?'

Marjorie looked at him sharply, but the sarcasm was no longer there. 'The job's had to go on hold. Ian Ericson was very understanding. I can go back any time I like. He agreed that this business with your father is far more important at the moment. Your mother's on the verge of a breakdown by all accounts; she can't cope with all this on her own. And Becky's having problems with the baby not sleeping day or night, so she can't do very much.'

'Hell.'

'And that's not nearly the whole of it,' she went on, straightening up from a tug on the bonnet lock. She checked the windscreen washing fluid and dusted her hands. 'As far as I can gather there've been some weird goings-on with that couple they hired – you know, the manager and his cleaner-wife? They seem to have had a hand in all this, somehow. But now they've vanished without trace.'

Phil's face had taken on a mask of stony resignation. 'I'll be ready in two minutes,' he said, striding into the house. 'Wait for me.'

Philip closed his side of the wardrobe and leaned his forehead against the door, struggling to get a grip on events. Having spent the most ghastly Sunday of his entire life wondering how he might yet persuade Jade that they could have a future together, in spite of all her arguments against it, and now to be dragged miles away from her before he could see her again . . . well, it was almost too much to endure.

Why hadn't he seen this coming? Or had he seen something like this coming months ago and tried to turn a blind eye? And why did some lucky devils sail through life getting away with murder when others like him were always brought to book? It was hardly fair.

He yanked open a drawer, grabbed an armful of clothes, and hurled it shut again. He didn't need a signpost to see where his life was now heading: in a minute he'd be on the road back to London to bail out his ailing parents; to act the dutiful son. Sucked up into his dull old life. Right back where he'd started . . .

Except that he wouldn't have Marjorie any longer: he'd burned his bridges there. He dropped the lid on a small blue suitcase, and paused with his hands pressing it down. Had he really messed up with Marjorie? How had it all come about? Things had got wildly beyond his control lately; that was about all he knew. He wasn't sure about anything else.

Oliver had set off for work leaving the flat in a hopeless mess. He'd not had a good night at all, having spent most of it torturing himself with thoughts of Jade in the arms of Philip Benson. He'd not fallen asleep until soft light filtered through the blinds, and soon after that the alarm dragged him awake. He'd ignored it, finally resurfacing so late that he'd gone through the flat like a whirlwind, reaching the office twenty minutes after his usual time and only achieving that by breaking every speed limit on his route.

To H J punctuality was a virtue, and Oliver felt he already had enough black marks against his name. He wished to goodness Marjorie hadn't blurted out the fact that he was still technically a married man. H J thought he was single and although most people wouldn't give a damn what he was, little things like this were everything to H J.

It was the biggest surprise of his life, therefore, when H J summoned him to his office and offered him instant promotion to Philip Benson's position, the latter having seen fit to hand in his resignation.

'You should, of course,' H J added, 'be reprimanded for incorrectly reporting your marital status to us, your employers, but we are prepared just this once to overlook the indiscretion.'

Oliver managed to look suitably humble. 'I'm sorry about that,' he mumbled, crossing the fingers that H J couldn't see, 'but I didn't think it so very wrong of me to put myself down as single, since my divorce was so nearly final. I realise now that I should have been completely accurate.' H J need never know that he had hoped to evade the Child Support Agency.

'I see.' H J wrinkled his nose at the word 'divorce'. 'Well, as I say, your work here has been exemplary, which is what counts most I suppose, and you deserve to be moved on. Congratulations and I hope your private life soon sorts itself out.'

Oliver knew better than to question what had been going through H J's mind since the barbecue or what investigations had been carried out into all concerned; he merely accepted that he'd been judged the innocent party and his ex-boss the culpable one. It certainly couldn't have helped the situation, could it, if one's wife was working with the enemy? Good old Marjorie Benson! He returned to his desk, happily whistling at the way things had turned out.

What was it all worth, though, without Jade? He sat down at his desk, suddenly sober. With no one to celebrate his success, her absence would hit him harder than ever when he returned to the flat.

But that evening, bracing himself as he turned the key in the lock, he expected to be confronted by the mess he'd left hours earlier, only to find neatness and polished order in its place. A smell of meat and onions wafted through a gap in the kitchen door and cooking tools were being clattered about.

His heart thumped. Surely Jade couldn't be here!

'Hi.' She greeted him shyly, sidling through the gap in the door.

'W-what are you doing here?'

'Cooking.'

'You . . . haven't –' he gulped '– come back?'

'I never really went away, you know.' She put her hands behind her back. With her hair hanging loose but held off her forehead by a band, and with her white apron tied round her waist, she reminded him of Alice in Wonderland. 'I only went to say good-bye to Philip. I . . . well, couldn't see our relationship going anywhere, quite honestly. For all sorts of obvious reasons. So I gave him the big heave-ho. That was on Saturday night. And afterwards I went to see Selina and my mother.'

'You've really – really come back?' he repeated. He couldn't take anything in.

'What's the matter? Don't you want me? I suppose I can hardly blame you if you don't.' Her face had begun to fall, but Oliver suddenly swept her into such an overwhelming bear-hug that tears were pressed from her eyes.

It was a long while before he let her go. Brushing

wetness from his face, he laughed. 'I really thought I'd lost you. I can't believe this is happening.'

'Silly. Don't you know I love you? Heaven knows why, but I do.' Her voice wobbly with emotion she cleared her throat and forced herself to become practical. 'Now come and sit at the table. We can talk about things over the meal. I've been thinking, you see, about your children, and how we can get them back.'

'Back?' He followed her, disbelieving. He must be in Wonderland too. The Mad Hatter or something. Soon he would wake up.

'Well, at least to get you decent access; but we can try for as much as you want.'

'But Jade, it all costs so much money, and – well – that's something we just don't have.'

'I know.' She looked away. 'I'm doing my best about all that, honestly I am. I know I've been hopeless with money. Anyway, this need not cost us a bean, because I can get good old Godfrey on to it; he'll do anything for me. Anything. And really, you know, he's a very clever lawyer; this sort of thing's his speciality.'

'But Jade, Jade, wait a minute.' He followed her into the kitchen. 'Supposing I did get them back – even for part of the time. How are we to look after them?'

'Oh, I'm sure we'll manage somehow. If that's what you really want.'

'Want?' Of course it's what I want.' Almost in a trance he helped her carry dishes to the table and poured out glasses of wine. 'But I won't hear of you giving up your law course. You weren't thinking of doing that?'

'It isn't going to be easy,' she hedged. 'Small kids need lots of attention.'

It sounded to Oliver as though she was wavering; perhaps motherhood sounded an easy option to her, and he knew how hard she had been finding the course recently. 'Look,' he insisted, 'you're not going to sacrifice any of your study time for the sake of my kids. I'd never forgive myself if you did that; neither would you forgive yourself either. You'll get that degree if it kills us.'

'Well . . .' Jade didn't look at all convinced. In fact her face had all the appearance of one choosing a suitable wedding gown, quickly followed by a trip to Toys R Us.

The thought of wedding gowns led Oliver to the memory of the blue sapphire ring in the jeweller's shop. Somehow, some day, he would get it for her.

'Do you think your mother might help us?' he wondered. 'She likes children, doesn't she? And she sounds like she needs to be needed.'

'She might help . . .' Jade looked surprised and hopeful. She would never have thought of it herself but this could indeed be a solution. Perhaps she could have the best of both worlds . . .

They sighed heavily in unison; apart from their horrendous money problems there was a whole new mountain to climb. And the going wouldn't be easy.

'Better get some of this inside us.' Oliver nodded at the dishes of food. 'So what have we got? I'm starving.'

She lifted a lid, smiling wryly. *'Boeuf en croûte*, of course.'

28

'I still can't believe it, Phil. It's an absolute disgrace!'

'I know, Chrissy, I know.'

'How people can *do* things like that? Poor old Mum and Dad. Ooh, how I'd like to get my hands on that pair.'

'Me too,' Philip agreed with fervour. 'But all we can do is leave it to the police.'

Phil and his sister were slumped over the breakfast bar in their parents' kitchen, airing their feelings about their father's so-called manager and his wife for the twentieth time in three days. They couldn't take it in that the two con-merchants had absconded with money from the business, prompting their father to have another stroke. That sort of thing only happened to people in newspapers.

Marjorie stood at the sink with a plastic apron wrapped round her middle, peeling potatoes into a stainless steel colander. She had half a mind on the pointless chit-chat; the other half was planning the evening meal. Someone had to keep their head and get on with things, she grumbled to herself, but why couldn't the others lend a hand?

Their brother Colin had been no help either. He'd breezed in for one day only, and Marjorie suspected he'd only managed that much because a business meeting had happened to bring him as far as Heathrow and the extra distance wasn't enough to put him out. That was the extent of *his* concern.

Chrissie had come quickly enough, to be fair, but now she kept peering out of the window. For several days a steady drizzle had been falling which meant there would be few visitors to her tea room and therefore no need for her to rush back to it. Her eldest daughter could just about manage the beds and breakfasts, she'd said, but not a sudden influx of people. So if the sun came out . . .

Marjorie glanced up from her peelings. No, not a glimmer of sun. It hadn't been seen for days. Now, should she make these into mash to go with the lamb chops, or should she slice them for *boulangère*? And would Sheila be sufficiently rested to want a share of the meal?

She turned to ask the others' opinion about their mother and realised that they had fallen silent for some time; now she'd caught them out, exchanging secretive nods and nudges.

Chrissy slid off her stool and stretched her arms over her head in an exaggerated manner. 'If you'll excuse me for half an hour, you two, I think I'll go and phone home.'

Marjorie swivelled back to the sink. She'd sooner peel another ton of potatoes than be left alone with

Phil. She hoped he would get up and leave her, the atmosphere was so heavy, but he asked her to sit down at the breakfast bar with him. 'Those can wait a while,' he told her. 'We don't need to eat until later.'

Marjorie didn't sit down. 'You've been talking to Chrissy, haven't you?' she accused him. 'About us, I mean. Our private business.'

'I didn't say a word about anything. Do you imagine I go around bragging about it? I'm not proud of what I've done.'

Marjorie's ears pricked up. This was a change of tune: he was actually admitting he'd *done* something. 'You know what Chrissy's like,' he went on. 'She's not daft, nor is she blind. You and I have hardly said a word to each other since we got here, and we've been sleeping in separate rooms, so she was bound to guess *something* had happened.'

'So what can she imagine we have to talk about, since we're so obviously estranged?'

'Everything, of course. We haven't discussed things at all. You haven't heard my side of the story.'

'You're joking! I've heard nothing but.' Marjorie discarded her plastic apron and leaned against the boiler with her arms folded. The appliance was rumbling to itself as it heated water – using oil or she couldn't have stood there – and was a vague comfort as it warmed her thighs. 'You saw a pretty young girl and you wanted her; couldn't wait to dip your wick. That's the beginning and

363

end of it. And hardly a novel occurrence.'

Philip winced. 'There's no need to make it sound vulgar.'

'Well! So sorry if vulgar doesn't suit. How about thoughtless, selfish and inconsiderate? Is that more to your taste? Or outrageous, despicable and vile? Pawgh! There aren't the words in the dictionary to describe how you've behaved towards me.'

'I know you must be upset.'

'Upset? Hmph! Try humiliated and furious. Or broken and dreadfully hurt.' She darted over to the kitchen roll holder and ripped off a piece for a handkerchief.

He nodded, looking crushed and pale; suddenly thinner inside his blue cotton sweater. 'OK. All those things. I do realise what I've done, you know. I've been able to stand back and look at it objectively these past few days, and honestly, Marjorie, I'm more sorry than I can say. I didn't mean to hurt you. I didn't deliberately go looking for an affair; certainly not with a slip of a young girl. It's just something that happened. A classic case. I don't know.' He shrugged, shaking his head. 'I suppose I was looking for *something*. I don't quite know what. A little excitement I suppose. A change of life. To feel like I'd really lived.'

He shielded his eyes, as though trying to block out the dismal weather and his present surroundings, so that he might recapture the bright golden summer and the crazy madness that had gripped him, and perhaps make sense of it all.

Marjorie lined up Sheila's spices so that all the labels faced front and stole a glance at him. She could almost feel a little pity for him, so harrowed did he appear, and was amazed at her reaction. That she should feel pity for *him*, when she ought to feel insulted that he appeared to have found her excruciatingly boring and not fulfilling enough for him! And he had hardly been a help to her either, with her own 'change of life'. On the contrary: he'd lost his wits over a beautiful young girl at a time when she'd most needed his constant support and reassurance.

But he was only human, after all. Could he help his yearnings any more than the next person?

'If it's any comfort to you I shan't be seeing her again,' he went on eventually. 'It's finished. Please believe that.'

She sniffed and put the handkerchief up her sleeve. 'That's really no concern of mine now. And it doesn't alter anything.'

But he went on having his say. 'I'm even pre-pared to admit that everything's been my fault.' He stood up and walked over to the sink where he stared out of the window. 'You were right from the very beginning, weren't you? We should never have gone away. I should have taken over the business and none of this would have happened. I could have chipped in with whatever redundancy money Spittals gave me, and Dad wouldn't have been ripped off by these charlatans. And he might never have had these strokes.'

She said nothing while he bowed his head, looking a picture of utter dejection.

'I'm sorry,' he said into the sink bowl, 'so sorry. More sorry than I can ever say.'

Marjorie closed her eyes. If only they could turn back the clock.

'And now I've lost everything. You. My job. The family business . . .'

'Your job?' Marjorie's eyes flew open. Had she managed to lose him his job after all? 'But surely they haven't really sacked you? I thought you were making that up. Why, none of what happened was anything to do with your work!'

He turned to face her. 'Oh, I dare say I could have walked back into H J's office and toughed it out. He hadn't really got grounds . . . I mean to say, there's so much of that sort of thing going on these days, no one would be in work if it were a sacking offence. Well, anyway, all things considered I've decided to jack it in. I've blotted my copy-book well and truly as far as he's concerned and my career's never going to be the same again. I'll never get to the top of the tree now.'

He laughed an empty laugh. 'I believe Knox is to be given my old job. Would you credit it? He's certainly come out smelling of roses. But doesn't his type always come out on top?'

Marjorie frowned. She was pleased for Oliver, of course. She'd always had a soft spot for him. But why did men have to be so hell-bent on coming out on top? It was all so ridiculous. Phil's inordinate bitterness towards Oliver, she recalled, had started on day one. She would never fathom out quite why.

'Is – is that what you really wanted?' she wondered aloud. 'To get to the top of the tree?'

Phil shrugged. 'Maybe that was part of my restlessness. Who doesn't want to be King Pin?'

'So . . . what are you going to do now?'

'Come back here, I suppose. Try and salvage enough of the business for us all to live on.'

Their eyes met and held. Who had he meant by 'all'? Marjorie was asking herself. But before she could mull that one over Becky burst into the room.

'Oh, Dad,' she breathed excitedly, 'did you really mean that? I couldn't help hearing what you said. Are you really coming back? Oh, that'll be brilliant, Mum! Terrific! Because I'm fed up to the back teeth with Steve's mum; she's hopeless at helping with Charlotte.'

She raised her eyes to the ceiling. 'D'you know, if I tell her to do one thing she goes and does the complete opposite? And I swear she's caused all Charlotte's sleeping problems. She picks her up when I don't want her to . . . but now I'll have you to –'

'Here,' Marjorie cut in quickly, 'let me take Charlotte upstairs to your gran. Seeing the baby takes her mind off things.' Let Phil explain to his daughter, she thought grimly, that things weren't as simple as he'd made out.

But this was a duty that Phil neglected completely. In fact, much to Marjorie's concern he

367

not only let Becky rejoice in the prospect of the family being back together again, he let the belief go unchecked in everyone else. By the time the evening meal was finished it was almost too late for Marjorie to back-peddle.

This is not fair, she told herself, struggling alone in the kitchen with the washing-up. Phil should never have put her in this position.

And her Cinderella role had begun to rankle in a way it never had before. She now saw that ever since her own parents had died she'd been the Benson family's drudge, overly eager to serve everyone for the privilege of being part of it. Becky, too, seemed to think she had only to snap her fingers and her mother would come a-running. In fact they all assumed she would drop back into her old role of general dogsbody as though nothing had changed at all. But it had. Oh, yes, it had!

Flinging off the plastic apron again, she marched upstairs, surprising Phil in his bedroom where he was hanging trousers in a press.

'Everyone's assuming that I'll be here,' she snapped as soon as she saw him, 'but I haven't made up my own mind. It's all very well you lot thinking you can put me down and pick me up again whenever it happens to suit you, like a useful old gardening coat or something, but I haven't had a chance to think things through yet.'

He had the grace to look ashamed. 'Yes. I know. I'm sorry. But I didn't know what to say.'

'How about telling them the truth?'

He slowly closed the trouser-press. 'Well . . . what is the truth?'

'I don't know. I'm asking you!'

'It's for you to say, really.' He came and stood in front of her. 'But look, isn't all this what you always wanted? Your family all around you, your new granddaughter close by, and both of us running the family business?'

The steam went out of her, all the fight. He was perfectly right, of course. Everything appeared to be going her way *now*. They might even be able to get back their old friends in time. The trouble was that, as with most things in life, as soon as you got what you wanted, you realised it was no longer what you wanted after all.

Seeing her hesitation, Phil took the opportunity to strengthen his position. 'If you like,' he said, trying to look nonchalant, 'I could try to get back our old house. It still hasn't been sold yet. We could sell the Brightwells house easily enough, I'm sure. Meanwhile we could perhaps get a bridging loan. Things might be a bit tight for a while, but it would all be worth it in the end, wouldn't it? Well, Marjie, what do you think?'

Marjorie fell silent, thinking about it. It was touching that he was prepared to do this for her, she supposed: a clear measure of his regret for what had happened. But . . . 'I don't know, Phil. I don't know.'

'I won't be expecting miracles,' he added quietly, 'I mean, as far as you and I are concerned. I know you're going to need time.'

'Time. Yes. I need time.' She nodded her head emphatically. 'Right now I need some sleep.'

'Of course.' He laid an arm lightly on her shoulder and walked her to the door, but he didn't dare risk embracing her or giving her a peck on the cheek. That would have been pushing things too far.

The old house showed further signs of neglect as Marjorie surveyed it from the road; closer inspection merely added to her dismay. At every turn she saw decay: flaking paint work, rusting handles, fragments of loose cement. It was hardly credible that such deterioration could have occurred during the short time they had been away. Had Marjorie not seen it for herself she wouldn't have believed it.

One quick glance into the back garden was enough to make her gasp. This was no longer her back garden – not the one she had planted and nurtured all those faithful years. Two of her conifers had died. The roses were diseased and flagging. The billiard-table lawn had become a wilderness of hay where now only newcomer weeds stood strong, lush and vibrant with their barbs and thorns on guard.

Marjorie stared about her in despair. If Phil ever managed to get back the house – and he was trying hard to do so – they would have a long struggle on their hands; an enormous effort to make. With the best will in the world could things ever be the way they were? Was it really only a matter of time? She had serious doubts.

Turning away eventually she continued her walk until she reached the telephone kiosk outside the newsagent's. Better to make her call out of earshot from the family, she decided, lifting the receiver.

She read the advertisements while she waited for Ian Ericson to take her call, but knew them all by heart by the time he deigned to come on the line. Even then he sounded every inch the brusque, harassed executive – far too concerned with his wheeling and dealing to be bothered with one of his wife's acquaintances. And when he discovered that that acquaintance was Marjorie his displeasure at the interruption increased.

He tried, though, to come across as the genial husband, still grateful to the woman who had saved his wife's life. 'Marjorie!' he boomed, with far too much enthusiasm. 'How are things with you? Your father-in-law all right, I hope?'

'Not too bad, considering, thanks – though recovery's going to be slow.'

'Now you just take your time, won't you?' Ian urged. 'No need to rush back here for the sake of the job. As I told you the other day, I'll keep it open for you, no matter how long you need.'

'It's very kind of you, I'm sure. And Stella's all right too, is she?'

'Out of hospital tomorrow, and very much looking forward to seeing you again soon. But as I said . . .'

'Yes, I know; I'm to take my time. But listen, I've been thinking.'

'Y-yes?'

Marjorie grimaced at herself in a reflective panel above the phone. Ian Ericson had had enough of her crack-pot schemes, his tone told her. Would he never be free of her? *Well, not yet*, she thought, crossing her fingers. *Not quite yet.*

'It's about the job that I'm phoning you, actually. Would it – er – be awfully cheeky of me if I decided to back out of it now? You see, having looked at it from all angles – well, I don't think it's what I want after all.'

'Oh,' was all he could say, but there was a world of meaning in that one word. Surprise. Acceptance. Relief.

'But,' she ran on before his balloon of euphoria dissipated, 'I wonder whether I could ask for something else in its place?'

'You mean, swap your wish for another one?' Now he seemed resigned. She could picture him slumped over his desk rubbing his hammer fist over his eyes, although she detected humour in his voice, as though he was finding the episode faintly amusing.

'Yes, you could put it that way. At risk of upsetting my Good Fairy, I've thought of something better. It's not exactly for me, though, although it would make me happy too.'

'Not exactly for you, eh? I think you'd better come out with it.'

'Right. Well it's this. I want you to buy something for Stella.'

'Buy?' Now he jumped to attention. This was much more up his street.

'She would really love a canal boat, you know . . . I suppose she's never mentioned it?'

'It's the first I've ever heard of it What would she do with a canal boat? She doesn't even go out of doors much.' He paused to think about what he'd just said, as though it had only just occurred to him. 'She used to. She was quite an outdoors type at one time.'

'Well, take it from me, she would like a boat. It would have to be long, I imagine – one with plenty of room. Oh, and she'd need some money to fit it out of course. Quite a lot of money, perhaps . . .' Marjorie's voice trailed away. Was Ian still paying attention?

He seemed to be lost for words. Then he said, 'Are you sure she wouldn't like a canal or two thrown in for good measure?'

Marjorie tittered obligingly, but she hoped he was taking her seriously. 'No, you can't buy canals, but I expect there'll be mooring fees, and – oh – all sorts of other things.'

'I see.' But clearly he didn't. 'And am I allowed to know *why*? I mean, what on earth will she do with this canal boat and moorings and things?'

'Ah, now. I suggest you ask Stella that. It's really for her to say.'

'Oh, I shall be asking her, most certainly. Right

away, in fact. I promised I'd pop in to see her about now.'

'And you *will* be buying her the boat?'

Wonderful. Marjorie rubbed her hands together as soon as she'd put down the phone. Ian Ericson had said yes! Pushing open the door, she stepped out on to the pavement and set off in the direction of her old hairdresser's.

A watery sun had begun to penetrate the recent rain clouds; the streets, shops and houses looked fresher and brighter already. But Marjorie didn't stop to admire them; she kept up her purposeful march until she finally reached the reception desk.

A clutter of appointment books, plastic pocket rain hoods and displays of hair products still littered the counter, she noticed, and the young doll-faced receptionist was, as usual, chatting at length to one of the stylists across the room.

'And what did he say about that, then?' The girl was all agog.

'Not much he could say, was there?'

'But, really, if I was you I wouldn't have–'

Marjorie cleared her throat so hard it hurt. 'Excuse me!' she rasped. 'Do I have to stand here all day to get some attention?'

The receptionist turned to her slowly with round, astonished eyes. 'H-have you got an appointment, Madam?'

'No, I haven't as a matter of fact. But as an old and valued customer, I'm sure Angie can fit me in.'

'Angie . . .' The girl drew her finger from the

appointments book. 'I-I'll go and see what she can do.'

Within minutes Marjorie was shampooed, wrapped in a towel, and sitting in front of a mirror.

'I must say these lights are truly awful,' she told Angie. 'They're hardly flattering to your clients. I don't know why something isn't done about them. Now, you won't cut the front too short, will you? And I want you to give it some *shape*. I expect it to fall into place when I wash it; not look like a hornet's nest.'

And it certainly looked better than a hornet's nest, she decided an hour later. She was back at her in-laws admiring herself in the hall mirror while Phil wrestled with a bank official over the phone. He seemed to have been at it for a while already, judging by the scattering of papers around him, and it was several minutes before he was through.

'That should do it,' he announced triumphantly, finally replacing the receiver. He beamed at Marjorie. 'Your hair looks good. Lovely. And it looks like we can go ahead with getting the house back!'

'Really?'

'Yes.' He grabbed her arms but thought better of it, well aware that she couldn't bear his touch. His betrayal was still too fresh in her mind. 'I'll go and tell Mum and Dad at once,' he muttered. At least they would be pleased with his news.

Marjorie stared thoughtfully after him, then turned and picked up the receiver. It was still warm from the heat of his success – a success, she realised with detachment, that might at one time have had her dancing on the moon but now touched her not in the least.

Soon she was through to Stella on her hospital bedside phone. 'Has Ian by any chance been in touch with you during the past hour or so?'

'Oh, Marjorie!' Judging by the excitement in Stella's answer, there was little doubt that Ian had already phoned. She was laughing and crying as she babbled to Marjorie, telling her everything she already knew. 'But why am I telling you this?' Stella sniffed. 'Surely it was all your doing? Only you knew of my dream. And Ian would never have thought of giving me something that he couldn't appreciate himself.'

'Well –' Marjorie smugly patted her new hair-do, but declined to bask in Stella's praise for too long. She quickly brought the conversation to more practical matters. 'Now how about this floating restaurant you were always talking about? You're going to need a hand. And I can pack a bag in a trice, you know . . .'

In fact she already had.